'UP THE GARDEN PATH, Sue Limb's first novel, is a
jolly comedy with a serious coda, a Feydeau froth that
turns into a *conte morale*, a move from the world of
thoughtless chauvinism and girlish acquiescence to the
moral uplands of feminist enlightenment. It is elegantly
written, fast, knowing, allusive, wise and exceptionally
funny . . . Ms Limb has a wicked eye for detail (of
personal quirk, of place and especially of squalor) and a
very smart turn of punning phrase . . . she's a talent to be
cherished, and a natural-born writer. UP THE GAR-
DEN PATH made me laugh out loud on a train going to
Harrogate: as far as I'm concerned that's a considerable
accolade'
John Walsh, *Time Out*

Up the Garden Path

SUE LIMB

CORGI BOOKS

UP THE GARDEN PATH

A CORGI BOOK 0 552 12561 X

Originally published in Great Britain by
The Bodley Head Ltd.

PRINTING HISTORY

The Bodley Head edition published 1984
Corgi edition published 1985

This book is set in 11/11pt Bembo

Corgi Books are published by
Transworld Publishers Ltd.,
Century House, 61-63 Uxbridge Road,
Ealing, London W5 5SA

Made and printed in Great Britain by
Hunt Barnard Printing Ltd., Aylesbury, Bucks.

To the one that got away

Up the Garden Path

1

Izzy pressed her nose to the glass: the whirling snow had blotted out Earl's Court. Unfortunately the effect would only be temporary. New Year. Time for a little resolution. All right, then, but where to begin? The body, perhaps. Izzy had been feeling so fat recently that it was like having somebody else in bed with her. She would have to shape up. But alas, so far her idea of exercise was reaching for the chocolates.

Then there was the untidiness. Izzy looked about her. It was only a one-bedroom flat, with a double bed for the vice and a bookcase for the versa, but Izzy had acquired dirty habits early and practice had made perfect. Izzy's mother had got up at the crack of dawn to scrub the farmyard and fold the cows, but the infant Izzy had ignored this example and played vile games behind the barn in the mud with little John Wilson, her partner in grime. Start as you mean to go on.

Body a wreck; home a fouled nest: what about her work? Izzy cast a cold eye on the piles of unmarked essays spilling out of their paper carrier bags. Plenty of room for resolution there. She would use visual aids and things this term, try not to fall asleep in assembly, and urge her class (4C) away from drug abuse and racketeering and towards joined-up writing. Oh yes, and she would open her girls' eyes to the absurdity of Cupid. His arrows would miss their mark. Izzy's girls would sigh no more for Steve Hirst (Upper Sixth, tenor sax and fatal eyelashes). They would be intent on fulfilling careers as plumbers and brain surgeons. After all, what did love bring but dust and ashes?

A tear fell down Izzy's nose and she ran to the cake tin. All right, so she was going to diet, but first she had to get rid of the cake. Besides, she had to eat something to get rid of the terrible taste of dust and ashes. Humble Pie, perhaps. Because Izzy's eccentricities over diet and hygiene, and her inadequacies as a teacher, were nothing to the black depths of her recent record as a lover. She was keeping such a low profile, her nose was practically on the pavement. Maybe she should have WELCOME printed on her back and aspire to the status of doormat. But it seemed a bit ambitious, somehow. Izzy snapped the cake tin shut. She would not eat. She would do her marking.

Lynette Taylor 4C   My Idele Christmas Pressent

My idele Christmas pressent is, that I would be discovred by a film directer. I would be working somwhere ordinery like a suppermarket on the till and this block would come in. hed be meddium tall with mid-brown hair cut meddium short and hazzel eyes and hed be wering a lether jacked and hed come up the till and say Twenty Sick Cut Please and a box of matchs and then hed suddenly lick see me propally and hed sort of blink and look agen and hed say Just a minit have you ever been a moddle? have you ever bin on the frount cover off a magerzine? And he woulde look a bit like Jeremy Eyerns only not so olde and not so big bages under his eyes, then we would go to Roam and live in a viller with a sorner and a swiming pull and we would have tow childern, a boy called Daren and a girl called Cheryl.

Izzy sighed. 'Why not think of being a film director yourself, Lynette?' she wrote at the bottom, and fought off the temptation to get herself a bit of cake after all. Ten more essays, she thought, and you can have a biscuit. Not till then.

*My idle Christmas presente wolde be a Mazerarti. I wolde
drive it rite up the M.1. at 120 m.p.h. and the pollice wolde
not cach me, then I wolde pick up tow hitchhicers grils one
bland one burnet and big bilt and we wolde drive up to
Scortland and at dinner time we wolde stop in a transept caff
and I wolde have a mixed girll with sosage backon egg and
chipes and a larger and lime and a snout.*

Izzy felt faint and got herself the piece of cake. It
wasn't the first time she'd regretted her choice of essay
title for 4C. 'It doesn't have to be a realistic Christmas
present,' she'd beamed at them, as inspirationally as
possible so near the end of term, 'it could be an idea, or
something that happens, or a change in the way the
world is – a complete fantasy, if you like. Get your
imaginations working!' So their poor young imaginations creaked and lurched amidst the debris of the
century.

Izzy stood by the window sadly eating her cake. As
for her own Christmas, well – even as the chocolate
icing melted in her mouth, she couldn't help reflecting
that she'd neither had her cake nor eaten it. She'd given
up the chance of a full-blooded Yorkshire Christmas
with her dear old mum, on the off chance that Michael
Tristram might ring. 'I might manage to slip away,'
he'd promised. 'I'm sure I'll be able to manage an
afternoon or something – maybe a couple of hours
sometime. I can say I'm playing squash. Dammit, my
love, I can't possibly survive without seeing you for a
whole two weeks.'

Two weeks had passed, and he had apparently sur-
vived. There had been a time, when Izzy had first
fallen in love with Michael, when she'd lingered in
Marks & Spencer's gazing fondly at the St Michael
labels in all the Crimplene suits. But after her two
Christmas weeks alone in that last outpost of the

11

Empire, Earl's Court, Izzy felt that Michael's halo had dimmed to a faint shine – no more than one might expect from, say, a particularly distinguished shampoo. Izzy heaved the heaviest sigh so far, and returned to 4C.

Tracey Field 4C   *My Idol Chrismas Present*

When I think off all the presence Ide like the one that relly stinks in my minde is whorld piece

Oh no, Tracey! Not right now, not on a full stomach. Izzy placed Tracey on the bottom of the pile.

Stephen Masters 4C   *My Ideale Christmas Present*

My Idele Christmas presente is, I woud meet an alierne hidding in my wardrobe their would be a grate bright shinning light comming off of him . . .

Stephen's alien went to the bottom of the pile too. Film directors, aliens, fast cars – was there no more to their dreams?

Izzy wondered for a split second whether to jettison the lot. Tell 4C their wretched essays had been lost in the snow, or caught up in a blazing inferno. She couldn't let them put this load of old rubbish into their CSE folders, surely. Whatever would the Moderator say? The Moderator was a particularly sinister sort of Examiner, and Izzy always imagined them as Calvinist figures, steel from the neck up and granite all below, even though she knew it was more likely to be that nice, ordinary Miss What's-her-Name who taught at a comprehensive school in Hackney.

Desperate for something different, she searched through the grubby pile for a particular one. Here it was. *Roger Razebrook 4C* it read in a small deadly hand, and in the space at the top of the page, *Man Utd Rule*.

Izzy would not dare to argue.

My Ideal Christmas Present

My ideal Christmas Present would be to do the biggest job as as ever been done, it would have to be in America, I plan it on my own but have a hard team behind me, It would be a Bank or a Security Firm, we'd brake in on Friday night, stay the weakened and leave on Sunday night with millions of dollers. Nobody would get hurt my blokes would all get fifty grand and I would go off to South America with the rest and live in a little village in the mountians with the Indians, And I would buy lots of things for the village a hospitle a schoole a swimming pool and a libry and in return they Indians would make me a blood brother and teach me all about their drugs and their life.

Ah, dear Razors! Crime and magnanimity so satisfyingly mixed. Izzy was just about to write some words of affectionate encouragement on the bottom of his essay when the phone rang. Her pen flew out of her hand, her heart leapt right into her mouth and she lurched across the room. TEACHER CHOKES ON OWN HEART, the *Standard* would proclaim. DOCTORS BAFFLED. FOUL PLAY SUSPECTED. Oh yes, it *was* foul play. And yet foul did also seem fair to Izzy's dizzy senses.

'Hello?'

'Hello, Izzy – it's Maria.'

Izzy said nothing for a split second, to keep the massive disappointment out of her voice.

'Izzy? Are you there?'

'Yes, yes, of course. Sorry. I sort of – sort of got my tonsils in a twist for a minute. How was your Christmas?'

'Absolutely vile. I don't know which was worse: the drunken bonhomie of Gwyn's tribe or my mother's hints about grandchildren. How was Yorkshire?'

Oh. Ah. Yorkshire. Izzy had told Maria she was going to Yorkshire, because she couldn't possibly tell Maria that she was staying alone in Earl's Court, on the off chance that a man might ring. In fact, Maria was ignorant of Michael's very existence. Izzy was so scared of Maria's disapproval that she had managed to conceal her affair for a whole two months.

'Yorkshire? Oh – er – it was lovely. My mum was on good form, and – um – the snow was nice.'

'Snow? I didn't know it had snowed at Christmas. I don't remember hearing about it on the weather forecast.'

Oh no – stupid Izzy. It had only just started to snow now, today, this very afternoon, January third – for the first time this winter.

'Well, we had a bit in Yorkshire – just a little light dusting – just in our valley, I think. It only – um – it only lasted a couple of hours, but it looked everso pretty.'

Crumbs.

'Anyway, Izzy, I didn't ring up to natter about the weather. I've got an urgent request. Can you come to dinner – right now?'

'Now? This minute?'

'Yes. I'm terribly sorry it's such short notice, but Gwyn forgot to tell me he'd invited them. So he's cooking and I'm sulking. I don't even know them. The bloke teaches with Gwyn at the Poly. Please come, Izzy. You know how good you are at talking and being nice to people. I'm exhausted. We only got back from Mountain Ash two hours ago. I've got Fiat-lag. I need you.'

'OK – of course I'll come.'

'Great. See you soon, then.'

Izzy was not dressed for going out: she was rat-tailed, grubby-jeaned and extremely sweatshirt. Still, she thought, if I bung some deodorant on, and a clean sweater, and run a rake through my hair, it'll do. She was rummaging in her chest of drawers for a clean sweater when the phone rang again.

'Izzy? This is Michael.'

Her heart leapt right out of her mouth and bounced around the room.

'Oh – Michael.'

Izzy's knees buckled and she sat down very hard on the floor. The furniture rattled.

'Darling! How are you? I'm so sorry I haven't rung before but it's been impossible. Listen, love, I've got to be quick – Louise is in the bath. She's suddenly decided to go out this evening because an old schoolfriend's just rung to say she's in town, and she's taking Jack because this woman's apparently got a son his age and they've always got on well – so I could come over, if that would be all right, darling.'

'Oh Michael – that would be marvellous!'

'OK, then – see you in an hour or so. Can't talk more now. See you soon, loveliest. Bye!'

Izzy threw herself down on the floor, pressing her cheek ardently to the rush matting. *Oh Michael Michael Michael* she whispered passionately to a small piece of cheese which had fallen down one of the cracks. It was appropriate enough. As far as Michael Tristram was concerned, Izzy certainly had the mouse's share.

But, oh God – the flat was in such a mess! The essays spilling out of the carrier bags, and littered all over the sofa; the washing-up lying about in pagodas, twitching portentously now and then; the tights unharvested on the floor, the apple core going gently brown on E. M. Forster, the aspirin dissolving slowly on the draining board. The smears of éclair on the fender.

And worse – her own person. Izzy ran to the mirror and did a brief spot check. Yesterday's spots were all still there – plus a new one, for luck. Or rather, lust, since a mere phone call from Michael was enough to send great pulses of hormone washing through her body. Thank God it was winter, and dark. Since they spent most of their time wrestling in the back of his car (parked in some dim mews) or disporting themselves in Izzy's artfully underlit flat, Michael had had few chances to view her face in cruel daylight. In fact, he probably had very little idea who she was at all.

She threw off all her clothes and turned on the shower. Under it she remembered Maria's dinner invitation.

'Oh Christ!' Izzy grabbed a towel and ran back to the telephone. 'Oh Christ!' She dialled. Poor Christ got a raw deal from Izzy. As one of the new pagans, she only ever blamed him for disasters.

'Hello!' Maria answered straight away, before Izzy had had a chance to work out what she was going to say.

'Oh Maria – I'm sorry – something awful's happened,' confessed the radiant Izzy.

'What?'

'I – I've suddenly started to feel incredibly sick. Really incredibly sick. And I've got these terrible pains in my stomach.'

'It's very sudden, isn't it?' Maria sounded suspicious.

'Yes, it *is* sudden, but that's how – that's how this particular bug strikes. One minute you're fine, the next you're in agony. My – my mum had it at Christmas.'

'You didn't say she'd been ill.'

'Oh, it's a very *brief* thing – I mean, it didn't spoil Christmas at all – it only last a few hours. But while it lasts it's terrible.' Izzy began to shiver. It was very cold, naked in the attics of Earl's Court. 'I'm really very sorry, Maria. Only I'd better not come.'

'No,' agreed Maria doubtfully. 'Ok. Take care of yourself. Get better soon.'

Izzy rang off in a glow of guilt and delight, and raced back to the shower. She scrubbed and sang like a little bird on a spring morning, because in an hour Michael Tristram would come bounding up the three flights of stairs and fall panting into her arms.

Everybody else arrived in this way, too – Izzy lived on the third floor – but with Michael it was different. He stayed panting in her arms until it was time to go away again.

But what a shame she had eaten so much cake recently! And thank God she had installed those dimmer switches! She knew she'd got a fresh pair of black stockings, and her patent leather stilettos were lying around somewhere, she was sure. She thought she could remember seeing them sprawled amongst the Brussels sprouts.

The phone rang again. Swearing and steaming, Izzy ran to get it. Now that her life was balanced on a perfect moment, any call was an intrusion. The phone no longer spoke as a household god from its shrine among the books, but as a black and spiteful Puritan determined to forestall joy.

'Yes?'

There were pips: it was somebody in a call box. Izzy frowned impatiently: who could it be?

'Izzy, darling – it's Michael.'

'Michael!'

'My dear, listen. I'm ringing from the phone on the corner of my street. I said I'd nip to the off-licence. You see, I'm sorry, love, but our plan's collapsed. When Louise got out of the bath and saw how hard it was snowing, she decided not to go out after all. I'm so sorry, darling.'

'Oh well.' Izzy was speechless. She seemed to have swallowed a football made of lead. All the songs dripped off her and soaked dismally into the carpet.

'I'm sorry, Izzy, love – really. Look, I've got to go now; someone might see me phoning from this box and put two and two together. Cheer up, sweetheart, I'll see you soon, I promise. I love you. Bye.'

'Bye.'

Izzy waddled slowly to the bedroom and got dressed in boring old jeans and jersey. Thick socks (once her

17

dad's golf socks) on her feet. Not for her, tonight, the nylon gleam of 10 denier, and her stilettos could moulder away with the sprouts. Izzy put on her warmest boots. She sat on her bed and stared dully at the carpet. A tear ran down her nose. Deep inside her, another sigh was unfolding, down at the soles of her feet. She hauled it up.

It was no use: she had been alone too long. She needed to go out to recover her spirits. Maria's dinner party, which ten minutes ago had seemed an unendurable obstacle, had now begun to glow with friendly light. Izzy looked round her flat. It had a forlorn look. She couldn't stay in, tonight, now. To the telephone again.

'Maria?'

'Izzy!'

'Maria – it's extraordinary, I know – but – I feel better!'

'What? But you were in agony a quarter of an hour ago!'

'Yes, it's odd, isn't it? I got up and walked about a bit, and then I – um – I just sort of had a huge belch and felt better.'

'Good God. How weird.'

'Yes. I suppose it was sort of like colic. Anyway, I'm all right now. So can I come?'

'Of course, of course. Great.'

Izzy felt very tired. All this lying was taking it out of her.

She sat and looked at the phone for a minute. She'd recovered her appetite already, and was looking forward to Gwyn's dinner. Izzy had only been off her food once in the past three years – back in November, when she'd first met Michael. They'd sat in the BBC canteen and gazed intently at each other across their chilling faggots. *This must be it*, thought Izzy. Even when she'd gone home, she'd been unable to force down more than a couple of biscuits, a yogurt and a banana. But now, well into the third month of her affair, Izzy's appetite was back to normal. The nausea of disappointment at Michael's second phone call had only lasted a minute.

All the same, it was all right for him, wasn't it: ringing up when it suited him. Of course, she could never ring him. That was strictly forbidden, though she knew his phone number by heart – and the address of his house, which she had never seen. Once she'd felt tempted to go up to Muswell Hill and just walk past – just once – but she'd dismissed this idea as too adolescent even for her. All the same – he hadn't even said when he'd see her again. Izzy stared at the phone.

She picked up the receiver, suddenly daring. If Louise answered, she could pretend it was a wrong number. She could ask for – let's see, she could ask for – Diane Clifton. Izzy had known a girl called Diane Clifton at school and the name had always appealed to her as the perfect alias: pure *Girls' Own Paper*. Izzy began to dial the forbidden number. Her heart, back in its usual place, began to hammer. Far away, in the unknown house, she could hear the phone ring.

'Michael Tristram.'

'Michael – it's Izzy.'

'Hello, Bill,' said Michael with frosty geniality.

'I take it Louise is right there in the room with you?'

'That's right. Is there some trouble about the filming schedule?'

'Oh God, I'm so sorry, Michael, but you rang off just now, and we hadn't arranged to meet anywhere, and I'm longing to see you – isn't there any chance at all of our meeting in the next few days?'

'Shouldn't think so, mate. Hang on, I'll get my diary.'

A pause. Izzy/Bill waited, her/his senses tingling. Michael's voice, under the assumed nonchalance, was tense and angry. Izzy felt guilty, rebellious, scared and full of love.

19

'Hello – Bill?'

'Yes?'

'How about a drink after work on Thursday?'

'Really? Oh Michael!' Her eyes filled with silly tears. 'Does this mean you'll come over to my place after work? Really?'

'Yeah – that'll be fine. See you in the bar, then, Bill. Try and get hold of Gerry – we'll need to ask him about the credits.'

'My God, Michael, you're as cool as a cucumber.'

'All right, mate – say hello to the wife and kids. Must dash. Louise is waiting.' And he was gone.

Izzy was shaking, but she had got her date. A little late maybe, but her ideal Christmas present. She dived into a vast old fur coat that smelt like a very ill dog, and had probably been one, once. Clever Michael! What a nerve he had! How elegantly he deceived: what an actor, what style, what poise.

It did not occur to the adoring Izzy that he might have had a lot of practice.

Frumpy in her rank old fur, Izzy emerged into the snows, her heart aglow, in the grand old tradition of British explorers. What did it matter if she looked frumpy tonight? St Michael was, for the present, safely tucked up in Muswell Hill, and as for the attendant lords waiting for her at Maria's – well, she rather liked the idea of looking frumpy for them. It was a tribute to her in-loveness. Like Hamlet, she disdained the refinements of dress. She was chic at heart.

2

Maria and Gwyn lived in Notting Hill. Not far away on bike or even on foot in summer, but today all the snows of January drove Izzy down to the tube. She arrived to find Maria chopping up aubergines. She excelled at getting the bitter juices out of them: perhaps they felt they just couldn't compete. At the other end of the kitchen Gwyn was surrounded by herbs, spices, saucepans and gristly bits of meat. Like many men, he enjoyed showing off his culinary skills – which usually involved transforming the visceral into the venomous. In the process he'd use a dozen saucepans, and leave white sauce all over the ceiling and bits of pork fat gleaming on the cooker, like the aftermath of some weird orgy.

'Hulloa darlin'! 'Ave a good Christmas, didyew? You look glorious!' He beamed benignly at Izzy's bosom. Perhaps he thought it the only part of her worth addressing. It must be said in his defence, though, that Gwyn was wall-eyed. It complemented his Byronic good looks: that touch of ruin that kindles a wantonness in beauty. It was Gwyn's proud claim that he could look at a woman's breasts with one eye and her legs with the other. Maria insisted that her husband was a feminist: Izzy privately thought that fetishist was nearer the mark. They were hardly into the first post-Christmas condolences when the phone rang.

'Let's hope they've got flu,' spat Maria as Gwyn went to answer it. She seemed more hostile than ever to her unsuspecting guests.

'Who did you say they were, Maria?' inquired Izzy gently.

'Search me. They're nothing to do with me,' Maria snapped. 'They're Gwyn's friends, not mine. No, they're not even his friends, they're only his colleagues, and he asked them to dinner when he was drunk at the pre-Christmas party, then he forgets to tell me until mid-after-bleeding-noon! On the way back from Wales! That we've got people coming round *tonight*!'

'Never mind,' consoled Izzy. 'They might be nice.'

'I don't care if they're as nice as apple-bloody-pie. It's being condemned to an evening with them, without warning, whether I want to or not, that drives me round the bend.'

'Well, let's go out, then. We could go to the pictures,' suggested Izzy. 'Let Gwyn entertain them on his own.'

'Oh, don't be so stupid, Izzy. How could I? That would be cheating. Come on, now. This is one of the grisly little rituals of marriage. You'll have to accept it – and permit me my grisly little groan.'

'Well, do shut up soon,' urged Izzy, beaming. 'It's getting boring.' And she ate a slice of raw aubergine.

'Hey, girls!' Gwyn returned from the phone like a conquering hero. 'Guess what? F'ntastic news, mon! My cousin Hywel's comin'. 'E came up from Wales yesterday on the train – 'E just rang up from some pub in Paddington, now, like, and 'e reckons 'e can be yere by nine.'

Maria's face was suffused with a murderous brightness and she plunged her knife into the heart of the wholemeal loaf. Izzy, another innocent bystander, was glad the loaf had been around.

'That does it!' yelled Maria, and Izzy relaxed. With Maria, *That does it* was always the prelude to collapse and acquiescence.

'What's he coming for?'

'He's been laid off – so he's coming to London to

look for a job. Great, isna'?'

'Where's he going to sleep?'

'Oh, I dunnoa – on the sofa? In the bath? Or maybe he'd like to couch up with yew, darlin' – on the nights I'm too drunk, like. He's always fancied you. Says you've got the best legs east of Neath.'

'Bullshit,' said Maria, with a face like ammonia, and went back to butchering the aubergines.

'You'll like Hywel, sweetheart,' Gwyn confided to Izzy, throwing an armpit around her. 'He used to play for Neath. And he's bloody good-lookin'. All the women are mad about him, mon. They used to stow away on his lorry just to get a glimpse of the back of 'is neck.'

'And he's your cousin?'

'Well, sorta. More like a second cousin, twice removed.'

'And twice replaced,' added Maria quietly. Gwyn went back to his culinary labours, and the women retired, with a bottle of wine, to the sofa.

'What's wrong with this Hywel bloke, then?' inquired Izzy.

Maria leaned back and closed her eyes. 'He's from the South Wales Coalfields, right? Known as the Pits. And tonight you'll find òut why.'

'Can't wait! Have another drink, Maria. It sounds as if you'll need it.'

'You know,' mused Maria, as the alcohol began to reach her remoter outposts and she relaxed into her doom instead of resisting it, 'you know – if there's less and less work, and more and more leisure, and more leisure means more dinner parties, I think I shall throw myself off the kitchen table.'

'Oh, come on. Dinner parties are fun, sometimes.'

'I would rather,' Maria chose her words with care, 'spend six Friday afternoons *in a row* with 5C than preside over the evening which is about to break on us.'

In the face of such hideous warnings, Izzy could only

fall silent, and nerve herself up for the ordeal. Still, Maria might be exaggerating. She'd won a scholarship at Oxford ten years ago for exaggerating, and it had suited her quite well ever since.

Maria was not exaggerating. Her foresight was extraordinary: as black as accurate. Bonnie and Dave arrived with priggish promptness at eight, bearing a bottle of nasty sweet wine. Bonnie (and by God, she was) glowed: Dave glowered, and that the first phenomenon in some way provoked the second was not for a moment in doubt. For at Bonnie's entrance so many hackles rose so high that for a moment the roof trembled. She was peachy, glowing, with her dinky little Fra Angelico curls framing her perfect, pretty, porky little face. Her itsy-bitsy lacey-printy smock billowed in the lamplight, and her convex cheeks gleamed. She was luminous with maternity.

'Puke!' muttered Maria at the pork, as she coaxed it out of the oven. Izzy, manhandling the ratatouille, did not dare to contradict. Though she was not quite sure whether Maria was complimenting the dinner or the guests.

As they ate, the conversation fell winded to the table, pinned and gasping beneath the weight of Bonnie's mighty, maternal monologue. '. . . it's so easily done isn't it – Sarah fell down today in the garden and got dirt in the grazes on her knees, but she was everso brave really, she didn't cry at all. Though I say so myself, she's got a nice little personality, and I don't think she'll be all that difficult when this one comes along.' (Here she patted her tumescent belly – not nearly hard enough, in Maria's view. You can't begin this discipline business too soon.) '. . . though you never know, do you? You just can't tell, they surprise you all the time, don't they? I mean, I did have a really close relationship with Sarah right from the start, she was on the breast for eighteen months . . .'

Not even the mention of mammaries could rouse

24

Gwyn from his contemplation of the table mats. And as for the wretched Dave, when the pudding appeared, he gazed into his chocolate mousse like a man who longs to dive into it and disappear for ever. By now Bonnie had launched into her aria *Great bargains I alone have discovered*, pausing once, in the midst of a paeon of praise to bulk-bought bog rolls, to ask Maria with sudden dramatic emphasis, 'What do you think of Marks and Sparks flan cases?'

Maria's brave old eyes flashed briefly in their aching sockets. 'I never think of them at all.'

Bonnie did not repeat her mistake. 'Oh, you really should try them,' she warbled gaily, 'I used to use them eversuch a lot, in fact I used to bake every first Monday in the month and stock the freezer, but we have to be a bit careful now Dave's got his ulcer, haven't you darling?'

Dave was manically smearing mousse into every corner of his plate.

'I always think it was that West Indian restaurant we went to that set it off, darling. We should never have gone there. Not that I'm prejudiced or anything; no really, I love them and their culture, they're so warm and full of life aren't they, but you can't be too careful, and—'

At this point Hywel Evans rang, or rather fell against, the doorbell downstairs and Gwyn hastened out to meet his cousin. Izzy guessed that Hywel was about to receive his warmest welcome ever, for Maria was gazing at the door with the paralysed desperation of the stranded missionary in the cooking pot. She felt more like the first course than the hostess: Bonnie was triumphing over the evening like a glowing vampire. The more the others wilted and paled, the more she shone, billowed and exulted. Could Hywel save the day? Had he brought his garlic and crucifix? All eyes were turned expectantly his way.

Izzy thought all Welshmen were small and stocky

like Gwyn, but when Hywel walked in, everything went dark. Gwyn was clinging to his cousin's huge frame like a flea on a racehorse.

'Great to see you, mon! Great! You're lookin' good – reely 'andsome, isn't he, Izzy? I told yew, girl.'

Hywel gangled pleasantly in the ionosphere, nodded to the assembled company and murmured ''Loa. 'Loa. 'Loa.' Then he folded himself down on to the sofa, with some relief, as if escaping from vertigo.

'I think yew've bloody well *grown*, mon! How's Neath? Couldn't get there at Christmas – I was too pissed to move. 'Ow's old Evans? Still banging his head against a brick wall?'

'Orright. Not much.'

This was the first of many gnomic exchanges, which were to veil South Wales in an even deeper mystery for Izzy as the evening progressed. Was Wayne still at it? Sort of. What about old Annie? Orright. And who replaced Owen in the team this season? Not that fuckin' useless Meredith for Christ's sake, oh no no NO! Had the Council made that sly old bastard up at Llanfair knock 'is bloody eyesore down yet? Yeah. Noah. Orright. Dunnoah.

Hywel, invited to clear up the last of the feast, placed both elbows squarely on the table, chewed like a cow and belched like a power station. At a quarter to ten he took his first initiative: an inquiry about the possibility of any 'serious drinkin' this evenin''. Gwyn immediately ran out into the night and returned loaded with six-packs. Somewhere, in an obscure dark place, the evening was being reclaimed. The gods of disorder were gliding back. Dave revived from his terminal depression and raised his eyes unto the Pils. Bonnie began to sulk, and secretly to conjure up a pregnancy ailment which would speedily remove them from the scene. Hywel lowered his lower lip at Izzy and inquired whether she was married at all.

'Not too much, like!' carolled Gwyn. 'Our luscious

26

Isabelle is up for grabs. Now's your big chance, mon. Get in there.'

'For God's sake, Gwyn!' Maria remonstrated, but he was already out of reach.

'What's the matter, girl? Yew think we don't know how to behave? Lissen. We're well brought up boys. Hywel's ma always belts 'im with a wooden spoon when 'e farts.'

Bonnie turned to Dave, and hissed, in a deafening martyr's whisper, that she felt one of her nasty thingies coming on. Suddenly the autistic Dave leapt into dramatic action. He threw back his chair and jumped to his feet. Izzy cringed, half expecting him to seize the chicken brick and brain his beloved with it. But no, nothing so rational was in store. He spoke.

'All right, sweetheart, we'd better be going.'

A quiet, measured, gentle voice. The voice of madness if ever it echoed among Maria's coffee cups. And so the maddened Dave helped his sickening sweetheart downstairs.

'Mind 'ow you goa!' yelled Gwyn after them.

'Nice-lookin' woman,' commented Hywel. 'Can't compete with present company, of course,' he added, leering genially at Izzy and then, with chivalrous inclusiveness, at Maria.

'We can do without these patronizing remarks, thank you,' said Maria, but smilingly. Speak for yourself, thought Izzy, and shot Hywel one of her extra-special looks. It would've fried the forelock off a weaker man. Not that Izzy was at all interested in Hywel of course. She was, as we know, in love with Another. But when you know that the Other is at this very moment in the arms of his beloved Louise (or Louse, as Izzy preferred to think of her) – well, a few agreeable sheep's eyes with a handsome Welshman couldn't do any harm, could they?

'My God, my God,' Maria intoned feebly to the dirty plates. She couldn't believe that Bonnie and Dave had actually been exorcised – and by Hywel! All things must have a use after all, she mused.

Izzy thought drunkenly of Michael, but then gazed at Hywel instead. He did have several things going for him. Height and silence for a start. Sometimes she thought her taste in men derived from an early fascination with church architecture.

Soon afterwards, she said she must go. Hywel looked hurt, but he would obviously be around for aeons, rather like Ely Cathedral. Izzy looked forward to a guided tour sometime.

'Don't forget the Japanese thing at eleven,' instructed Maria.

Izzy and Maria had agreed to sign on for a course of strenuous Oriental aerobics. Izzy wouldn't forget. She needed the exercise.

'I'm so fat!' she wailed, walloping her beam.

'Rubbish, darlin',' cried Gwyn. 'You are what can only be described as truly delectable to my tired old eyes at least. We like women with a bit o' flesh on them, don't we, Hywel?'

'I think yew're bewtiful,' intoned Hywel reverently.

So, just in time to catch the last tube home, Izzy went away, still in her grubby jeans and sweatshirt, but on the whole, slightly more pleased with life.

Back home, she surveyed her delicious eyrie with its faithful mess. Ah, the freedom: to go to bed when she liked. To stay up all night if she liked. To play music if she liked, and the music she liked, if she did. She got undressed slowly, reading a copy of *Vogue* (she must remember to hide it next time Maria came round). She must also remember to do the washing up. And the washing. And the marking of the essays. And wipe the bits of éclair off the fender. But for the time being she would go to bed, in her delicious freedom. In bed, she stretched, she sighed, she left a candle burning, she indulged herself by staring into it, and seeing, in its depths, Michael Tristram's tiger grin. And then, in the midst of all this pleasure, she felt a stab of pain. She was, after all, alone.

3

It had been Maria's idea to go to the Japanese exercises. She'd waved a pamphlet at Izzy. It was only twenty quid for eight sessions.

'This is what we need,' she promised. 'Japanese exercises, taught by the Master, Hideki Shehito.'

'Headachy what?' had been Izzy's initial response, and she was still far from enthusiastic about the scheme. But Maria reckoned it would improve their physical tone and their spiritual welfare. She was attracted by systems, disciplines and philosophies. But then, she had always been a clever girl, unlike Izzy, who'd scraped a bare Third at Birmingham University. Izzy would've been happier about philosophies if she could have eaten them. As it was, she accepted Maria's advice about her spiritual welfare, and about many other matters, much too uncritically. Sometimes, though, she did healthily conceal things from her, as we know.

As she stumbled out into the January morning, slipping on frozen slush, this exercise business seemed rather a silly idea. Maria was waiting outside the church hall: early, as usual. Izzy was not late, for once, but then she hadn't realized that the church hall, tucked away in the backwaters of Ladbroke Grove, would be so easy to find. She would be late next time, in her complacency.

'Hello.' Maria's eyes were bright. She looked as if she were in the grip of an idea. 'Got your leg warmers? I bet it's freezing in there. This is just what we need, Izzy.'

'You keep saying that,' complained Izzy. 'What I need is to go back to bed.'

'No, don't be so wet. This will be the making of us. Shake off our stupid Western assumptions. The Eastern attitude to exercise is much more in tune with Nature. None of this jogging nonsense. This stupid macho squash-playing.'

Izzy felt rather hurt. Michael played squash regularly – though not as often as his wife thought.

'We must try to shed the blinkers of our Western late-capitalist bourgeois conditioning. I wish this bugger would hurry up, I'm freezing to the pavement.'

They looked around for the Master, but there was no sign of Hideki. A wan crowd of enthusiasts waited, muffled, on the church steps.

'Can't we go in and warm up?' Maria asked a nearby girl.

'He brings the key,' was the gnomic reply. So they waited, shivering.

Somewhere across the distant traffic a clock struck eleven, and up the steps came a small Japanese man, his face impassive, the muscles in his jaw working slightly. He did not greet his disciples; he did not look to left or right. He produced a key from the depths of his pale green tracksuit and unlocked the door. Before going inside, he leaned over and spat out a piece of chewing gum into a pot of dwarf conifers. Not exactly in tune with Nature, thought Izzy, as she followed him inside, mingling with his flock.

The church hall was icy cold and smelt of long-past jumble sales. The Master switched on the neon lighting, kicked off his flip-flops and walked barefoot without flinching across the permafrost of the stone floor. Izzy began to feel a deep sense of foreboding. But it was too late.

They warmed up with some exercises traditionally performed by Shinto priests at dawn. One consisted of holding your hands high above your head and crying, 'Haigh!' and then thrusting them down to knee level

31

and howling 'Chua!' You had to do this every second or so, on and on and on, and you had to do it with your eyes shut. 'Haigh-Chua! Haigh-Chua! Haigh-Chua! Haigh-Chua!' Izzy dared not peep. They sounded like an ancient train puffing its way up a mountainside. 'Haigh-Chua! Haigh-Chua! Haigh-Chua! Izzy carolled. Arms up, arms down, arms up, arms down. When was the Master going to tell them to stop? Where *was* the bloody Master anyway? Gone off to the pub? An elegant little Oriental trick to sneak off for a snorter, leaving a roomful of silly English trendies going Haigh-Chua! Haigh-Chua! with their eyes shut in a freezing church hall. Izzy opened half an eye. All she saw was a few square feet of mouldy wall. Haigh-Chua! Haigh-Chua! Oh, she thought, if only I was that wall. Oh wall, oh wall, oh sweet and lovely wall, fall on this Chink; his time has come to die.

'All Light,' announced Hideki, a month later. They stopped, and Izzy could feel her body split apart and roll off in opposite directions into far corners of the room. She knew Maria was behind her somewhere, but she didn't dare turn round to look.

'Now, exercise of bleathing, arso tladitionary performed at temple at daybleak.' What was wrong with these wretched Shinto priests, getting up at dawn and flogging themselves to within an inch of their lives? Why couldn't they sit and stare blearily at the wall and toy limply with their muesli like everybody else? But no. They had to rise onto tip-toe, draw in an immense breath, then hold it and count to two hundred. *Two hundred?* thought Izzy, teetering slightly on the tips of her toes. *Two hundred?* Without releasing your breath? You must be joking.

She found that by holding her ribcage expanded and slipping tiny sips of air in surreptitiously around the edges of her nostrils she could cheat quite easily at this one, unlike Haigh-Chua! When the Master reached his two hundred, and fell forward off his cast-iron toes with a great tearing gasp for breath, all his followers fell with him. Including Izzy. She was, if not anxious to oblige, eager to escape detection. She would lie, cheat – anything – anything to get her to one o'clock without dying. The Master had other ideas.

'Risten to body,' he intoned. 'Your body ter you what it want.'

Izzy's body wanted to stop all this nonsense at once and go and have a cup of chocolate in a sunny café somewhere.

Ah, no! *Die, English Dog* seemed to be the order of the day, as the tiny tyrant launched into another series of spine-shattering exercises. This time they had to hurl themselves on to the floor and sink their teeth into their own backsides. The Master picked his way daintily among his tortured aficionados. He paused by Izzy. She made a superhuman effort to bite her bum.

'Velly stiff back,' scolded Hideki, and gave her a slight kick in the kidneys. 'No force. Risten to body.'

Blooming heck, thought Izzy, *and I paid twenty quid for this. I must be completely off my rocker.* If indeed, after all this, there was any rocker left.

After more exercises too horrible to mention, they sat in a circle and the Master taught them the first line of a Japanese song. It was something about the mayfly hovering above the almond blossom, and it went, 'Chghoua – hng – Ch Hau'ng – T'ang-gggggghue-choimmmmmn-mnnnghuaw.' When the Master sang it, in his curious cracked nasal voice, his whole face buckled and grimaced, and it sounded like a message from the windiest precipices in the world. When Izzy sang it, she had to translate it in her head into a silly little rhyme about Chua and Chang having a gang-bang or she couldn't even remember the words. If they were words. It all seemed so strange, they probably weren't even words at all. Her feet were certainly no longer feet. She'd only been sitting on them for five minutes, but already they'd turned into a couple of rather bad-

33

tempered hedgehogs.

At last, at last, one o'clock came.

'OK. Is enough for today,' said the Master, bestowing on his victims a dinky nod.

Is enough for the next three thousand years, thought Izzy, pulling on her darling old warm socks. The delicious, comforting woolly feel of them almost made her cry with relief. She wanted to crawl right inside her left sock and curl up there, and never come out again. Maria appeared at her side, shoes and socks all correct, her face a pale mask, but a heretic raging in her eye.

'Jesus Christ!' she burst as they walked out into the welcome frost. 'What *was* that? Revenge for Hiroshima? My God, Izzy, I don't think I can walk as far as the nearest caff. I'll have to die right here on the pavement.'

'The worst bit,' mused Izzy, 'was not being able to stop while it was going on. Not being able to say, Gosh, sorry, I didn't realize it was going to be like this – or, Sorry, I've just remembered I've left the oven on, and just rush out. Or even just rush out.'

'Ah, well, that's crowd psychology, isn't it? That's how these totalitarian dictators get to power. They know how to manipulate crowds by fear, so that even if you have a healthy impulse to protest, you don't, because you're afraid of what the rest of the crowd will think of you. Thank God, there's a MacBurgers.'

Whatever else may be said about MacBurgers, at least they do serve hot chocolate – even if it is in paper throw-away cups. To Izzy and Maria, who at that moment possessed paper throw-away legs, it seemed a fitting place for their convalescence.

'Why do we let ourselves in for things like that?' wondered Izzy, kindly taking part of the blame.

'Oh, I don't know. Human beings enjoy suffering, I suppose.'

'I don't.' Izzy settled comfortably into sipping her

chocolate, happy for the first time that day. She allowed herself a brief thought of Michael – not more, for Michael was one of the things she concealed from Maria. She'd have to tell her one day, of course – and how she longed to tell. For until we tell our friends of our love, it lacks an important dimension: our sense of its insignificance.

The sun came out. A beam shot down through the steamy café and landed on Maria's cropped head. Her black hair gleamed, and she was looking happier by the second.

'I love these beams of sunlight when you're sitting in cafés,' Izzy basked. 'It makes sitting drinking chocolate so much more naughty when you know that outside some poor fool's playing tennis, or jogging.'

'I may have been rather hard on jogging,' admitted Maria. 'But I'm sure the East does hold the answer. It's Japan that's all wrong. A nasty, militaristic oligarchy, now I come to think of it. I should've realized.'

'What does oligarchy mean – I can't remember. Anyway,' continued Izzy, not really interested in oligarchies, 'I'm beginning to feel wonderful.' Her body was beginning to hum, as if released energies, long dammed-up, were at last a-flowing. 'Yes, you know, Maria, I'm beginning to feel absolutely marvellous.'

'It's the chocolate.'

'No, it isn't – it's Headachy's exercises, I'm sure. My body feels sort of winged. Wonderful. Don't you feel it?'

Maria wouldn't, yet. Instead she was looking rather closely at Izzy's complexion, which the sunbeam had thrown into alarming relief.

'How's your love-life?' she asked abruptly. Izzy was dropped on.

'Er – well, OK. Nothing special, you know.'

'Same old guys? Ben-now-and-then and the cynical dentist?'

'Well, no, I haven't seen the cynical dentist for a while.'

'Who is it, then?'

'Who's what?' Izzy blushed, and looked as guilty as possible. Even guiltier than necessary, really. What a good job it was Michael, not Izzy, who had to deceive a spouse, with the many agilities it demanded.

'Who's the man of the moment? And why aren't you telling me about him? Is he married?'

'Of course not,' blustered Izzy. 'Don't be daft. Would I go around with a married man?'

'You bet your sweet life you would. I just hope it's not someone at school. It's not that new pottery bloke, Dick, is it? I know he's sweet on you, Izzy, but really—'

'Ugh, no! Not Dick! Never, ever!' Izzy was genuinely insulted. To compare modest Dick with Michael was high sacrilege.

'Well, who is it, then? It must be someone you're ashamed of. Is he too old? Or too young? Or a bike-boy? Or does he make you dress up in suspender belts and all that junk?'

'Don't be silly,' evaded Izzy, realizing that the time had come. She really was rather proud of Michael, and would enjoy revealing his identity. All the same, something in her cringed. She knew Maria all too well.

'Oh, all right, if you must know. Do you remember that bloke who came to do a programme for BBC Schools last term? They filmed some of my 2C drama.'

'No.'

'Oh, come on, Maria, you know you remember. You said he was dishy.'

'What – the one with the bald patch?'

'Well, yes, if you insist, he does have a bald patch. But he does also have wonderful shoulders and magnetizing green eyes and he's very fit – not a trace of a paunch.'

'OK, OK – you're not trying to sell him, are you? So when did all this start?'

'Er, well – at the time, really. More or less at the time.'

'And you've been carrying on for over two months, and I never knew!' Maria sounded miffed.

Izzy felt partly guilty, partly triumphant.

'Just wait till Janet hears about this. She always said how transparent you were, Izzy. You're a dark horse!'

'No – you mustn't tell Janet. You mustn't tell anyone. It's a big secret.'

'Oh yeah? And why, may I ask? No – don't tell me – he's married.'

'Well, yes, all right, yes, he is married. But, Maria—'

'So it's the good old secret affair, is it? Honestly, Izzy, you must be mad. When did you last see him?'

'Oh – some time before Christmas. Well, it's hard, with the school holidays and things.'

'So he's got kids, too?'

'One. A boy called Jack. He's six.'

'Oh, Izzy, Izzy! Ask yourself: is he worth it? He's never going to leave his wife, is he?'

'Well, we're playing it by ear.' Izzy was struck by how naïve and familiar it all sounded in public. 'We just want to give it time. To sort of find its own shape.'

'Which means he won't leave his wife. Let's hope he won't, anyway. You know my feelings where kids are involved, Izzy.'

'I know.'

'Look at it quite simply and dispassionately. The whole thing's a can of worms.'

'Well, marriage is a stupid and disgusting idea in the first place.'

'Is it? What would you do, if your media whizz-kid was free? You'd want to live with him, right?'

'Well – yes.'

'Then what if you had a kid? Just stay living together?'

'Oh, I don't know,' shrugged Izzy wearily. Hideki's exercises were beginning to wear off, after all: she had a grinding sense of her own inadequacy. 'I don't want to think about it – not like this, at any rate.'

'Oh no, of course not. You just want to perpetuate this dreadful system in which you count for nothing, you just pander to his vanity, he gives you an hour or two when he feels like it, he's in this wonderful position of having his cake and eating it, with two women at his beck and call. I bet you even wait in sometimes, on the off chance that he'll ring.'

'Come off it! I'm not that far gone. Anyway, it *is* hard for him. It's awful for him. It's an incredibly painful situation all round.'

'Don't give me that. People get what they want. If they get suffering, that's what they really want.'

'That can't be true.' Izzy's argumentative powers were beginning to flag.

'You're being used, Izzy, and you're abusing and deceiving another woman. This is not right, surely?'

'So women deserve our loyalty, always, automatically, in preference to men? What about Bonnie last night?'

'Oh God – don't remind me. Some people like to torture, and some to feel pain, that's all.'

'But it's the institution of marriage that's wrong, surely, Maria! It's marriage, in some way, that's ruined Bonnie. Her maternal role and all that. The flipping freezer and stuff. Marriage is the enemy, isn't it?'

Maria toyed with her empty paper cup. 'Well, we do live in the world, Izzy. We have to work with what we find. But we must try to be honest.'

Izzy had the feeling that they were both being dishonest – driven to it by their desires and needs, but she couldn't put her feelings into words. But she knew what was next on the menu – an advertisement for Maria's marriage.

'That's the thing about Gwyn and me. All right, we're both fallible human beings. We have rows, we get on badly – God knows the saucepans fly often enough. But at least we're honest.'

'Are you?'

'If Gwyn wants to have an affair – *when* Gwyn wants to have an affair – he'll tell me. And vice versa. And I'd respect that and control my jealousy – if I felt any. It's the only way to handle it.'

'Well, I admire you,' lied Izzy. 'I wish I had your guts. I couldn't share Michael. I'd scratch his wretched wife's eyes out if I had the chance.'

Really, though, Izzy pitied Maria – for not, apparently, feeling the same all-encompassing passion as herself. *My jealousy – if I feel any*, indeed! Did anything like blood flow in Maria's veins?

They left the café, and parted at the tube, feeling chilled and unsatisfactory.

'I didn't mean to get at you just now,' mumbled Maria. 'Don't take it to heart. It's only 'cos I care for you.' And, leaving, she gave Izzy the curt nod of true love. Izzy, still feeling bruised, sought her train. She hated that kind of argument. Maria loved arguments, had relished them at Oxford: for her they were a kind of painless flexing of muscles. Izzy had never got the hang of them, always felt attacked, and ended up either in a rage or depressed. She was depressed now, because she felt that in many ways Maria was absolutely right, but that she was somehow leaving out something vitally important. What was it? Izzy puzzled over it, and was only soothed when she got home, and awarded herself an extra slice of chocolate cake. A consolation prize.

She found Maria's view of jealousy unimaginable. Maybe Maria and Gwyn had been married for so long that they had lost all passion, and with it possessiveness. Izzy simply could not imagine being without her jealousy. Sometimes she could hardly bear to hear Michael uttering Louise's name; it sounded so like a caress on his lips. And the fantasies she'd evolved for Louise's annihilation! Izzy was a tender-hearted creature, who'd trap a spider under a cup and release it out on to the roof rather than kill it. She was even kind to wasps, opening the windows and asking them politely to leave. And as for mice – well, she'd invented the Liberal's Mousetrap to deal with that little problem. A cereal box, baited with muesli, artfully stationed by the skirting board. When a scrabbling came from within, she pounced – but only to carry the box carefully downstairs and release the bemused mouse outside the back of one of the all-night delicatessens in the Earl's Court Road.

Faced with the robust health of Louise Tristram and her little son, however, Izzy was ruthless. She'd gone in for car crashes at first. A mangled, charred ruin on Muswell Hill, with kindly ambulance men murmuring, 'She couldn't have felt a thing.' But Izzy's better nature did assert itself, and Louise's subsequent deaths became more and more comfortable. A mysterious illness, which made her feel absolutely wonderful, and the very next moment, stone dead. A tile blown off a roof in a gale which decapitated Louise, walking below, on her way back from Harrod's where she'd just spent a small fortune – an inheritance from a great aunt. 'Death was instantaneous,' crooned the coroner, each time. Louise ate a tin of bad salmon which eased her into a gentle coma and thence into the next world . . . Louise's house blew up, ten minutes after Michael had left for work, because of a faulty gas valve, killing Louise, Jack, and the gerbils in a split second . . . Louise was vapourized by a passing UFO . . .

At length Izzy dreamed up a more humane and satisfying solution. Louise would run out on Michael.

She would have an affair with the Director of the Art School where she worked part-time. No – she would go further afield. She would run off with a French explorer and disappear for ever into darkest Africa, taking Jack with her. He would have a wonderful childhood there with all the scorpions and things. Much more wonderful than if he'd stayed in boring old Muswell Hill with his balding dad. And certainly more wonderful than if he'd been blown up by a faulty gas valve.

Tormented by guilt because of her fantasies, Izzy called the Gas Board in to have a look at her own valves. It would be just like life, she thought, to get blown up yourself for having such thoughts. She was sometimes aware of an Eye watching her every move. Not God, or anything crass like that, of course. 'OK, OK,' she'd say to the Eye, 'I will start behaving well soon. I'll just finish this cake first.' Sometimes, Maria seemed to take on the role of the Eye. Izzy couldn't decide if she wanted Maria's cleverness exploded, so they'd feel more like equals. On the other hand, Maria's unfailing wisdom somehow made it easier for Izzy to be self-indulgently foolish.

And boy, was she self-indulgently foolish on Thursday afternoon! She expected Michael at six, but her preparations began at two. Well, actually they began that morning, when she went out and bought herself a new dress in the sales. It was ridiculous, really: Michael never seemed to notice what she wore. Indeed, he usually tore it off her within thirty seconds of entering her flat. But Izzy didn't so much buy new dresses for him as to celebrate with herself her sense of occasion at seeing him. So she bought the dress. It was brown velour, very clingy, and she had to remember to hold her stomach in when standing sideways to the object of her affection. If only she could have held her bum in, too. This cake business would have to stop.

At two, Izzy embarked on a frenzy of clearing up. At

last the apple core and E. M. Forster parted company: though the book retained a small poignant stain to commemorate their liaison. The fender lost its smear of éclair. The tights were whisked away. The Hoover devoured the microscopic debris of Izzy's life: the crumbs, the flakes of skin. Of her skin and of Michael's skin. They mingled in the depths of the machine. The flat became a boudoir: freesias added their scent to the hyacinths, and the lights were turned down low. The cushions were plumped up, and the sofa and bed cleared for action – though Michael often disdained them both, preferring the challenges of the kitchen table, the bathroom windowsill and, on one memorable occasion, the stairs outside her door (they were dark, and Izzy's was the last flat). He was waiting impatiently for summer, for Izzy had a balcony.

At three Izzy sank into her bath, looking like Albert Schweitzer as she was wearing a great white moustache of bleach-cream. (You shouldn't really use it in the bath, but Izzy hadn't read the instructions properly.) She shaved her legs, pumiced them, gave herself a face pack, plucked her eyebrows, washed her hair, and painted her toenails red. Then she had to spend a long time soothing her irritated and angry eyebrows, legs and upper lip. If she had thought of Hideki's instructions to Risten to Body, she might have heard a few home truths about Michael Tristram. Yet if her body resented all the plucking and bleaching and shaving that went on for him, it certainly also reacted to his presence, his voice, even the very thought of him, in a remarkable way, producing juices, electric shocks, tingling, and occasionally, at moments of greatest excitement, the sense that she was falling over a black and velvety precipice, down towards Paradise.

At five she was ready: the black suspenders in place, the glassy-smooth Hanes stockings (American imports and wildly expensive – but Michael paid), the French knickers and the stiletto heels. For though Michael

42

Tristram was a man dedicated to natural brown rice and natural wholemeal bread, though his Muswell Hill garden was innocent of all fertilizer save horse manure, though his floors and doors were natural wood and his curtains sun-bleached cotton, when it came to women what he wanted was the pale, protected flesh, the sinister black lace, the crippling shoes. Izzy apparently understood. Unlike Louise, who was addicted to stripey woollen vests and the repulsive, neutering leotard. Actually, Izzy didn't understand at all, and flew back to her own woolly vests and leotards the minute he disappeared. But while he was with her, she collaborated. She thought it was the way to win his heart entirely. Silly Izzy. And she had read such a lot of books, too.

From six till six thirty she would've paced up and down her flat, if she could've walked at all in her stilettos. Instead her nervousness led her, disastrously, to pick her spots. When at last she realized what she was doing she gave a shriek of horror, ran to the bathroom, plastered more make-up on, and then turned the lights down even lower. What a wonderful investment those dimmer switches had been! At last, at six forty, the doorbell rang. His voice, distorted yet ineffably, desperately his, on the intercom: sounding like a sex-crazed Dalek. His feet thundering on the stairs. Her heart galloping as she teetered towards the door. She flung it open.

'Izzy.'

The room whirled, it whirled. Let us not blame them. Izzy's feet were not on the floor. It had taken two hours to dress and make up: within a minute her dress was in a crumpled heap in the hall, and her make-up had been eaten away. She could hardly breathe: he seemed everywhere: closer than her own blood, and as riotous. He inched his way towards the kitchen: ah, it was the turn of the kitchen chair. He sat on it, and drew her down upon him. The herbs and spices danced in her vision, at first, but then she had to close her eyes. She did not want a random label to spoil her delight. One does not want to catch sight of Sage and Onion Stuffing at such a time.

Afterwards, lying on the sofa in the scent of freesias (he had brought some more), she let her eyes feast on him. His own green eyes glinted at her. True, his hair was thinning, but so what? It was blond: he was tanned: he was tall. Besides, like Gwyn's squinty eyes, a small imperfection is the final delight. His beautiful square hands stroked her legs. Or did they stroke the Hanes stockings? They said little, and Izzy noticed that the longer their relationship continued, the less time they spent talking. It certainly was very carnal. And there was a lot of time spent looking.

'We ought to talk more,' she ventured gently. He ran his finger up her arm, along her shoulder, up her neck, along her jaw, and over her lips.

'Your lips,' he whispered, 'are the most sausagey I've ever seen.'

'But – don't you think we're a bit too – obsessed by our bodies?'

'Certainly not. In fact—' He paused, and moved closer, close enough for their breaths to beat gently on each other's faces. '—in fact my body thinks that's enough talk for the time being.'

Izzy listened to her body. It agreed.

4

All good things must come to an end: and so, sometimes, must the bad ones. The appalling Christmas holidays gave way, in the end, to the mis-named Spring Term. That term in which the sixty-two varieties of flu rage, the Deputy Head contemplates suicide and the earth seems sunk for ever in its iron sleep. Izzy and Maria taught in Islington. Izzy got the tube to Notting Hill, where Maria picked her up and drove with her usual horrifying dash down – or rather against – the Euston Road. One of the disadvantages of teaching in Islington was that the sun was in your eyes both on your way to school and your way home. Maria greeted this as a sign of the hostility of the universe: for Izzy it was an excuse for exotic sunglasses. In January, of course, there was more often than not no sun at all, only a kind of dismal veil of fog and fumes.

'How's what's-'is-name – your media man?' asked Maria with a most conciliatory smile, especially for 8.15 a.m.

'Michael. He's OK. I saw him on Thursday,' recorded Izzy proudly, yet conscious that to boast about a mere glimpse of the man she loved betrayed the poverty of her situation.

'Are you seeing anyone else, Izzy?'

'Well – not really. I've seen Ben a couple of times, but he's been on tour recently. Besides, I don't really feel like seeing anybody else.'

'Well, I think you should,' nagged Maria, swerving

alarmingly to avoid a sudden bollard. 'I don't think you should just hang around and be at his disposal, as if you were some kind of service – bastard!' This last endearment was addressed not to Izzy, nor even the absent Michael, but to a pushy Cortina.

'If you had a couple of other guys around, and he knew about it, I think you'd find things a lot easier.'

Izzy couldn't disagree. She could barely utter a sound that was not a prayer for survival. She'd forgotten, over the holidays, just how desperate Maria's driving was, and was now eating her purse in an effort to stay silent. Still, Maria was her friend, and what's a few shreds of leather between incisors?

'You could take up with Dick,' suggested Maria generously. 'And Hywel's obviously on the rampage and fancies you like mad. *Steamin'* was the word he used yesterday to describe his state.'

'It's very unlike you to try and fix me up with men,' wondered Izzy, thinking *Let me get there in one piece, Lord. I'm sorry about all those fantasies of child- and wife-murder. Punish me. Punish me, Lord. Only let me live.*

'Well, I know you, Izzy. You still appear to need the buggers. Your consciousness, if I may say so, hasn't yet been raised.'

'I think it's been lowered.' Izzy was half guilty and half defiant. 'Anyway, if you despise men so much, why are you living with one?'

'I use them,' boasted Maria. 'Anyway, I never said I despised them all. Gwyn is a good comrade and he's fun, and he mends things and anyway, why am I justifying my marriage to you?'

'I don't know,' said Izzy. 'Or perhaps you were justifying it to yourself?' She was rather pleased with this last thrust, and hadn't really expected it to sail so confidently out of her mouth.

'I don't know,' admitted Maria. 'But I've got to start thinking about History now. It's the Upper Sixth first lesson and my Dutch Republic is decidedly rusty.' They fell silent, avoided a bus by a millimetre, and Izzy discovered the excellent stratagem of closing her eyes. She wished she had thought of it before.

By some miracle they arrived, and entered the jostling tumult. School smelt different, somehow: slightly cleaner, as if the ferocious old tramp who passed for a caretaker had finally got around to scraping the worst of the chewing gum, blood and cabbage off the floor. There was that fresh but deadly atmosphere of the first day of term. Those members of staff who led lonely or thwarted lives were sitting up perkily in the staff room, telling silly jokes. Those who one would wish to know as friends were slumped, pale and defeated-looking, against the radiators. The afore-mentioned Dick, a pottery teacher from Derbyshire, who had been new last term, looked up as Izzy came in, and blushed. Izzy pretended not to see him and went straight over to the coffee machine. Presently First Bell rang out its brutal summons and they trooped off to their classes: some slinking like condemned men to the gallows, others strutting off like petty Hitlers towards certain triumphs.

Izzy strolled along, dreaming of seductions. She knew that what Maria had said was right. Her Christmas had been frittered away in idle waiting, on the off chance, to see a man she hardly knew, who belonged to somebody else (Izzy believed in *belonged to*). So why shouldn't she cultivate other lovers? Why not? It would certainly be more fun than consciousness-raising sessions and feminist theatre groups – the sort of thing Maria would resort to, in her position. Izzy liked seductions, and was quite good at them. The problem was, would she be too much in love to try? A distant sound broke upon her reveries: the fracas of her class, 4C (C for Comyn, not Cretin), engaged in its courtship displays, grooming rituals and territorial disputes. As the door opened, she could not make out how they managed to do so little, so loudly. They were much

47

given to libidinal lounging on the windowsills. The air was torpid with hormones.

''Ello, Miss Comyn! D'jer 'ave a nice Christmas, Miss? Like yer jeans Miss like yer pixie boots. SHRUP Gary! Watch out Miss. 'E's put a plastic dogturd underya desk. Immature ent 'e Miss ay.'

They grinned at her with a mixture of affection and contempt. She grinned back in self-defence. They were quite a groovy bunch of yobbos once you got over the initial shock of their appearance. Skinhead, acne-festooned Wayne Drinkwater, for example, or the towering, scarfaced Mark Newman, 'The Thing from the Swamp'. Or the vast restless bulk of Stephen Masters, who possessed the most camp and gossipy tongue in the school. As for her favourites (of course teachers have favourites – how do you think they get through the day?) – well, they sat together by the window, their chairs tipped well back, reading girlie mags and playing cards.

On the left: Jonathan James, blond, meltingly handsome in the brownshirt mould, almost totally illiterate and absolutely totally depraved. ('He's a dirty bugger, sir – he jerks off into the vacuum cleaner,' his little brother had confided to one of Izzy's colleagues.) On the right, with light green hair, an earring, a couple of tattoos, and a career of thrillingly daring crimes already behind him: Roger Razebrook, universally known as Razors.

By night, and always undetected, he Broke and Entered: by day he Thieved and Racketeered, but surprisingly often he turned up at school and always behaved like a perfect gentleman: carrying Izzy's books, silencing Stephen Masters' shrill monologues with an economical, 'Shut it, bumface,' and often requesting that Izzy should read Ted Hughes' poems to the class. The only thing that surprised her was that Ted Hughes hadn't already written a poem about

Razors himself – along with all the other pikes, tomcats and foxes.

The girls, of course, were all secretly at his feet. And count Izzy in – only she adored him so much that dissimulation was impossible, and she dropped her books and grinned foolishly at the mere sight of him. When he spoke (which was not often) the girls went quiet and giggled. And yet he appeared to have little interest in any of them. God knows why, for the girls of 4C were quite criminally beautiful. Yes, all of them – it was as if the normal thunderbolts of adolescence had been somehow turned aside and melted by their sheer grace. Never mole, hare lip nor scar, nor mark prodigious such as are despised in discothèquery upon her Vestals did she see. At least, she hoped they were Vestals. She had her doubts about Lorraine. But then Lraine came from an unusually flamboyant Broke Nome.

The beauty of Izzy's girls provoked in her some pride and not a little envy. At their age she had been barrel-chested, splay-footed, whacking-thighed and greater-spotted. And was so still. Her only outstanding features were all too much so: a baroque bosom and what Michael had referred to admiringly as sausagey lips. Her bust was the bane of her life. She wished people would avert their eyes from it, but this would often necessitate going right around the corner. She was stuck with it – and no amount of caftans and fluorescent socks (to distract attention away to other areas) was going to work.

Mind you, I could try slimming a bit, she thought, admiring her stable of fleet, sleek girls as they whispered their scintillating secrets while the boys thumped and lumbered among the desks. ('Phwaugh, Miss – Dooley's dropped one – open the winder, Newman!') Yes. She would definitely take herself in hand, eat less cake, do Headachy's exercises, stop killing Louise, and recruit some new lovers. More alluring New Year's Resolutions flooded in.

The 'class counselling period' drifted to its close, with Stephen Masters performing a fey monologue about some New Wave group called the Dusseldorf Delicatessen. Scarface Newman was cleaning his fingernails with a knife so huge, Izzy did wonder whether she ought to confiscate it. But then, he *was* performing a semi-hygienic act with it. Ah, the moral debates and paradoxes faced in the classroom every day.

Later that morning she met her class again, for their English lesson.

'Miss, can we go out an' sit on the field?'

'Nah, it's freezin' you berk.'

'Yer goolies 'ud drop off.'

''E ent got none anyway, Newman!'

'Shut yer face, poof!'

Izzy waited elegantly and sardonically (she hoped) for the barrage to die down. JJ and Razors lorded it silently at the back, chairs at 45 degrees, picking splinters out of the desks and flicking them at each other in a sophisticated, half-hearted way. The lesser boys went on fizzing and fussing. It became clear that her silent reproach wasn't working.

'Stop this bloody racket!' she roared suddenly, like the lion in MGM.

'Ooooh, language, Miss, reelly!' simpered Stephen Masters.

'Shut yer face, Masters,' came Razor's icy tones from the back of the room. Instant silence. Who would not wish to prostrate themselves before such a creature? thought Izzy. Who would not wish to load his merit richly? Starting at the green hair and working downwards. (Not the Headmaster, for a start. 'Razebrook is a thoroughly evil influence,' he told her once, full of obvious envy.) Her class waited, totally silent for a split second of attention. What was she about to impose on them? Writin'? (Ugh NO, Miss – me hand's worn out

can't write Miss and we know why eh Newman.)
Readin' pomes? (Agh NO Miss this pome's stupid it
don't rhyme.) Drarmer? (Oooooh GREA' Miss can we
do that play about the 'aunted 'ospital?)

'I want to have a discussion today,' she began.
Pandemonium instantly broke out. It was almost as bad
as the House of Commons at Question Time. Time for
another roar, obviously. She tensed her tawny tonsils.

'WE'LL DO WRITING INSTEAD UNLESS YOU
ALL BE QUIET!'

Relative peace.

'I want to talk today about marriage. Is it a good
thing? What do you think about it? *One at a time and put
your hand up first!*'

'My mum and dad's divorced, Miss.'

'And mine.'

'And mine.'

'I end never goin' to get married,' JJ drawled slyly
from the back.

Izzy seized on this.

'Why not, Jonathan?'

''s daft. I mean, yer get landed, don't yer? You marry
some old girl, right – two years later you've got a
coupla kids, no money. Same old borin' routine, sit at
'ome an' watch telly, get fat, never see yer mates.
Finished, ent yer?'

'Does everyone agree with Jonathan? *Stop that, Garry!*
Yvette?'

'No, Miss – you don't have to have children right
away, do you 'cos you can get conceptives, Miss, and
anyway, I'm going to stay at work after I'm married.'

'Is that the best way for a woman to plan her future?
Get married but stay at work? Stephen?'

'No, Miss, it's all wrong these women they've got all
the jobs, Miss, and it's the men, the men what's
unemployed and if all the women stayed at home
everybody'd have a job.'

Chorus of protest from the girls.

'Do all the boys agree with Stephen? *I won't tell you again, Gary!*'

'Women should stay in their place, Miss.'

'And what's that, Mark?'

'Bed.'

Storm of sniggering. Patient sighs and he's-an-idiot expressions from the girls.

'If you're unhappily married, is it right to leave your husband or wife? *Gary, just get out of here, I've had enough!* What things would you consider?'

'Kids, Miss, if you've got kids, Miss, it'd be wrong. You've got to stay together, Miss, if you've got kids, ay.'

'Nah, it was great when my old man moved out. He used to fump us. And me mum 'ated 'im.'

'But what if there aren't any children?'

'If there ent no kids, I'd go.'

'Is it always wrong to have a relationship with someone else if you're already married?'

'No, Miss, no not if your 'usband was cruel and beat you up, Miss.'

'''E'd beat you up more then, wouldn't 'e? Stupid cow!'

'If my ole girl was messin' aroun' wiv another bloke, I'd kill 'er.'

'So you wouldn't mess around with other women, either, I take it, Wayne?'

'Oh, well, that's different, Miss, ennit?'

'Na it 'taint.'

'Yes 'tis.'

'Only a scrubber would mess around wiv a married man.'

Crumbs, thought Izzy.

'What about you, Roger?' Razors eyed her lizardly. 'What are your views?'

'Well – it's a fing of the past, ennit, marriage? I'd live wiv a girl if I wanted to.'

'Yeah,' exulted Skinhead Newman, 'then you can

take off any time you want, and she can't do nuffink abaht it.'

Razors did not even condescend to look at him.

'Nah. 'Snot like that. You can't jus' run away from problems. You gotta try and sort 'em out. Uvverwise you'll never get nowhere will ya?'

Izzy gazed at Razors in rapture. What wouldn't she give to live with him in a sleazy flat over a caff. So he was fifteen and she was twenty-eight: so what? It might seem like a big age gap now, but in a few months, when he'd reached his sexual peak (Izzy wouldn't be reaching hers for years yet) it'd be magic. They'd stay in bed all day and then he could nip out and nick some supper from Harrod's And they'd 'sort their problems aht'. They might even have a child. Yes, a daughter with green hair and an earring. A real urban sizzler. Give her a tortoise and she'd reach for the tin opener. That sort of child.

To make room for this most satisfying fantasy, Izzy got the class to jot down their ideas on paper for the rest of the lesson (*Oh no Miss SNOT FAIR I ent gotta pen Gerroff Gary Shrup Lraine Miss he keeps DOING IT.*) At length, though, they settled. Izzy's thoughts still raged. At this stage of the lesson, she knew, she ought to be walking tenderly amongst them as they wrote, gently questioning them as to the progress of their dad's paroles, smoothing their troubled brows and persuading them to give up their glue tubes and turn to Jesus. But on this day Izzy felt unhinged. So she sat on the radiator and cooked up Mark 2 of the fantasy, which dispensed with the green-haired daughter, and introduced instead JJ, joining them as a ménage à trois and starting up a rock group called Mad, Bad and Dangerous to Know.

I must stop fantasizing about my male pupils, thought Izzy. My duty lies with the girls. Ah, the girls! There they all were: their Silvikrinned hair glinting uniformly (except for Lraine with her greasy quiff): all slender as grasses. Izzy knew that at the end of the lesson they'd all come up and swarm round her table and whisper confessions about Love Bites, Miss, and That Queer Bloke Who Lives in the Caravan and how Caryn Taylor had stolen Yvette's boyfriend and Lorette's mum had to have an operation. Trying to get them talking in class, though, had been a struggle. At puberty the boys seemed to become more themselves, Stephen Masters getting fatter and camper and JJ slyer and more handsome, and Razors cooler and sharper like a Fox's Glacier Mint, and bloody Gary Smith more and more bloody insufferable. But the girls seemed to groom themselves into a group identity, luscious and elegant and conscientious-about-work and serious-about-boys. Except for Lraine, who scowled in a nicotine-scented sulk. Izzy knew that Yvette was a tempestuous tragedy queen and that Lynette was a romantic depressive who lived in a dark night of the soul, and that Tracey was a tight-lipped athlete with a deep contempt for men. But the detached observer would never have guessed, because all they ever presented in public was the correct and shining image. They were preoccupied with their physical beauty. They were like groomed greyhounds, and marriage was the hare. Lraine had muttered something once about wanting to be an engineer, but Lraine was regarded as an aberration. No, marriage was their mirage, and they never guessed what thirsty work they'd find it.

Lunch came – hitherto the high point of Izzy's day, but the new Izzy averted her eyes from the Bakewell Tart and took her grated carrot, as the saying goes, like a man. She followed Maria blindly through the gobbling throng, and when they arrived, saw that she'd chosen a table adorned with Dick, slightly muddy from his morning's exertions. He beamed at them, and Izzy was alarmed to see that his glasses had steamed up. The table also held Janet Worth (Biology – the one who'd thought Izzy was transparent. Ha! So much for

Biology.) and Mr Brinsford, a delicate little old man who taught Modern Languages but whose personal presence had more to do with Ancient Silences.

'Izzy!' Dick was palpitating behind his foggy glasses. 'Did you have a good Christmas? How was Yorkshire?' Two sentences (albeit short), without a hesitation, was good going for Dick.

'Well—' Izzy was already sick of carrot, and regretting all the lies she'd told. She'd told Dick that she was going to Yorkshire at Christmas so he wouldn't pester her. She'd told her mother that she had to stay in London to mark A level scripts. To avoid spilling the Michael-beans, she'd told Maria she was going to Yorkshire. To Michael she had lied that she had to be in London anyway, to teach some private pupils (so if he could possibly snatch an hour or two—). Sometimes she couldn't remember which story had been offered to which sucker. To herself alone she had admitted the awful truth: she was hanging around in London on the off chance of glimpsing the elusive Mr Tristram, husband of Louise and father of Jack. And that made her sucker-in-chief. Perfide Amor.

'Yorkshire was gradely. Pass the salt, please, Jan,' was all she could manage.

Dick was encouraged. He was easily encouraged. He had spent his Christmas in Tottenham, doing a lot of work. During the autumn he'd built himself a kiln and over Christmas he'd simply worked for days and days: crouched over his wheel, his stubby fingers coaxing into the world mugs, jugs, bowls, vases. Dick wished he could make more exciting things. He knew a woman who made tall boots – porcelain boots, high-heeled ones. Vases for the very weird and fairly rich. It made Dick go hot to think of those boots. But, at the moment, nothing made him go quite as hot as Izzy. And here she sat, beside him. At last.

He'd missed her over Christmas. She'd never given him a thought, of course, but he'd given her several. As he stroked and squelched and rolled and pummelled his grey, silken clay, as it surged between his fingers, as it rose into glistening columns on the wheel, he'd longed for Izzy like an old donkey longing for green grass. He'd had girlfriends before: back in Derbyshire there'd been librarian Mary. But she'd been as cold as his clay, and as pliable, and as available, and even at the time Dick had felt listless towards her. In fact, he'd come to London partly to avoid her. Now, Izzy was something else. Indifferent to him, certainly. Romping with flesh and high spirits. Not too nastily clever like her friend Maria. Nice. Gentle. And red hot.

The minute he'd first seen her he'd felt the twinge that can make your life a misery. That had been back in September, and Izzy had been wearing a striped T-shirt and jeans – her usual school uniform. But the jeans were very tight, and the stripes had galloped so wantonly. On her little feet were dainty little boots. In her ears, several interesting earrings, including one which looked like a fly. Her blue eyes were not large, but they were slanty. Her hair was short, so Dick could see her neck, about which he was especially mad. And as for her lips – well, here they were right now, gleaming with oil, a speck or two of lucky old pilchard clinging to them. When Izzy bounced around the staff room, Dick rocked in his socks. To the casual observer, Izzy was a bit pneumatic, but nothing special. To Dick, she was Aphrodite.

'Was it cold up there?' he inquired: about Mount Olympus, Yorkshire, wherever she had been.

'Up where?' What was he on about? Izzy had, at this moment, been thinking of her last afternoon with Michael. The bruises were fading. She felt sad.

'Up in – in Yorkshire.'

'Oh, yeah, it was great. Walks on the moors and all that.' If only she could go for a walk on the moors with Michael. He knew the names of all the birds – one of his many unfortunate attractions. His dad had been a village schoolmaster in Gloucestershire: he'd grown up as a bit of a farmer's boy. Izzy had scanned the Ordnance Survey map for the name of his village, so besotted was she. It was called Bussage Frampton. Bussage Frampton! What a kissy, rampant, tumbling-in-the-hay sort of name! If only she and Michael could hurl themselves into a private haystack behind the wood at Bussage Frampton!

'I did a lot of work at Christmas,' Dick volunteered, having waited in vain for her inquiry. 'Made enough coffee cups to – to – um – feed an army.'

'Did you? How lovely. What colour are you going to paint them?'

She didn't just want to romp in the hay, though. She wanted to do all the other things with Michael, the ordinary, wifey things. Like wake up with him. Clean her teeth with him. Have a leisurely breakfast. Have any sort of breakfast. Watch telly. Potter in the garden. All those delicious things you can do when time is yours, lots of it, stretching away for years. Izzy's heart gave a self-pitying lurch.

'I don't paint them. I glaze them. I've got a nice ash glaze. Ash makes – fantastic glazes, y'know.'

'Does it? Oh, good. You know what they say. *Oak out before the ash*—' Izzy's voice tailed off. She could see a cottage, with a huge garden around it. There was jasmine round the door and a huge fig tree against the sunny wall. Indoors was a lovely kitchen with stone flags on the floor, and she, Izzy, was baking. Yes, BAKING. Wearing a clean apron, with all her ingredients ranged neatly before her. There was the most delicious smell of scones, and at her side, two small children jumped excitedly up and down. The boy – yes – *Tom*– had his father's green eyes and fair hair. So did the girl – um – *Sophie*. But you could tell they were Izzy's children too because they both had the sausagey lips. They grabbed some scone and ran out of the kitchen. Izzy's eyes followed them into the sunlit garden, to where Michael was sitting under the apple tree, working on his scripts. And Izzy needn't bother to go out and hurl herself at him because *she was his wife!* Bliss.

'It's not that sort of ash.'

'What, Dick?'

'Not – not that sort of ash. It's burnt wood.'

'What is?'

'The – my glaze. For the coffee cups. Would you – er – would you like some, Izzy?'

'Oh, yes please. That'd be great.' Half-heartedly Izzy addressed herself to her wretched apple. Mr Brinsford picked at his Bakewell Tart, grew faint-hearted, and left it. Izzy glared at him. Such men do not deserve to live. Unlike Michael – ah, Michael. She and Michael were in a railway carriage, on their way to the seaside, their babes Tom and Sophie on their knees, when the old lady opposite leaned over and said, 'Shall I bring them round for you? Say, Wednesday evening? They'll be finished by then.'

'What, Dick? Sorry?'

'The mugs. I could deliver them on Wednesday, if you like. Say – at about seven thirty? And maybe you'd like to – you'd like to go out for a – a – um – a bite?'

'Oh, yeah, OK.'

Just then a fight broke out – nothing serious, just the usual fight between the mafiosi gangs of the third year. Dick sorted it out, felt pleased (even though the girls concerned – yes, girls – were decidedly weedy) and then he walked off towards the Art Block, feeling rapturously happy. He thought he'd worked wonders. He'd got a date with Izzy. He felt so happy that he gave Darren Shaw a clip round the ear-hole, which was long overdue. Izzy, alas, had not seen his heroic stand on behalf of law and order. She'd already forgotten about Wednesday evening and would cancel it, on some pretext, later. She was back at her cottage with the apple trees – she had only ten minutes left there before

4L would intrude on her time and attention.

4L were the same age as her own dear 4C, but whereas 4C were all of human life, 4L were an O level class and had therefore postponed human life in the interests of higher things. They were polite, ambitious and self-concealing, and at present battling their way through *The Tempest*. Izzy had been reading Prospero (well, why not – it had made an old *poseur* very happy) and on this particular afternoon they had reached the very last scene. She should have finished it off last term, but Izzy found it hard to time things properly. And now she confronted Prospero's Epilogue speech, in which he reveals the frail insufficiency of the lonely human individual. No man is an island and all that. Reaching deep into her ribcage for a saturated-fat, gold-top Gielgudian voice, she began. The sublime simplicity of it all rolled off her tongue like best ball-bearings, though at times she was aware of the faintest of shuffling sounds from the back of the class. Reaching for their hankies, no doubt.

> 'Now my charms are all o'erthrown,
> And what strength I have's mine own;
> Which is most faint: . . . Now I want
> Spirits to enforce, art to enchant;
> And my ending is despair,
> Unless I be reliev'd by prayer,
> Which pierces so, that it assaults
> Mercy itself and frees all faults.
> As you from crimes would pardon'd be,
> Let your indulgence set me free.'

Izzy closed the book. A breathless silence. Their faces, pale, moved, met hers. Then, from the back, a hesitant voice piped up.

'Please, Miss, Helen's been sick.'

That night, Maria's Volvo seemed winged. Izzy

couldn't explain their safe arrival in any other way. Not that she noticed the driving so much: she was thinking hard.

'Maria,' she ventured at length, 'do you think it's a bad sign if you spend too much time fantasizing? I mean, if reality seems constantly to be breaking in, like a – sort of like an unwelcome intruder? I mean, is it a sign that your life's all wrong? Or do you think a bit of fantasy's all right? Maria?'

'Eh?' Maria jumped. 'What? Sorry, Izzy, I was miles away.'

Miles away in Tottenham, Dick let himself into his house, deep in a fantasy about Izzy naked and some gooey brown earthenware clay. Dick's fantasies confined themselves to modest lust: he left the Cotswold cottages to the real hardened escapists. He hastened straight to his shower and turned it on. Not a cold one, you understand. He didn't mean to exorcise his fantasy by it; rather to join in himself. When you think about it, it is really quite a scandal that the education of the nation's children is in the hands of such people.

5

'Izzy – this is Michael.'

'Michael!'

He often phoned around 5.30 p.m., by which time Izzy had arrived home from school, and his secretary had gone.

'Can't talk for long – you understand. Listen, my dear, I'm afraid it'll be very difficult for me to see you for the next couple of weeks. We're doing some filming, for one thing, and Louise is in a funny mood so I'm having to get home early and stick around.'

'Oh. Well. All right. What more can I say?'

'Look, don't be bitter, please, sweetie – don't. We'll have plenty of good times later – I promise! I miss you like hell – Could you manage a lunch next week?'

'A lunch?' A lunch during the school term? She teaching at Islington; he working at White City or, worse, Ealing? Was he mad?

'Yes, I suppose I could manage a lunch.' If Michael was mad, Izzy was madder.

'Thursday, then – that's the best day, because I've got to go to BH in the morning. So I could see you somewhere round Oxford Circus. How about Ben Trovato's?'

Ben Trovato's was a seedy restaurant tucked away behind Oxford Street. Izzy and Michael met there because it was too horrible even for BBC employees to frequent. There was something exotic and exciting, though, about its extreme darkness, the papier mâché cavern-effect of its walls, the blood-red stumps of candle guttering atop the sad mountains of old wax, the extreme insolence of the service. Izzy would be there at one, even though back at school there would only be half an hour left before afternoon lessons. There was only one way out: she'd have to skive. Or to be more precise, she'd have to stage an illness.

For Izzy, who'd hardly had a day's illness in her adult life, this was quite a challenge. She vaguely remembered having measles and mumps, as a child. Or rather, she remembered the delicious meals on trays which her mother had carried upstairs for her. She'd been tempted to malinger away in bed for ever, and even nowadays enjoyed eating in bed more than eating anywhere else. But this was hardly a help when planning to fake an illness. She'd have to stage her collapse around 11.30, she reckoned, in order to get out of school early, get down to Oxford Circus early, and change, in the ladies' loo, into Something More Uncomfortable. Izzy felt scared, and excited. Would she be convincing? Or would the Big Bad Headmaster – the Eye in the Sky – see through her ruse and put her in detention?

Flurries of snow swirled outside her window, but on the appointed day she nevertheless packed the Hanes stockings, the stiletto sling-backs and a light blue, elegant, crêpey dress in a groaning carrier bag. Thank God for her huge old fur coat, she thought, diving into it. Her ordinary school uniform of thick sweater, jeans and little boots was all right for 4C, but not for Michael. Someone had once said she looked like a fat little elf-boy in her pixie boots. An elf boy. Hmmmm. Michael wouldn't like that. He wanted his women to be women, complete with click-clack of footstep and the small electric whisper of nylon leg crossing leg.

Izzy carefully laid the first stages of her plot in the car.

'I feel really grotty this morning,' she moaned to Maria.

'Listen,' snapped Maria, 'don't you complain to me about your bloody health. I had to have four aspirins this morning before I could even face getting up.'

'Oh dear. What was it – another migraine?'

'Yeah. Had it all night. Sick three times. So don't talk to me about being ill. You don't know the meaning of the word.'

Izzy was silent, justly rebuked. She wondered why Maria had so many migraines. She was asthmatic, too. Izzy had read somewhere that headaches and asthma resulted from suppressed rage. But it didn't seem to her that Maria ever suppressed her rage at all. Or perhaps she had even more rage than she habitually showed? That was a frightening thought.

At school Izzy shivered ostentatiously by the radiators instead of joking by the coffee machine. Until Dick arrived, of course, nobody noticed.

'Hey, Izzy,' he faltered, 'you're not looking your usual – I mean, do you feel all right?'

'Not really,' whined Izzy, gratified. 'I think I've got a chill on the stomach.'

'Oh dear. You poor thing. Don't you think you should go home? The best place for you is – um – in bed,' he concluded, and gave a sudden, violent blush.

'Oh no.' Izzy decided it was time for the English bravery. The stoicism for which the race is famous. 'I'll be all right. It's nothing.'

'It doesn't look like nothing to me,' persisted the anxious Dick.

Izzy had a sudden glimpse of him as her doting husband: he'd confine her to bed at the first hint of a sniffle, wait on her hand and foot, and keep all her friends at bay. It was really rather an attractive prospect. But now she shrugged off his assiduities. She had the distinct feeling, that morning, that he had damp hands.

'You're shivering,' he remonstrated. 'Really, Izzy—'
But she was saved by the bell.

At break, she decided to bring things to a crisis.
Down in the ladies' loo she fished a tin of talcum
powder out of her bag. She was just patting it on her
obstinately rosy cheeks when the door opened. Izzy
fled into a cubicle. Then someone else came in – it was
Jan the biologist and Mary Greenfield, martinet-and-
mother-figure of the English Department. Izzy knew
they'd be gassing away about the weather all break, so
she dabbed a few more furtive fingerfuls of talc on her
cheeks, hid the tin and emerged feebly.

Neither of them noticed her beautifully staged
frailty, so she leaned her brow against the wall above
the wash-basins and groaned weakly.

'Are you all right, Izzy?' asked Jan.

'Yes, I've just been sick, that's all.'

'Oho – morning sickness, eh?' hinted Mary. 'Have a
glass of water.'

'Sit down and put your head between your knees,'
suggested Jan. It was what she always prescribed for ill
people, no matter what was wrong with them: broken
leg, malaria, tumour on the brain. It wasn't offered so
much as a prophylactic as to fold them up safely out of
the way. Izzy declined to put her head between her
knees. She knew, if she did, she'd get talcum powder all
over her jeans.

'You should be tucked up in bed, my girl,' announced
Mary sternly. 'It's bound to be bad if our Izzy goes
down with something.'

'Yes, that's right,' mused Jan, 'you're hardly ever ill,
are you? Are you sure you don't want to put your head
between your knees?'

Izzy was sure, but she nevertheless allowed Mary to
organize her invaliding-out: telling the Deputy Head,
arranging covers for her classes. In the corridor they
met Dick.

'I'm going home,' faltered Izzy.

'Oh dear. I wish I could drive you home, but I've got a double lesson with 3Y now.'

'It's OK,' smiled Izzy wanly. She was actually beginning to feel ill, so intense was her performance.

In twenty minutes she was on the tube, the Victoria Line rocketing her boisterously towards her assignation. Oxford Circus was thick with feathery snow, and bargain hunters barged rattily into one another on the skiddy pavements. Down in the ladies' loo Izzy donned her pale blue crêpe dress, the stockings, the shoes, the works. She hogged the mirror for a full fifteen minutes, slapping on not just her usual Michael faceful but some extras: rouge, mascara, green frosted eyeshadow. Partly in honour of the occasion – their first lunch in public together for many weeks – and partly to combat the extreme gloom of Ben Trovato's. She did want Michael to be able to make out the dim outline of her face.

Then, through the slush, to the restaurant. After five yards her feet were sopping wet, and the tops of her thighs were frozen – locked in Siberian garters. Snowflakes melted on her lashes and caused havoc with the mascara. Some flooded into her eyes and began to sting. So, remorselessly, did Nature strive to undo what Art had so precariously achieved. She finally burst into Ben Trovato's twenty minutes early, ordered some white wine, and tried to still her fluttering heart. She hadn't seen Michael for over a week, and her body and soul were in urgent need of a transfusion. His figure would loom in at the door; there'd be snow on his shoulders and in his hair . . . Izzy closed her eyes, sipped her wine and wished they were on holiday together in Siena.

An hour and a quarter later, Izzy gave him up. She was by now quite drunk, and extremely angry. The waiter had at first pestered her to order, but then, as her abandoned role began to develop, snottily ignored her. A solitary woman, obviously stood up and snivelling into her Soave, is not good for business. Ben and his fratelli were extremely relieved when she finally lurched out, having consumed almost a whole bottle of wine and a few of his stalest crusts. Izzy limped home, shivering and sobbing by turns. At Marble Arch she realized she'd left her pixie boots, jeans and sweater behind in a carrier bag in the most infernal corner of the ill-starred trattoria. They were probably already part of some diabolical lasagna. Izzy didn't care: they could wait. It could wait. Everything could wait. Especially her. Boy, could she wait! For hours and hours. Nobody could wait better than her. The Dumb Waiter, that's me, she thought. Sniggering drunkenly to herself, she steered her way through the Earl's Court slush and fell into bed with her shoes on.

Several hours later she was awoken by a repeated ringing at her doorbell. She stumbled through the darkness to the intercom.

'Hello?' she grunted. Go away whoever you are.

'Xzabelle? THXZK IXXK GPXTZ, DXRLYKN, ANX HXTPL.'

Izzy immediately recognized these Aztecs as Gwyn and Hywel. After three years in her present flat, she spoke fluent squawk-box. She let the Welshmen in, and sat down heavily on her sofa.

'Izzy! What yew doin' all dressed up, girl? You jus' been asleep? Yew look all crumpled, like. Maria tol' us you was sick, so we come runnin'.'

'We've come to cheer you up,' droned Hywel, looking at her legs, which he had not seen before.

'So Maria's coming, too?'

'She'll be yere any minute, mon. Jus' parkin' the car.'

And even as they spoke Maria rang, and was admitted. She stared.

'What on earth are you wearing, Izzy?'

'What? Oh, this.' Izzy gave a long shuddering sigh.

'I thought you were supposed to be ill.'

'I am ill,' snarled Izzy, with vehemence and, at last,

some truth. 'I've been sick four times this afternoon.' Did four sound too many? She realized she'd said *four* because she'd wanted to out-sick Maria.

'Well, do you have to tart yourself up to be sick, or what? What's-his-name isn't coming, is he?' pounced Maria.

'No he bloody isn't.'

'Then what on earth are you all dressed up for?'

'Well, it's a long story,' sighed Izzy, reaching into the black void for a long story. Any story. For a moment she toyed with the idea of staging a dash into the bathroom, followed by a few blood-curdling retches, if only to give her time to think. But no, she didn't have the energy.

'It was because I'd been sick.'

'What, were you sick on your old clothes? Where are they? I'll wash them.' Maria looked hopefully around, but of course Izzy's clothes were miles away.

'No, no,' protested Izzy feebly. 'No – but because I'd been sick so much, I thought – I might have lost a lot of weight – so I thought I – I thought I might just be able to get into this dress at last. So I thought I'd try it on.'

'What with? A shoehorn and some Vaseline? No, my love, you've still got a few pounds to go before you can appear in this little number decently in public.'

'Really?' Izzy was genuinely shocked.

'I think she looks bewtiful,' intoned Hywel.

'But, look, Izzy – it's all crumpled – you must've *slept* in it, for God's sake.'

'Ah. Yes. Well.' For the first time ever, Izzy wanted to murder Maria. Such is the fruit of adultery and deception. Not only do you want to kill his wife: you want to kill your best friend.

'Oh, Maria, leave off, can't you? I'm supposed to be ill, not on trial. Yes, I did sleep in the bloody thing. I came over faint when I was trying it on, so I went back to bed and I was too feeble to get undressed.'

'Ah, poor little darlin'. Let me go out and get you

some chips, that'll soon make you feel better,' crooned Gwyn. It seemed to Izzy the first sensible thing that had been said. But Maria disagreed.

'Don't be stupid, Gwyn – chips would be disastrous. Go on, Izzy – get undressed and get into bed. I'll make you some hot milk, if you think you can keep it down.'

Even as Izzy was wrinkling her nose in disgust, the phone rang. A good few minutes too late, in Izzy's view.

'Hello,' trying to sound frail.

'Darling! It's me. My dear, I know you must be absolutely furious with me. I'm so sorry about lunch today. Will you ever forgive me? Only my PA fell down some steps at BH just as we were going for lunch – she broke a bone in her ankle apparently – anyway there was a dreadful old hoo-ha about it and I couldn't leave the poor girl there, could I? Then, finally, just as I'd got her all sorted out and seen to, who should bear down on me but my boss, with a face like thunder, and proceeded to tear me off several hundred strips. I was already half an hour late for you when he turned up, and by the time he'd finished, it just wasn't worth coming – I reckoned you'd have given me up by then. Please, Izzy, say you forgive me – I can't bear to think of you waiting for me there all that time.'

'Oh, it's all right,' sighed Izzy. How could she say anything at all with Maria's sharp ears a yard away? Could Maria hear what Michael was saying? That was the question. He did tend to blast away on the phone, like the SAS.

'You sound really pissed off. Oh, my darling little Izzy, please don't go all cold and hostile on me. Say you forgive me, my dear – say it, please. Louise has just gone to the off-licence – she'll be back in a minute. How long did you wait?'

'Oh, not long.'

'What did you do?'

'Nothing much.'

68

'Please don't be like this, Izzy. It's unbearable.'

'I'm not.'

'You are. Oh, God, I feel awful. You feel awful, and there's nothing I can do. I've no way of even getting to see you for days. It's hopeless. I do love you so much. Do you love me still, despite everything?'

'Of course,' said Izzy sullenly. She was fighting the urge to hurl the whole telephone at the wall. It wasn't Michael – he sounded as if he'd had a really awful time – much worse than her own day. It was just this endless, stupid maze. Izzy was stifled. She wanted to scream.

'No, darling – please say it to me properly, once, before I hang up.'

'I don't think so. Goodbye.' And she put the receiver down. At the other end, Michael was teased and tantalized as never before. He wanted her unbearably. It never occurred to him to imagine that she was with someone else. He always imagined her as alone when she was not with him.

'Well,' said Gwyn, 'let's get this shoa on the road, orright? I make some supper. Hywel goes out to get some beer, you girls sit aroun' and look bewtiful.'

'I think you should go to bed, Izzy.'

'I don't want to go to bloody bed!' bawled Izzy in a sudden eruption of violent, homicidal rage.

Maria looked astonished. 'Well, bugger you, then. I was only trying to be helpful.' And she walked out. Izzy burst into tears.

'Don't mind 'er, darlin'' consoled Gwyn. 'She'll be back in a minute, orright? She'll jus' walk roun' the block for a bit, to cool off, like. I expect she's gone to get the beer. C'mon now, sweetheart. Stop cryin'. Where's your eggs? I'll make you a nice omelette.'

Izzy sat on the sofa, and Hywel took off her patent-leather stilettos, and lost no opportunity of stroking her ankles as he did so.

'Christ!' he murmured. 'These tights is magic, mon.

Come yere, Gwyn – 'ave a feel.' But Gwyn was singing and cooking so loudly he didn't hear.

'They're American stockings,' said Izzy, with some pride.

'Noa. Never.' Hywel gazed with awe at the delectable objects. 'Y'doan't say. *Stockin's*. I can't take this, y'knoa. It's turnin' me on too much, like. Yew're an incredibly attractive woman, y'knoa, darlin'.'

'Hush!' scolded Izzy, nodding at Gwyn and enjoining tact. There was a rug on the sofa. She drew it over her legs and snuggled down. At last, at last the day was beginning to make sense. Hywel craftily eased himself under the rug, too, placing her feet in his lap.

'I'll warm yewer little tootsies up,' he promised, with a dirty leer. Izzy giggled. More was warming up than her tootsies. They lay back like contented cats. Gwyn was frying some onions, and he'd found a reggae programme on the radio. Its soothing heartbeat lulled Izzy, and what Hywel was doing to her feet under the rug filled her with a sense of delicious absurdity.

'I didn't knoa I was a foot-fetishist, like,' he whispered, with a lewd wink. God, what a handsome hulk he was! As if to salute her, he belched loudly.

''Urry up with my dinner, mon, I'm absolutely ravishin'!' he urged. Scrambled eggs with cheese and onion soon winged their way over. Oh, the delight of it all.

'Come on, you dirty buggers, stop all that perverted nonsense under the rug! Or I might 'ave to join in, like!' Gwyn boomed.

The food tasted heavenly. The warmth of the cushions, of Hywel's lap-of-the-gods, and the easeful reggae soothed Izzy into blessed stupidity. Suddenly she realized that Maria hadn't come back. Oh dear.

'Never mind her, sweetheart – she'll cool down. She's 'ad a bit of a bad time today what with 'er migraine. I expect she's gone off early to bed, like.'

'But that's worse – I forgot she'd had a migraine, and

70

I yelled at her.'

'Noa, noa, don't fret, now. I's all right. I'll sort 'er out. Doan't worry, right?'

Izzy nodded. She wished Maria could be here, though. Then things would be perfect. They were pretty good as it was. Gwyn and Hywel didn't seem to care if she was ill or not, which made her bloom and sing. Under the blanket, she and Hywel were in rude health. She thought, briefly, of Michael. If only she could have times like this with him. But it was impossible: it would always be desperate, snatched, unfulfilling. She closed her eyes. Time may have passed, or not. She wasn't sure.

'Look yere, now.' Gwyn eventually stretched and got up. 'I've got to go off and see somebody. Now, Izzy, girl, I'm leavin' you in very, very unsafe hands. I trust I make myself clear, like?'

Hywel looked indignant. 'Doan't listen to 'im, darlin'. I'm 'armless. My intentions are everso honourable. I'm a reformed character.'

'Get 'im to do the washin'-up, at least, for Chris' sake, Isabelle. We've never managed to get 'im to do it yet. You're a bloody great drone, mon!' He thumped his cousin affectionately. 'An' when are you goin' to get up off yewer arse an' look for work I'd like to knoa?'

'Not tonight,' grinned Hywel.

Gwyn gave Izzy a smacking kiss, went to the door, where he paused. 'Dirty bastards,' he grinned, and was gone.

Izzy and Hywel stayed as they were for a while. Why move when everything was so deep and warm. Eventually Hywel stirred, and turned his great glistening brown eyes on her.

'How you feelin', darlin'?'

'I feel great.'

'Your tummy orright, is it?'

'To tell you the truth, Hywel, there's nothing wrong

71

with me at all.'

'Great news. Great news, mon.' And a slow smile broke across his dark and devious face.

Time ticked on. The reggae programme gave way to the news. Hywel got up and turned it off.

'Noa news is good news,' he grinned. Then he returned to the sofa, knelt by Izzy and rubbed his face gently against her hair.

'It's still snowin' outside,' he remarked. Then he lowered his face to hers and gave her the most languorous kiss she had ever received. On and on it went, his tongue exploring lazily like a creature full of sun and sleep. She felt nothing about the heart, as she did with Michael. But she did seem to be turning into a mermaid. She was definitely growing a long serpentine tail. Hywel's kiss drifted away. Now his breath was an ocean in her ear.

'Hywel – I'm – I'm in love with this man. This – this BBC man. I—'

'I doan't mind, darlin'. I love yew anyway. Come on, now. Be nice to me. I 'aven't touched a woman for months.'

Izzy smiled at this. He had obviously touched a good great many women as recently as last week. Another huge kiss broke over her, and she went under, swirling among the whirlpools of his breath. The sofa was beginning to creak.

'I'm tryin' to rape yewer sofa,' he confessed, sliding a snakey hand under the rug.

The phone rang.

'Let it ring,' urged Hywel, deep in her neck. But Izzy at the moment could simply not bear it to ring. She struggled free: she seized it.

'Yes?'

'Hello, Izzy. This is Dick.'

'Oh, Dick.'

'How are you feeling? I hope I haven't – disturbed you.'

'Not at all. I'm much better. I'll probably come to school tomorrow.'

'Will you? Oh, good. It was just a twenty-four-hour thing, I expect.'

'Yes, I suppose so.'

By the sofa, Hywel was undressing. Izzy watched, hypnotized.

'I've been thinking, Izzy—'

'Yes? What?'

Hywel was naked. He stood and stretched, and then came towards her, monstrously Priapic.

'Would you like me to bring those mugs around tomorrow?'

'OK.' Izzy would have agreed to anything. Hywel knelt at her feet and slid his hands up her legs.

'And – um – would you, maybe, like to – er – to have a bite to eat somewhere?'

'Oh yes, sure, that would be lovely,' Izzy promised between clenched buttocks.

'Shall I come round at about – say – seven thirty, then, if that's convenient?'

'Yes. Sure. See you then. Bye. YOU PIG!'

Izzy crashed the phone down, and Izzy herself crashed down. Not for nothing had Hywel played for Neath. His silken tackle he reserved for the ladies.

'Not on the floor,' pleaded Izzy. 'Let's go to bed.' He carried her there, as if she were feather-light. Which was some achievement. Presently Izzy felt as if she were part of the mechanism of a fat gold watch, and she wanted to go on thus, in this oily ticking, voluptuous, endless, for ever. And nearly did.

'I don't think I can take much more of this,' she breathed faintly an hour later.

'There isn't much left,' warned Hywel. He was right. Instantly, with a shudder, he was asleep. Izzy took a little longer. Gently she sank down to join her heart, which had slumbered throughout the whole episode. She felt easy, soothed, serene. But the happiest

73

soul in the Greater London Area that night was Dick, and nothing could lead him to sleep. At 4 a.m. he gave up the attempt and went off to make some jugs.

6

At school next day, eleven people asked her if she was
feeling better, and Mary Greenfield confided that she
thought she was going down with it herself, but she
thought she could hang on till the weekend. Being ill
in your own time, not your employer's, is the
hallmark of the Great of Heart. Izzy placated Maria
by saying she was sorry she'd been so bad-tempered
last night, but she'd been feeling ill. Maria gave the
same apology.

'Still,' she added, 'I couldn't help noticing that
Hywel wasn't stretched out on my sofa this morning.'

'Ah, no,' grinned Izzy brazenly. 'He was stretched
out on mine.'

'Wonderful bedside manner he's supposed to have.'

'Yes.' Izzy giggled. Things were all right again. She
thought of her last glimpse of Hywel: fast asleep
under her quilt, his cup of tea untasted beside him.
Well, why shouldn't he have a lie-in? After all, he
was in some senses a night worker.

When Izzy arrived back at the flat at 4.45 p.m.,
however, he was still there. Still under the quilt. Still
motionless, his long dark lashes nestling on his cheeks.
Good God, had he *died*? WELSH FOOTBALL STAR
DEAD IN TEACHER'S BED: FOUL PLAY
SUSPECTED.

'Hywel!'

He awoke instantly, gave a deep sigh, and beamed at

her. 'Hulloa, darlin'. What's the time, now?'

'It's nearly five o'clock, Hywel. You've been in bed all day! Get up, you great fat slob, I've got someone coming soon. You must make yourself scarce.'

'OK. Trust me, darlin'. Tell you wha', though – a cup of tea might go down orright.'

'Oh, might it, indeed? I've been working all day, you know. I think in the circumstances *you* might make *me* one.'

But of course it was Izzy who made the tea. And the fry-up which seemed the only thing that would get Hywel out of her bed. Once he could smell the bacon sizzling he crowbarred himself out into Izzy's goatskin rug, where he got dressed with a remote ponderous deliberation. He reminded Izzy sometimes of a beautiful dinosaur. It was getting on for six: Dick would be here at seven. But why shouldn't Hywel be around when Dick arrived? It might be quite a good thing – not exactly the Ultimate Deterrent but a useful shot across the bows. OK, Dick, Miss Comyn will have dinner with you, but don't get any big ideas, right? As far as you're concerned, the orange blossom, the champagne and the confetti are right over the horizon. This could be the start of something small.

Dick washed long and hard at the prospect of his date. He had even bought new underpants in Izzy's honour, and his recently-scrubbed scrotum tingled within them like a haggis which feels its Hogmanay has come. Dressed only in these underpants, he surveyed himself in the long mirror inside the old wardrobe in his bachelory, rather ripe Tottenham bedroom. With his John-Lennon-type owly glasses on, he could see quite clearly that he looked ridiculous. Without them, he could see nothing. Yearning for experience, he was paralysed with self-loathing.

And yet his star was riding high. *Taurus, your big chance has come*, announced Patric Walker, Astrologer

Extraordinaire, in the *Standard*. *Seize the opportunity which presents itself*. And Patric wasn't kidding. For even as Dick got into his beat-up old van, slamming the door gently to dislodge the minimum of rusty flakes, Izzy was thinking of him. She'd even gone into the bathroom and was rolling unguents into her armpits in order not to offend him. That was all, though. A brief glance in the mirror confirmed to her that her school make-up would do perfectly well for Dick. So would her school clothes. (Her second-best school clothes – she must remember to retrieve the others from Ben Trovato's this weekend.)

Dick parked his van, carefully lifted out the box of mugs, and strolled around Earl's Court for a while, as he was half an hour early. He'd never been to Earl's Court before. All he knew was that he might see some Australian transvestites if he was lucky. Dick was very lucky. The Australian transvestites seemed positively frumpy beside some of the exotic creatures parading about. Earl's Court may once have been British, but now it scarcely seemed even a protectorate. Eastern women veiled from head to foot in deepest black peeped out from pillar-box slits. Others wore black cardboard masks. Rastas cruised around with their tall jelly-bag hats: punks with pink coxcombs spat dextrously into the gutter. Dick was alarmed and excited. He made his way to Izzy's door fifteen minutes early and placed a trembling and only slightly muddy finger on her doorbell.

'YPLAXTKZK!' barked a sinister little box by his head. Dick jumped.

'It's Dick,' he told it, doubtfully.

'CXTPKM XYXTN!' it enjoined. There was suddenly a loud, angry buzz, and the door seemed to jump in its frame and open for him. He stepped inside, his heart hammering. He felt he had crossed some mysterious threshold and was on his way to a spicy kingdom. Would his modest mugs be welcome? He hugged them to his chest as he climbed the endless stairs.

He arrived breathless, to his chagrin. He did not want Izzy to think he wasn't fit. But the fact was, he wasn't fit. Besides, Izzy's stairs were so steep and so many that even the fit arrived breathless. And some pilgrims even had to pause and lean against the wall halfway there – there was a greasy mark on the wallpaper to show the place. Dick paused for breath, but Izzy opened the door straight away.

'Hello!' he gasped, thrust the mugs into her arms, and stepped inside, feeling both faint and triumphant.

But horrors! What was this? A huge and handsome stranger was sprawled on Izzy's sofa, reading *Vogue*. Dick's world went black. His hair, suddenly, did not fit but was three sizes too tight. His new underpants were full of bees. He was near to murder.

'This is Hywel – Hywel – Dick,' smiled Izzy, and started unpacking her mugs.

'Hulloa!' said the stranger, and courteously swung his legs off the sofa to make room for Dick.

'How d'you do,' nodded Dick, and stubbornly (and, he hoped, rudely) sat down instead on a silly little stool.

'Oh, look, Dick's made me some lovely mugs!' rhapsodized Izzy, sitting down herself beside Hywel. Disaster! Dick was much mortified as he looked at them sitting there together, their elbows – he couldn't help noticing – *touching* – as Izzy unwrapped the mugs. This stupid stool was making him feel like a garden gnome. He had to peer at the world over his square, ugly knees. Wretched, wretched. What wouldn't he give to go back to the beginning of the evening and start again. What wouldn't he give to go back to the beginning of his life and start again.

'Grea'!' The hideously handsome giant took one of Dick's mugs and cradled it in his enormous hand. 'Yew a potter, like?'

'That's right.' Dick was much relieved to detect, in

Hywel, thought processes even slower than his own. 'What do you do?' Male model? Ponce? Izzy's gigolo?

'Nothin' much at the moment, like. I just been laid off. I used to drive lorries, in South Wales. But I come up to London to look for work.'

'Hywel is Maria's cousin-in-law,' explained Izzy, and immediately set about making them all a cup of tea, to christen the mugs. 'He's staying with Gwyn and Maria,'

'Tell you what, tho',' pondered Hywel. 'I'm thinkin' of movin'.'

Dick thought of suggesting Katmandu as a place where unemployed lorry drivers might find work, but held his tongue.

'I got this mate, see, lives down in Streatham.'

'Why – don't you like being at Gwyn and Maria's?'

Hywel knotted his brow with a desperate effort at concentration. 'Noa – it's not that. But I feel – I dunnoa – sorta in the way, like. I been there a fortnight already. There's a – there's a sorta funny feelin' 'angin' about sometimes. I dunnoa. But I think I'd best be movin' on, like.'

Knowing Maria's private views about Hywel's presence, Izzy could only be glad.

'I hear Streatham's – um – very nice,' said Dick helpfully. Perhaps Hywel would like to go off there right now?

'Really, Dick? Where did you hear that? I'd heard Streatham was a hole.'

Dick did not know anything about Streatham, but it did not sound nearly deep enough to drop Hywel off into. Dick was to learn more of Streatham, and be reassured.

'I don' mind livin' in a hole. It'd be safer, like, if the bomb drops.'

The tea was brewed, the mugs were praised anew, and at length Hywel's departure seemed, even to himself, to be due.

'Well, darlin',' he said, heaving himself up and permitting himself what looked to Dick like a full-blooded embrace, 'must goa. See you soon, like. I'll ring you tomorroa.' Thus, innocently, did Hywel worm his way into Dick's big apple.

The *darlin'*, the promise to phone, and above all the unnecessarily salivary kiss, all stung Dick like hornets. Paralysed and cramped on his stupid dwarf's stool, he found he was almost looking forward to getting over Izzy and resuming his life of solitary wedging. What a painful mess of things women make. His Uncle Herbert had been right.

But Hywel was gone, and now Izzy turned to him with a placatory smile.

'Now he's gone we'll open the wine,' she sparkled, with a conspiratorial wink. She sensed that Dick was desperately in need of kindness. 'He's a nice boy, Hywel, but it's a shame he's got nothing to do – he just hangs around the few people he knows. Come and join me on the sofa, Dick, that stool's a bit uncomfortable.'

Dear, delightful Izzy! In an instant Dick was sinking into her warmed cushions, a glass of chilled wine in his hand, and her words soothing his prickly heart. Uncle Herbert's warnings were fading from his memory. *Wommen, lad? Leave well alone. Ye'd have more rest wi' a bagful o' snakes.* Was Izzy being treacherous? She'd said, 'He's a nice boy, but . . .' Dick went snuffling after that *but* as if it were the finest truffle. What a pearly word. He turned it round in his mind, admiring its shine. *Nice boy* wasn't bad, either. Dismissive. Patronizing. Dick tasted the wine, for a moment wished it was beer, but then pulled himself together. Things might yet be all right after all.

Izzy, curled up at her end of the sofa, regarded Dick benevolently. How shyly his eyes gleamed behind his glasses – like little chocolatey buttons. He'd washed his hair. She could tell: it shone like muddy fur. He was not unlike her dear old teddy bear. What a kind light twinkled in his eyes. So what if it was mixed with lechery? Izzy liked lechery. It was a sign of life. Besides, she knew quite well that Dick would die for her, whether his passion had been requited or not. Would Michael die for her? He wouldn't even risk a telephone call for her, most of the time.

Idle small talk about school trickled to and fro, and Izzy's eyes, wandering with some interest for the first time over Dick's body, decided there was no evidence of a paunch. Solid, but not saggy. So far so good. The social work she was contemplating could not take place under any old conditions. A paunch would disqualify the recipient utterly. Izzy was very hard on paunches, and the paunches had often regarded this as unfair, given her tolerance of so much else. Dear Dick! Paunchless, devoted, shy, and bursting with lust. Who would not have taken pity on him? Certainly Izzy did. Her night with Hywel had left her feeling benign. She might provide a service for the elderly and infirm, in due course. Feels on wheels.

'Let's go and eat,' she smiled. 'We can put the wine in the fridge and finish it when we come back.'

When we come back! Dick's heart lurched with joy and terror. They went out to eat. Dick hoped the food would not be too foreign.

The meal – Italian – was good. Luckily the background music was so loud they didn't have to talk much. When they did, there was always school. And Dick was such an *ingénu* as regards London – having lurked in Tottenham for most of the Autumn Term – that Izzy found herself in the flattering position of experienced young woman-about-town, handing out Metropolitan wisdom to her humble provincial swain. Dick appeared to know nothing about anything – not even all the marvellous pottery which awaited him in the museums and galleries. During the Christmas holidays Izzy had torn herself away from her lonely phone vigil for long enough to see an exhibition of pre-Columbian figurines. The catalogue was even now lying by her bed, with Hywel's neglected tea still standing forlornly upon it. Dick was quite genuinely interested in the pre-Columbian figurines. All the same, he couldn't quite believe that the votive Earth-Mother figures Izzy described could possibly be as beautiful or fruitful as her shapely self.

Izzy wished, rather, that he wasn't quite so keen on her. All the same, she accepted the adulation with grace, since it was offered. Recent events had been a comfort. She chose not to think of that other execrable Italian restaurant where recently she had played so disgraced a part. Dear Dick! He would never keep her waiting, not for a split second. In fact, he'd be downright early, poor devil. Izzy drank some more wine, feeling, as the evening wore on, that this social work business wasn't going to be quite as easy as falling off a log, after all.

'Well – um – eleven thirty.' Dick gazed passionately at the table. 'I s'pose I'd better – er – be on my way.' He knew about the wine waiting back in Izzy's fridge, but he wanted to offer her, at this point, an escape route. He was sure that his humble presence must by now have become irksome. Surely it couldn't be that this goddess was game for more dalliance?

'Oh, come on, Dick, don't abandon ship yet. There's that wine to finish. Or would you like some coffee?' For a moment, there, she thought he was going to chicken out. Or was he just being ultra-considerate? Yes, that was it. How sweet.

Dick, usually the potter, felt himself at this moment to be the clay.

Back in Izzy's flat, he became stupefied with terror. His coffee cup shook in his hand. He had declined the wine: he felt quite intoxicated enough as it was, thoroughly befuddled with temptation and opportunity.

'I shouldn't be drinking this coffee,' confessed Izzy. 'It'll keep me awake all night.'

Dick had one of his sudden blushes. 'Nor me, really. It makes me – er – gives me wind,' he concluded seductively.

Time ticked on, and the conversation ground to a howling silence.

'Ah well,' he croaked, terminally, after an epic pause. He rose unsteadily to his feet. Izzy got up, too, and they stood eyeing each other in dismay as their *mésalliance* vanished before their very eyes.

'Hold me!' commanded Izzy in desperation and hurled herself like a prop-forward into his arms. There, she breathed, the worst's over – though his heart was hammering away so fast she thought he might have a coronary. He thought so, too. A coronary or diahorrea. His vision had clouded over and his ears were singing, just like that time when he'd woken up in the middle of the night after the Bad Cauliflower. He held on tight to Izzy, all right. She was all that stood between him and the black spaces of unconsciousness. After they had been locked in this iron embrace, like a seized-up engine, for several minutes, and it was beginning to hurt, Izzy reckoned it was safe to wriggle slightly and put her face up to be kissed. To her relief, he had obviously done it before. But ah, reckless Izzy: never with such joy, such anguish.

Dick's blushes were spared, and his new underpants remained unseen, for at this point Izzy wisely switched out the light. A dark and steamy struggle ensued. So excited was Dick that there was a moment when he feared he might plunge into the abyss of impotence but, just in time, he thought hard of his first glimpse of Izzy, last September, in her joyous striped T-shirt, and rose to the occasion. Then, he only stuck his finger in her eye once, and by and large, what was meant to happen, did – in about four seconds flat.

'Ooooops – sorry!' he gasped.

'Don't worry, Dick,' soothed Izzy. 'That always happens. We've got the whole night ahead of us.' She wished he had not said *Oooops sorry*, though.

By half past one Dick was beginning to get into his stride. By half past two he was becoming insatiable.

'Not *again*!' groaned Izzy. 'Please, Dick! Go to sleep, for God's sake!'

Dick obeyed.

Hours passed. Dick snored, increasingly provocatively, it seemed to her. Last night, with Hywel, she'd sunk effortlessly into the warm arms of the unconscious. Tonight it was a struggle. She got hotter, turning and twisting like a chicken on a spit. Dick seemed to be boiling up like a steam engine. She crawled to the edge of the bed and tried to doze there, an explorer on a precipice. By 5 a.m. a rising nausea had her in its grip. She got up, took three aspirins, and finally slept.

The phone broke in. Izzy awoke. She jumped up, caught her foot in the bedclothes as she sprang out of bed, and struck her head violently on the wardrobe. Through stars she saw Dick's vast inert bulk stir slightly and plunge back to sleep. She seized her dressing gown and ran to the phone. And for once, it was the voice she most longed to hear which spoke. And for once, she was not a little dismayed to hear it.

'Izzy – my dear! A most extraordinary thing has happened. Louise just decided on the spur of the moment to go to Godalming for the weekend. Her parents live there. She's taken Jack. So I'll be right over, my darling.'

'Do you mean – you can *stay?*' gasped Izzy. This had never, before, been remotely on the cards.

'Yes. I can stay. I did promise to do some decorating here, but I can invent some excuse. Oh – Izzy – let's stop wasting time, talking on the phone. Let me ring off and rush right round there and squash the breath out of you.'

'Oh – don't rush,' faltered Izzy. 'Er – since we've got all weekend, I mean, I'm hardly awake yet, I'm afraid.'

'Don't get up! Don't move a muscle! Just stay right

there in your dear little pot-bellied bed and I'll jump into it with you in half an hour.' And he rang off, before she could temporize further.

Back in the bedroom, she surveyed the snoring Dick. Michael's suggestion to go back to bed did not seem to fit the bill. Instead she threw herself at Dick's stupefied torso. Could she decently get him out of the flat in twenty minutes? Could she indecently do it?

'Dick!' she rattled his shoulder savagely. 'Dick. Wake up. You must wake up. Dick! Dick!' Dick gave a faint snort, stirred, smacked his lips, and sighed back into sleep.

'Wake up, Dick, you berk! Wake up, for God's sake, don't just lie there like a pig, you pig! Get up, for Christ's sake – wake up! Are you in a coma, or what?' Her harridan bawling and desperate clawing eventually had an effect. He opened an eye.

'Izzy!' he cried, in rapture at the sight of her exhausted scowl. He swept her into his arms. She rolled over him, helpless, as he licked and kissed.

'Dick!' she gargled as best she could with his thick tongue wrapped around her tonsils. 'Get off! It's no good! You've got to go! There's no time for this!'

But Dick's hands had already torn off her dressing gown and were grabbing hungrily at new territories. Her resistance only seemed to inflame him more. He was deaf, blind, and inexorable: a Chieftain tank of lust rolling with stupid fixity towards its goal.

'My mother's coming, you stupid bastard!' Izzy made a supreme effort, freed one arm, and hit him very hard over the head with the catalogue of pre-Columbian figurines. Dick stalled, and blinked, then looked round as if he expected to see an outraged matriarch at the foot of the bed.

'Where?'

'She's not here yet, but she's on her way! She just rang to say she'd be here in ten minutes! I'm sorry, Dick, but you must go! She's a Methodist!'

This terrifying detail appeared to galvanize Dick. He put on his glasses and hurtled from the bed in a frantic search for his scattered clothing. Izzy suddenly could not bear the sight of him, and fled into the bathroom, where she showered as she had never showered before. Too bad if Dick wanted to have a pee before he went. Let him pee in the street. Everyone else in Earl's Court did.

Standing under the scalding stream, Izzy scoured and scrubbed with loofah, sponge, pumice stone, rubber duck – anything she could lay her hands on. Dick's ablutions in anticipation of their gaudy night were as nothing compared to her purifications after it. Presently though she realized that she could never wash *enough*, and sensibly stopped short of outright flaying. Pink and tingling as a ham on heat, she wrapped a towel round herself and, after listening guiltily inside the bathroom for a few seconds, emerged.

He had gone. He'd made the bed for Michael (something Hywel, with all the time at his disposal, had not done for Dick). The window was thoughtfully open just an inch – enough to blow away all traces of pong. The coffee mugs were washed up. Relief poured through Izzy. She'd feel guilty later, she knew. But Michael was about to burst in on her. What were the priorities? She could feel guilty later. Now she needed eyeliner. Black-eyed and wearing only her Chinese dressing gown, she arranged herself sitting up in bed reading the catalogue of pre-Columbian figurines. The bell rang.

'MXTCHXKL,' said the squawkbox. She pressed the door-release button, opened her own front door, then hopped back to bed and seized the catalogue. Everything seemed perfect – she plumped the pillows a bit – then suddenly she saw something alien and light blue hanging from the lampshade. Good God! Y-fronts! She grabbed them – and even as she did so she heard Michael's hearty pounding on the stairs – and stuffed them, in panic, under the pillow that was to be his. *Damn you, Dick,* she thought uncharitably, *can't you even keep a grip on your own underpants?* But then she smiled a smile, her very best. For in the doorway, covered in delight and carrying a huge bunch of flowers, stood Michael.

7

'Well.'

'Well.'

With these quiet words, Izzy found herself somewhere else. He didn't dive at her, but leaned against the door-post, just looking. The scent of the flowers filled the room.

'Good morning.'

'Good morning.'

With her heart beating in her fingertips, Izzy wondered what on earth she'd been up to in the last few days. She seemed suddenly to be awake, and alive.

He was wearing his old leather jacket, his battered corduroy trousers (that badge of the intelligentsia), his Fair Isle pullover (knitted by Louise'. mum – but Izzy didn't know that). And he was wearing his fatal old grin. The one that sent his whole face into curious crooked angles, and turned his green eyes into a slanty Tartar's. Or a tiger's. These green eyes feasted on her now. She felt her skin begin to glow, and her senses shimmered. Her room seemed full of danger.

'Would you like some breakfast, Michael?'

'Not so fast! First I'm coming in there with you.'

'Oh no, you're not.' Izzy jumped out of bed and skipped past him, snatching her flowers as she went. 'We've got the whole weekend – so first I'm going to have breakfast, and put these flowers in water, and talk to you.'

He followed her to the sitting-room-cum-dining-room-cum-kitchen. How joyfully she shook the flowers apart and jammed them in an old coffee jar. And how unlike Louise – who would have spent five minutes arranging them in an elegant vase. Izzy put the kettle on, got the cups and plates out, singing, and enjoyed ignoring him. He found it charming. He found this whole flat charming: Izzy's created universe. It was like a child's room. Huge paper kites on the ceiling, dancing silver motorcars hanging in a mobile, children's drawings on the walls (by her nieces in Edinburgh). A few battered old toys lay about: the leather elephant, a sensitive soul whose skin was polished by years of embraces, and Father Bear, a dirty old devil with a hole at the end of his snout into which Michael often shoved a Gauloise. When Michael was around, Father Bear sometimes performed acts of unspeakable lewdness upon the hapless elephant. There were a few pot plants, but they were mostly dead. Izzy had killed them all, even the hardiest, by enthusiastic overwatering or absent-minded neglect. Michael soon learned to bring cut flowers instead. His wife Louise only had to look at a lemon pip and it burst into luxuriant life. Ah, the wonderful variety of women!

He had brought some croissants. Izzy grabbed them greedily.

'I love croissants,' she beamed. 'I love the way they make you feel slightly sick for the whole of the rest of the morning.'

'Only the very best sort do that, my dear,' boasted Michael. His, of course, were the very best sort. He laid the table, washing and drying the cutlery as necessary.

'These are lovely mugs.'

'Yes. Dick made them for me. He's the pottery teacher at school.'

'Dick, eh? He's madly in love with you, I suppose?'

'Well, he fancies me like mad, at least,' Izzy shrugged modestly.

'Sensible man. Still, I'd better not find him round

here, ever, or I'll break his bloody neck.'

Michael tucked into his croissants, little guessing how close he had come to such a provocation. Pouting demurely, Izzy poured the tea. It was Earl Grey – Michael's favourite. A taste he'd picked up at Cambridge, and then, briefly, in the theatre, where he'd also picked up his slightly camp intonation, his 'my dears' and 'darlings'. He occasionally my-deared or darlinged a male colleague, which had given rise, at times, to a false hope. For Michael was as straight as the Mall.

'My dear, this jam has a film of mould on it.'

Izzy was shocked. But then, her usual breakfast was All-Bran. It was at least two months since jam had passed her lips.

'Oh, gosh – sorry – scrape the top off, it's probably all right underneath.'

To Michael it was a pleasure to do so. A most delightful pleasure to be here at all, in his mistress's warm little flat, nestling up against its skylights, with the pigeons making love outside on the crumbling ledges and the mice romping quaintly behind the ancient fridge. But would he feel the same if he shared it with her all the time, instead of returning, as he always did, to his large, elegant, Muswell Hill house? It was a question he had never asked himself. Though Izzy had often imagined living with Michael, the thought had never crossed his mind at all. His house was on his mind, though.

'Listen, darling, before we sink without trace into this most wonderful weekend, I must tell you now that sometime I'm going to have to go back and do a bit of decorating.'

'That's all right, I'll come and help you.'

'God, no! Old Mrs Harston next door has got eyes like lasers.'

'Oh, all right. Why have you got to do it, though? I

90

thought Louise was so house-proud she redecorated every year.'

Michael winced slightly at this return of his distortions.

'Not really. There's these two rooms up at the top we've been neglecting, you see. We never use them except to store junk. We fling the odd unwanted Christmas present in there. You know the sort of thing: carved beechwood sea-lions, pictures of Great Uncle Charlie in fireman's uniform. It's where the skateboards go to die.'

'You're so lucky to have so much room!'

Michael felt a twinge of guilt. Izzy's whole flat would fit into the larger of his two attic rooms.

'Yes – well, Louise decided it was a criminal waste of space, so we're doing them up a bit and then she's going to find a tenant for them. Good idea, really – it'll give her an interest.'

'I thought Louise was an artist. You make her sound like a bored housewife.'

'Well,' he smiled patronizingly, 'I think Louise would decribe herself as a bored housewife rather than an artist at the moment. In fact, she often does. No, I didn't mean it in that sense. I just thought it would be jolly convenient if a handsome lodger turned up and she fell madly in love with him.' Michael often pretended to Izzy that he'd like Louise to take a lover. He also pretended it to himself. It would assuage his guilt. But if it actually happened, what would his reaction be? He wasn't so sure.

But Izzy's busy imagination had already translated this chance remark into a whole screenplay. A towering Swedish neurosurgeon arrived on Louise's doorstep, was rapidly installed in the attic, took to working nights and hanging around the house in the daytime. Izzy was fairly sure neurosurgeons had to work nights now and then – or perhaps he'd better be an obstetrician. Yes, that was better. Izzy knew that after the birth of Jack, Louise had suffered After Effects. Well, over a bottle of gin, the obstetrician explored Louise's after effects, and pretty soon they were in each other's arms. Izzy offered the obstetrician a professorship at Uppsala University. He accepted, and he sailed away into the midnight sunrise taking Louise and Jack with him. (Lots of nice creepy-crawlies in Sweden for Jack to stuff into his jam jars.)

'What are you thinking, darling?'

Izzy looked up with a mischievous twinkle. 'I'd just married Louise off to the lodger.' How excellent it was to be able to tell the truth for once.

Michael rather wished she hadn't, though. His laugh was hollow and he changed the subject as soon as he could, to work (his, naturally – though he wouldn't forget to make tender inquiries as to the progress of hers, in due course). Michael often wished he was a Muhammadan. Having to discard one wife in order to equip one's self with another was barbaric. In fact there were lots of things about Christianity which he found barbaric. To have Louise and Izzy both, whenever he liked, that was his fantasy. And that wasn't all. The girl who'd broken her ankle at Broadcasting House would be there, too. Oh, in some inferior, serving-maid capacity, of course. She would never challenge Louise's and Izzy's sovereignties. But at times it would be nice to look on her flecked hazel eyes, so large and candid, and what Michael imagined must be her pearly young bum.

They talked, and the delicious morning unrolled. Michael was very entertaining about his work. His imitations of the various dear old lushes who kept Schools TV ticking over always reduced Izzy to hysterics. She was also vastly entertained by his account of himself as the overworked, underpaid, oft-propositioned, fumblingly incompetent Enfant Terrible of the Department. Actually, it was substantially true, though Izzy thought her Michael must be the most brilliant TV producer who had ever sprung on an unsuspecting BBC. But the truth was that Michael was imaginative but slipshod; entertaining, but short on detail. His scripts were never ready on time, his promises forgot, and BBC video cassettes regularly surfaced in his toolshed or cat basket at home. Michael reckoned it was his PA's job to keep track of such details, and to some extent she did a miraculous job in fending off disaster. She probably adores me, he flattered himself in his worst moments, thinking of the odd expression in her hazel eyes. He did flatter himself. She was violently in love with a Turkish geologist called Aziz and rarely gave Michael a thought that was not contemptuous. Whereas Izzy rarely gave Michael a thought much short of veneration.

'I'm so sorry about that débâcle at lunch the other day, darling,' Michael mumbled, looking abashed.

'Oh, that's all right. I understand. Don't go on about it.'

'Things are so difficult at times.'

'I know. You don't have to tell me that.'

For a moment Michael was pulled up by her tone, and tried to imagine her life. Poor little Izzy, living for her glimpses of him, waiting, in this lonely little eyrie of a flat, for his rare phone calls, fantasizing about marrying him, neglecting herself when he wasn't around, dismissing other suitors with a wistful declaration of her love for him, going to her lonely bed night after night, often to dream about him (she told him of those dreams). Dear, devoted little Izzy: all the flowers in the world wouldn't be enough for her. He reached across the table for her hand and gazed fondly at her.

Michael did feel himself to be Truly in Love with Izzy, and he was right. Talking with her was good, and easy. Eating with her (now they'd recovered their appetites) was a delight. Going to bed with her was the most delicious bliss – such as he'd never known with anyone else, incidentally, in his long and adventurous career. But most of all, just sitting and looking at her seemed to transport him into a trance of joy. A colleague of his at work, the egregious Bob, had once seen Michael and Izzy lunching together in the BBC canteen (before Michael had realized public lunches were a bad idea) and, smiting Michael on the shoulder next day, had boomed, 'You lucky bastard, Michael! A lovely trollopy little mistress like that *and* a beautiful wife.' At which Michael had cringed and yet exulted. Quite a few things in life had that effect on him.

'Come, little pusskin,' he cajoled, toying with Izzy's paws. Who has not at some time or other heard themselves say such things? 'Come – it's time for bed.' It was nearly noon, but with Michael and Izzy, any time was time for bed.

With world enough and time, for once, Michael contemplated an endless afternoon in Izzy's bed. Izzy, though game, was suffering the after-effects of Dick's gaudy night and couldn't help thinking that a trip to the zoo might be a better idea. But, as usual, appetite conquered discretion.

Towards three o'clock, when a return bout was being arranged, Izzy's doorbell rang. They froze in mid-caress.

'Who's that?' asked Michael. Izzy, ever generous, did not ridicule him for this inanity. Whoever it was was safely out on the street, three floors below, and could jolly well stay there.

'They'll go away,' reasoned Izzy, and went back to her navel engagement. But the doorbell rang again. And again. Their impulses of delight drained away, and they sat listening in Izzy's bed, two guilty hideaways.

'Whoever can it be?' wondered Izzy. Her flat did not overlook the street at the front, so they wouldn't be able to peep down at whoever it was going away.

'One of your many admirers, no doubt,' joked Michael, though a little pale. The bell rang again – a terrifying, long-drawn-out summons, the ring of a madman. No one had ever rung Izzy's bell like that before.

'I don't *know anybody* who rings the bell like that,' she marvelled, and got out of bed and began to dress in a fumbling, hasty way.

'What are you doing, Izzy?' cried Michael in alarm. 'You can't answer it!' He was suddenly haunted by the idea of his Louise down there, an avenging fury, pressing the bell and pressing the bell until the end of time.

'But what else can I do? It's obviously something important.'

'But you can't let them in! It might be someone who knows me.' Michael, too, got out of bed and pulled on his trousers. They paused, half-dressed, in a brief and promising silence. But then it rang again: a sinister series of short bursts, followed by a terrible, nerve-shredding long-drawn-out one which drove Izzy to cover her ears and yell, 'Shut up!'

Michael finished dressing. They looked at each other, and waited.

'It can't possibly be anyone who knows you, Michael,' Izzy reasoned. 'I don't know anybody who knows you, do I? It's obviously got to be one of my friends – and it must be pretty important.'

'Well, all right, but look – I'll go and sit in the bedroom. You just get rid of whoever it is as quickly as you can.'

'All right,' agreed Izzy, moving towards the intercom.

'Wait a mo!' Michael panicked. 'I must have a slash first.' Tension always played havoc with Michael's bladder. When he retired into the bedroom, he took an empty milk bottle with him in case the tension got too much again. With the bedroom door firmly shut, Izzy spoke into the intercom.

'Hello. Hello. This is Izzy. Who is it?'

There was no answer. They had gone.

Michael came out of the bedroom and they both sat down in an atmosphere of strain and mystery. It was as if the guilt and danger of their relationship had taken shape and in this threatening incarnation had hammered at the doors of their safety. They were shaken. It disturbed them, and it would not be easy to rediscover the magic weekend. Michael lit a Gauloise, Izzy made them some more Earl Grey, since it was nearly tea time, even in the real world.

'What shall we do tonight, Michael?' she asked, begining to recover a sense that the world, might, after all, be beckoning them with pleasures rather than pursuing them with punishments. 'Shall we go to the theatre? Or a movie? Or to hear some jazz?' She knew Michael liked jazz. But then the phone rang.

'Oh Christ. Let's put it off the hook, shall we?'

'OK, I will, only I must just answer this one first. It might just explain the other business.'

Izzy's intuitions, as usual, were bang on.

'Izzy? This is Maria.' Her voice was strange, throttled. 'I *thought* you were in! I came round just now and rang and rang, but there was no answer. I'm ringing from the tube.'

'Ah, it was you. Well, you see, I've got Michael here with me.'

Michael scowled.

'Oh God, I'm sorry, Izzy. I didn't mean to disturb you. But – oh God!' Maria seemed to choke, and grow incoherent.

'What is it? What is it, Maria, for goodness' sake? Has there been an accident, or something?'

For Maria to burst into tears was hitherto unknown.

'No – I've – I've left Gwyn.' Another burst of sobbing.

'Come round at once,' ordered Izzy, and put the phone down.

Michael looked angry. Before he had a chance to

remonstrate, however, Izzy seized the initiative.

'Don't worry, it's just my friend Maria.'

'What's happened?'

'She's left her husband. She's very upset.'

'Oh God! Why couldn't she leave her bloody husband next weekend?'

'Don't be callous, Michael.'

'I'm sorry, Izzy, I don't mean to be unsympathetic. I'm just being selfish. All I see is our weekend disappearing down the drain – the only weekend we'll probably ever have.'

'Oh, that's the score, is it?' Izzy's eyes flashed. Her role had never been quite so clear, before. 'I'm sorry. I'd been under the impression that we were in love, and that things might change, and that we might be able to – to get something together between us, eventually.'

Michael ran his fingers through what remained of his hair. It was a despairing gesture, and it always increased his despair, by reminding him of his baldness: his destiny: ugly old age, and beyond.

'Look, we can't go into all that now, darling,' he urged. 'I'm just being melodramatic, saying it's the last weekend we'll ever have – I mean, the only weekend. Of course we'll have other weekends. Of course we will.' But it had been said. 'Only look, Izzy, try and cool her down and sort it out so we can get rid of her and have the rest of our time together – please.'

'I'll try. Of course. I'll try.' Izzy was wide-eyed and angry with everything. 'But I can't promise anything – I can't just chuck her out. She's my friend, Michael – and she's left her husband, for Christ's sake.'

'OK, OK,' Michael lit another Gauloise. 'Damn, I'm running out of fags. Shall I go? Or shall I lie low in the bedroom? Or what?'

'No – that'd be silly, hiding in the bedroom. Stay here. It'll be all right.'

But it wasn't. Maria burst in looking like some wretched creature from Greek tragedy. Her eyes were red, there were great rings under them, and she carried two huge suitcases.

'My God, Maria, did you carry those up the stairs! You should've said – Michael would've come down and given you a hand.'

'I don't need any bloody man to give me a hand with anything, thank you very much,' blazed Maria. Michael immediately felt it was time to go, but Izzy detained him with a look.

'Sorry to be so rude, but I am quite out of control,' gasped Maria. 'Got a fag?' Michael gave her his last one. She inhaled deeply, and was immediately seized by a bout of desperate coughing.

'Should you be smoking, Maria?' ventured Izzy. 'After all, your asthma –'

'Don't start that!' snapped Maria. 'I can't stand being lectured. Give me a break, Izzy. Can't I even have a miserable little cigarette in peace on the day – ' here she burst into tears – 'on the day I – the day I leave Gwyn?'

Michael rose to go. To Izzy, Maria's crying, though a novelty, was easier to deal with than her anger, but Michael could never stand the sight of a woman's tears. Perhaps because he had so frequently provoked them in the past.

'I'll go, love,' he murmured to Izzy. 'Give me a ring if you get the chance. I'll be at home all weekend. Maybe I'll get that ruddy painting done after all.' Thus, with a wan joke, he went.

Maria was much too beside herself to realize that she'd just ruined a beautiful weekend. But after all, her own sorrows were on an epic scale. For a while she just cried, and Izzy did not know what to do, so she made more tea. Maria ignored hers. Izzy drank hers. It gave her something to do.

At length Maria's sobs subsided, and she began to stir her tea. A healthy sign, thought Izzy, but Maria went on stirring and stirring, and stirring and stirring, and then finally broke her hypnotic trance, and in a fairly normal voice, said, 'I'm terribly sorry about all this, Izzy.'

'Don't be daft.' shrugged Izzy. 'Do you want to talk about it?'

'Yes, of course I do. That's why I came. I just don't know where to start.'

'Well, why on earth has all this blown up, Maria?'

Maria controlled her trembling lip with desperate courage. 'Gwyn – has been – has been having – affairs with other women. For years. Behind my back.'

'Good God!' Izzy was astonished, not so much by the revelation, as the fact that Maria should have thought it so unlikely, and have been so devastated at its discovery. When she came to think of it, the *fact* was not at all surprising. Gwyn gave off all the signals of the straying husband: the glad eye, the opportunist grope, the double-entendre. But the very ostentation of the signals had deceived Izzy (and no doubt Maria) into thinking it was all a joke.

'How did you – discover it?'

'A letter. Isn't it silly? Isn't it standard? A letter in his pocket, the stupid jerk. He asked me to take his trousers to the cleaners. Naturally I cleared out the pockets. And in one was a letter from a girl at the Poly.'

'How odd. It's almost as if he wanted to be discovered.'

'Oh, I don't know. He's drunk so often, and of course that makes him forgetful. But when I confronted him with it, there was the most extraordinary unburdening. Instead of just admitting this one little fling – and passing it off as a little fling – he sort of panicked and began admitting to all these other affairs, going back for years. Ever since—' here Maria's voice grew choked – 'ever since the summer we were married. And that was with my best friend from college.'

'Well,' vowed Izzy, half joking, 'he's certainly never

laid a finger on me.'

'Are you sure?' Maria looked sharply at her.

'Of course I'm sure,' flared Izzy. 'Do you really think I'd have an affair with your husband? I know you think I've got no morals at all and have an insatiable appetite for adultery, but I do have some principles, you know!'

'Sorry,' apologized Maria wearily. But her mind was elsewhere. 'It's just that when you discover that three of your friends have been messing about with your husband behind your back, the whole world seems riddled with deceit.'

'But, Maria—' Izzy was trying hard to arbitrate – 'didn't you say recently that you wouldn't mind if Gwyn had affairs with other women?'

'I said we'd got an understanding that he'd tell me about them, and that would be OK.'

'Well, he has told you about them.'

'Whose side are you on? He's supposed to tell me about them one by one as they happen – not in a bumper package five years later! I've been deceived, Izzy – that's what hurts. Not the fact that he screwed other women. It's the fact that he lied to me about it, time and time again. I thought I was living one life but in reality there was another one going on I didn't know about. I thought he was my friend, my mate, my comrade, but really he was lying to my face, humiliating me, making a fool of me. My life with him was a mockery – an absolute mockery. He took away my life by lying to me. How could I say that I possessed my own life when I didn't know what was happening in it? I've been utterly betrayed and my peace of mind has been destroyed for ever. I shall never trust another man as long as I live.'

'Come on – surely that's not being very fair to men?'

'I don't intend to be bloody fair to them. As far as I'm concerned, they're not fit to be treated fairly. They deserve everything they get, and much more.' She was

100

pale now, with a clenched calmness which terrified Izzy.

'Um – do you want something to eat?' she ventured. 'There is a chicken in the fridge. We could roast it.'

'I'm not very hungry,' sighed Maria. 'I don't feel like eating, thanks.'

'Well, what do you feel like?'

'Like committing murder.'

'Come on, Maria. Don't be so melodramatic.'

'I could kill him,' said Maria in a very matter-of-fact voice. 'I could kill him. He's made a mockery of my life.'

Izzy was silent. She was deeply shocked and felt for her friend, but she was also beginning to find it just a bit tiresome.

'Izzy—' at length Maria's thoughts rose from their homicidal depths to more mundane matters. 'Izzy – could I stay here for a while, and sleep on your sofa, while I work out what to do and where to go?'

'Of course you can. You needn't ask.'

Izzy went ahead and cooked the chicken anyway. It would have been hers and Michael's, and indeed, he had bought it, and was even now sitting down savagely to beans on toast in Muswell Hill. She toyed with the idea of ringing him up and inviting him over, but it seemed inopportune, with Maria radiating hatred for men all over the hearthrug. After all, thought Izzy, Michael's deceiving his wife, too. Maria might kill him as a proxy. Meanwhile, in Muswell Hill, Michael started to paint his attic, and found it rather soothing. He also had a brief fantasy about the voluptuous Iranian girl who might turn up as lodger. Izzy and Maria watched TV – although Maria seemed to gaze beyond it, into some world of her own, some ruined landscape. It was her past, and she was taking leave of it.

8

Izzy made up a bed for Maria on the sofa. She wanted to phone Michael, but felt intimidated by Maria's grim face. Maria seemed to be evolving into a piece of furniture. She sat about, motionless, staring through the walls. Izzy, who could usually cheer people up quite easily, was utterly defeated and felt her spirits drain away out of some deep plughole of the soul, till nought remained but emptiness and scum. Once she'd made the bed up, though, she had an idea.

'Maria – let me sleep on the sofa. You have my bed.' With Maria safely stowed in the bedroom, she could manage a private phone call to Michael.

'Nonsense, Izzy. I wouldn't dream of it. I'll sleep here. This will be fine.'

'But I *want* you to sleep in my bed. I really do. Then you can lie in tomorrow and I won't disturb you.'

'I don't want to lie in tomorrow. No, really, Izzy, I'll be perfectly all right here.'

Izzy now discovered what the phrase *gnashing of teeth* meant. Actually, her whole body seemed to be gnashing slightly.

'Well, look, Maria, the thing is, I want to ring Michael, and so—'

'Oh, that's it, is it?' observed Maria coldly. 'Why didn't you say so? OK, fine.' And she walked to the bedroom. She paused at the door. 'If any man rings for me, you can tell him to go boil his head.'

By the time Maria hit the sack, it was midnight. Too late to ring Michael? Izzy thought not. But the phone rang for a long time before she heard his voice, bleary and impatient.

'What is it?'

'Sorry, Michael, I didn't realize you'd be asleep.'

'It doesn't matter. How are things?'

'Fairly bad, I think. But I might be able to see you tomorrow morning. I could send Maria out for a walk or something. Or maybe she'll go out anyway. Could you come round, say, at eleven?'

'But, Izzy – is this on the off chance? I mean, my dear, might your harpy of a friend be hanging about? I really don't want my head bitten off – or my bollocks.'

'I don't know. I really can't say. She might be. But I'm sure she'd push off for a while if you turned up.'

'Well, look – let's leave it that you'll ring if an opportunity seems about to present itself, OK?'

'Oh, all right then. I'll ring you anyway – just to say hello.' Izzy felt rather dashed. Michael seemed to have less resilience than necessary. And he shouldn't have called Maria a harpy. Sadly, Izzy went to bed, or rather, to sofa.

At 1.30 a.m. the phone rang so harshly in the night that Izzy jumped out of her skin. The phone was right by the sofa. She seized it.

'Hello?'

'Lissen – Isabelle – lissen, darlin' – tell that wife of mine to get 'er arse over to the phone, now.'

'Certainly not, She's asleep. It's the middle of the night.'

'Fuck the night! Jus' get Maria to the phone, right? We got to stop all this nonsense. I gotta talk to 'er, now.'

'Don't be silly, Gwyn. Go to bed. You can talk to her in the morning, if she's willing. Which I very much doubt.'

'Why's that, then? What's she bin sayin'?'

'She said that you could go and boil your head.'

At this Gwyn seemed convulsed with laughter. 'Yew English girls! You're scrumptious, mon! Lissen, tell 'er to come yere. I got something to say to 'er.'

'Gwyn, I've told you – it's too late. Try in the morning. I'm going to put the phone down and leave it off the hook. Now GO TO SLEEP!'

As she snuggled down again, Izzy wondered that, while Maria seemed fatal about the bust-up, Gwyn seemed so frivolous. Overnight, Maria had turned to stone. She sat like a statue at the breakfast table, stirred her coffee endlessly, and ate half a piece of dry toast.

'Do you feel like going out today?' ventured Izzy. 'It might do you good. It's a nice day. We could go to Kew and have a look at the hot houses. Or maybe go to the zoo.'

'I hate zoos. All those cages! No – I'd rather stay in and read, if it's all right with you, Izzy. I feel exhausted. I can read in the bedroom if you like. Do say if I'm in the way.'

'Of course you're not in my way! Don't be so daft! Only I do wish you'd eat something.'

'Oh, don't go on about that. You're worse than my mother. My mother!' Maria turned, if possible, even paler. 'God, Izzy, I've got to tell my mother.'

'There's no need to rush into things like that, surely. Hang on a bit. You might change your mind. You and Gwyn might patch things up. It might be all right, after all, you never know.'

'Oh, things are going to be all right,' said Maria calmly. Izzy's hopes rose. 'But as for patching things up – forget it. There's been far too much patching up as it is.'

She settled herself down in a corner, on the floor, with some cushions – as if by leaving the sofa unoccupied she was minimising her invasion. In this curious refugee-like crouch she laboured over a letter to her parents. Izzy thought it strange that she should write to them, not go and see them to talk it over. She didn't know much about Maria's parents, except that they were antiques dealers who lived in the countryside outside Oxford. Izzy's

104

mum, the window of a Yorkshire farmer, lived in a cottage near Haworth. Come to think of it, Izzy mused, I must go and see Mum soon. A weekend up there would be nice. She missed her mum's shortbread.

The phone rang again. It was Gwyn. He insisted on speaking to his 'daft bitch of a wife'.

'I am not here,' insisted Maria.

'Sorry, Gwyn, she's not here.'

'Don't give me that, girl. I fuckin' *knoa* she's there. Jus' stop all this nonsense and get 'er to the phoane.'

'Maria is *not here*, Gwyn. Now please stop bothering me. I'll get her to ring you next time I see her.'

'Oh, noa, noa, noa.' Gwyn gave a wail of despair. 'I can't stan' this, mon. It's crewelty to dumb animals. It's jus' ridiculous, runnin' off like that and refewsin' to face mea. We got to sort this out, now.'

'Look, Gwyn, I'm very sorry about all this, but I can't help you at the moment.'

'But—'

Izzy put the phone down. 'Look, Maria – aren't you ever going to talk to him? I mean, have I just got to go on saying *She's not here*, or what?'

Maria gave a cold shrug. The phone rang again. 'Let it ring,' she ordered.

'No, I can't – it might be Michael.'

But of course it was Gwyn, and Izzy had to hang up on him again. This time she left the phone off the hook.

'Now for some peace,' she sighed. 'I suppose I'd better mark my O level essays.' It was very, very far from being the weekend she'd looked forward to.

An hour later, her front doorbell rang, and the squawk-box uttered its usual bark.

'OK. Come in,' instructed Izzy, and pressed the door-release button. Maria looked up in alarm. 'Don't panic,' grinned Izzy, 'it's only the electricity man come to read the meters.'

Izzy's front doorbell rang.

'But, Izzy,' faltered Maria, 'it's Sunday.'

Too late. Gwyn sprang in.

''Ulloa, ladies! Read yewer meters, like?'

Maria jumped up, betrayed.

'Oh, crumbs,' said Izzy.

'Get out!' yelled the wronged wife.

'C'mon now, girl, calm down. Izzy, put the kettle on, there's a darlin'.' Gwyn grinned, ostentatiously relaxed.

'Well, damn you, if you won't get out, I'll bloody go myself!' Maria strode for the door. Gwyn caught her wrist as she passed him.

'Steady on, girl! You're not goin' nowhere. You an' me's got to 'ave a talk, like, an' Isabelle yere can be ower witness.'

'Don't drag me into it!' cried Izzy. 'I'll just make you a cup of tea and then I'll go.'

'Let go of my wrist. LET GO OF MY WRIST!'

'Not till yew promise not to run off.'

'Why the hell should I? Why the hell should I promise you anything? I owe you nothing. Let me GO!'

Izzy, deeply embarrassed, put the kettle on, and tried to ignore the matrimonial mêlée.'

'Now, come on, girl, don't be childish, let's jus' sit down an' 'ave a cup of tea an' talk it all out, like.'

'Damn you! Why the hell should I? I've had enough of you and your lies. I hate you. Let me go. LET ME GO!'

But Gwyn's grip was all too strong, and he saw nothing wrong in resorting to his brute strength. Maria's temper snapped, and she bent down and sank her teeth hard into his hand.

'Ow! You bitch! Gerroff!' He let her go, and she shot away across the room and banged her head against the wall. A Van Gogh painting came crashing down beside her, and one of Izzy's Chinese kites floated down from the ceiling. Maria leaned against the wall, blinking and stunned, then her face crumpled into tears and she rubbed her head. Gwyn bounded to her side.

'I'm sorry, darlin' – I didn't mean to hurt yew, honest, sweetheart. Come yere, darlin'. Yew'll soon feel better, now.' He endeavoured to embrace her, but Maria flung him off, stormed to the kitchen end of the room, and turned on him.

'Get out! Just get out! We don't want you here! You drive me mad! You're a devil! I hate you! Go away!' Her face was bright red, her eyes seemed about to fly out of their sockets, and her voice was a horrifying broken screech. Gwyn stood staring at her for a moment in awe, but then recovered himself.

'Orright, I'll goa. I'll goa. But jus' before I do, like, I want you to promise me that you'll see me – later, when you've calmed down. We gotta talk this owt, darlin'. I do love yew, y'knoa.' He took a step towards her: conciliatory, appeasing, looking curiously vulnerable with his cross eyes and his stray curls. Maria hurled the grater at him and hit him squarely between the eyes.

'Shit!' He was astonished, and angry. 'I'll smack your bloody arse for that, girl.' And he dived at her. Maria threw the ketchup. It smashed on the wall behind him. He seized her: she walloped him repeatedly with the chopping board. He ducked, swore, and flailed at her.

'Stop it! Stop it, you lunatics!' shrieked Izzy. 'If you must kill each other, go and do it somewhere else. You're wrecking my bloody flat!' They paid no heed to her. Izzy could bear it no longer. She ran out and downstairs to the second floor landing, then paused and listened. There was a sudden squeal, then Maria burst out and slammed the door behind her. A muffled roar: the door had obviously hit Gwyn in the face. Maria ran down the stairs towards Izzy: Izzy's door was flung open again and Gwyn shot out, tripped and fell downstairs on to his wife. Maria wriggled free, gasping like an old dog, but Gwyn stayed where he was. The fall had hurt him more.

'Ow – Christ, Jesus Christ, Jesus, my fuckin' ankle! Shit!' Maria ran back upstairs and into the flat, slammed the door, and locked and bolted it. A brief lull ensued. End of round one. To Maria on points. Gwyn's nose was bleeding, and as he stood up, gingerly, he winced at the pain from his ankle.

'Oh, Izzy,' he moaned, in self-pitying wail (perhaps, for once, justified), 'Izzy, girl, I've broken my bloody ankle. Gis a hand.' He seemed to indicate that she should help him upstairs. But Izzy was suddenly angry herself.

'Are you mad? Maria's never going to let you in. Just go home, Gwyn, and stop making such a fuss. You're not badly hurt. Stop being so silly and childish.'

'Not 'urt? Not 'urt? Listen to it. You've got a heart of stone, girl. I'm destroyed. You bloody women – you fight like fuckin' dervishes.'

'Oh, shut up! I'm fed up with both of you. You've ruined my weekend and you've wrecked my bloody flat. Just sod off, Gwyn, can't you? Sod off?'

The spectacle of the gentle Izzy thus transformed by fury was unusual enough to impress Gwyn. He limped off downstairs, whingeing in a pathetic way to himself.

'Beaten up by a pack of women. So this is what my life's come to. Supposed to be the weaker sex. Fuckin' murderers. So much for gentleness. So much for for-giveness—' At the bottom of the stairs he paused and gave Izzy a last half-defiant roar.

'You ent seen the last o' me yet, tell 'er!'

Izzy mounted her stairs feeling exhausted. Thank God the people on the floor below hadn't appeared. Let's hope they were out. Of course Izzy cared what the neighbours thought. Sex was all right, but violence was against all her deepest instincts. She rapped at the door.

'Let me in, Maria. It's all right, he's gone.'

'Are you sure? You're not tricking me, Izzy?'

'Oh, God!' Izzy exploded. 'Let me into my sodding flat, for Christ's sake, Maria, and STOP MESSING ME ABOUT!'

Slightly abashed, Maria complied.

If Izzy was messed about, that was nothing to the state of the flat. Tomato ketchup was everywhere, her best kite torn and trampled, her Van Gogh smashed, broken crockery everywhere, and overturned bottles and jars pouring and oozing. If only Izzy hadn't been in the habit of leaving the tops off things. She looked at it all and sighed deeply. Maria followed her gaze, and registered for the first time the results of the fracas.

'Oh dear, I'm terribly sorry, Izzy.'

'It's all right,' shrugged Izzy. 'After all, your marriage doesn't break up every weekend, does it?' And they set about clearing up.

On their way to school next day, Maria warned, 'Not a word of this at school, Izzy.'

'OK,' agreed Izzy, but it set her thinking. Presently she inquired, 'But if you – split up with Gwyn for good – you'll tell the people at school, eventually?'

'If they ask. If I think it's their business.'

'But for the time being, not a word?'

'Not a word.'

Izzy sighed. 'We do seem to need this secrecy business sometimes, don't we?'

Maria gave her a sharp look. 'Sometimes it protects your aching heart.'

And sometimes, thought Izzy, it makes it ache in the first place.

The minute she joined 4C for registration she felt there was something wrong. It wasn't on the surface: the boys, as usual, foghorned about, thumping each other playfully. But something was up amongst the girls. They provided the submerged atmosphere, so when there was Female Trouble the classroom might sound the same but it smelt different. This morning there was sulphur in the air. Izzy could not detect its source, however.

Razors had been missing for several days now. The rumours flew. He'd been recruited by an American gang operating in Chicago. He'd been arrested and was being held for questioning about a bank robbery. About a series of bank robberies. He'd gone off to Berlin to mastermind a drug-smuggling racket. Towards the end of registration, however, the door opened quietly and he was suddenly there, strolling modestly in, ever the Perfect English Gentleman in his green hair and earring. The whole class went still with anticipation. Izzy was agog – so much so that she could feel her gog right up against her tonsils.

'Roger!' she exclaimed. 'Where have you been?'

'Had a slight cold, Miss,' he murmured politely and slid into his chair. Then the bell rang for first lesson. Izzy picked up her bag and walked off towards her tryst with the Lower Sixth. She had only gone a few steps however, when the most ferocious din broke out behind her. Squealing, screaming, the jarring shriek of chairs, and the ear-splitting crash of overturned desks. She flew back.

Sharon and Lynette were fighting like wildcats: hair, teeth, nails, with the boys delightedly urging them on and the girls painfully crying to them to stop. Izzy knew she had to outvoice them all, and reached down to the soles of her feet for a huge breath. Some of Hideki's recent exercises suddenly revealed a practical value. *Bleathe thloo sore of feet* he had instructed, and in doing so Izzy found from somewhere a roar bigger than the Apocalypse.

'Sharon! Lynette! STOP THIS AT ONCE!'

They fell apart instantly, panting, ashamed, defiant, their hair all in knots, their hands trembling.

'Now the rest of you, go off to your lesson. Sharon, Lynette, just stand still and calm down.' The rest of the class filed reluctantly out, and shut the door behind them.

'Now, you two – what is this all about?'

Silence. Lynette tossed her head. Sharon glared out of the window. They were obviously going to continue dumb like this for ever.

'Sharon, go off to your DS lesson now, and come to the staff room to see me at break. Lynette, you stay where you are.' It wasn't that Lynette was the more

110

wicked, but her tongue was probably looser. Sharon, sulkily, walked out and slammed the door.

'Now then, Lynette, what's it all about?' Silence. 'Come on.' Silence. 'You can tell me. I won't tell anyone else. But I won't have my girls murdering each other the moment my back's turned.' Silence. 'Come on, Lynette, you're a sensible girl. I know you are. You wouldn't turn into a wildcat just over nothing. What was it?'

Lynette's pout relaxed slightly. 'It's Tony Fisher, Miss.'

'Tony who?'

'He's left school, now, Miss. He works at Grundy's. I've been going out with him for six weeks.'

'Yes?'

'Well – well last Friday Miss he said he'd go to the disco with me but then he rang up just before Miss and said he couldn't come 'cos his granny was ill and they'd got to go and visit 'er in orsepital Miss so I went to the disco on me own Miss wiv the girls like and Dawn and Tracey was there and they said they'd seen him down Wimpy's with Sharon. So I run off down there Miss but they wasn't there no more. Then on Saturday I rang him again and asked if I could come round and he said he couldn't 'cos 'is mum wanted 'im to go down Brent Cross wiv them Miss, so I said what about this evening and 'e said all right Miss but he sounded sort of odd anyway I said I'd meet him outside the Ope and Anchor at nine—'

'Come to the point, Lynette.'

'Yeah Miss yeah well anyway he never turned up Miss 'e stood me up and he never done that before so on Sunday I rung 'im up again Miss but he said he was too busy to see me 'cos 'e 'ad to work on 'is bike. So I went for a walk down the rec and John and Dave said they'd seen 'im with Sharon too, and just as I was walkin' 'ome I seen them Miss they was on his motor bike and they went past me they never saw me 'cos it was dark and everything but I recognized 'er boots Miss, then this morning she came in wiv love bites all over 'er neck so I decided to do 'er Miss.'

The next class was by now massing outside the door, staring through the glass with flat noses squashed up close, and rattling the door handle. Izzy felt an enormous weight descending on her.

'Oh well, Lynette, I can't possibly sort this all out now. You bring your books and come with me. You can sit and work in my sixth form class and we'll talk again about it at break.' Izzy knew that if she sent Lynette off to join Sharon in the Domestic Science lesson the saucepans might well fly. The DS teacher was new, tentative, and looked as if butter wouldn't melt in her hotplates. Trailed by the dismal Lynette, Izzy made her way to the Lower Sixth.

They were reading their own books when Izzy arrived – not Shakespeare, she noticed. They gave Lynette a few snotty looks and settled with that sixth form indifferent over-schooled weariness to the *Troilus and Cressida*. Lynette, sitting at the back, had to write a piece called *The Best Way to Sort Out Arguments*. Izzy hoped Lynette would have some good ideas. She certainly had none. Lynette stared out of the window and bit her nails. If only I could do the same, thought Izzy. But still, there was always the escape into Literature. But wait – *Troilus and Cressida?* Wars, wars and lechery? Could she face it?

'We won't do *Troilus and Cressida* today,' announced Izzy. 'Get out your Wife of Baths – I mean, your Wives of Bath – I mean – well, you know what I mean.' Not a smile, of course, from this ashen-souled set.

'But, Miss – you said—'

'Never mind what I said. We'll do Chaucer instead.'

'Please, Miss Comyn – I haven't brought my Chaucer.'

'Nor have I, Miss.'

'Nor have I.'

'Oh, all right then, *Troilus and Cressida* it must be. Where were we?'

'Act Five, Scene Two, Miss.'

'All right. Carry on reading – same parts as before.'

Jennifer Jackson, a pink-cheeked and virginal Queen's Guide, cleared her delicate throat:

'Troilus, farewell! one eye yet looks on thee,
But with my heart the other eye doth see.
Ah! poor our sex: this fault in us I find,
The error of our eye directs our mind.
What error leads must err. O! then conclude
Minds sway'd by eyes are full of turpitude.

'What's turpitude, Miss?'

At break Izzy flew to the coffee machine where Maria was already drinking deep, looking much perkier. She had just been talking about the Civil War, which always cheered her up. Too bad it hadn't done much for 5M. Never mind. Dick bore down on the coffee machine, too. Izzy felt he was someone she'd vaguely known once, and about whom she'd forgotten an important fact. Maria slid away.

'Well, Izzy,' he inquired tenderly, 'how – um – how were things?'

'Oh God, Dick, absolutely awful, you've no idea.' Come to think of it, just how *did* Dick know? Izzy was puzzled.

'Was she difficult?'

'Well, you'd be difficult if you'd just walked out on your husband.'

'Oh, my God, Izzy, how terrible for you! I hadn't realized – I, er, that that had happened. Was it sudden?'

'Yes, completely out of the blue. This weekend.'

'Stone the crows. Jesus.' Dick was running the gamut of his emergency vocabulary. 'And at their age, too.'

'Well, they're not thirty yet, Dick. Besides, I don't think any marriage is safe at any age.'

It was Dick's turn to look puzzled. 'Izzy – did you say

113

'– um – not thirty? Who?'

'Maria and Gwyn, of course.'

'Oh lor' – you mean *Maria* and *Gwyn* have had a – a bust-up?'

'Yes. Who did you think I meant?'

'I thought – I thought you meant your mum and dad.'

'My *mum and dad*? Listen, Dick, my dad's dead.'

'Oh, Gor' – I'm sorry – I've got hold of the – I've got hold of the wrong end of the stick.'

Just then there was a very loud knock at the staff room door. Mary Greenfield flung it open.

'Don't you *dare* knock on the door like that!' she trumpeted. 'Who do you want to see? Who? Don't mumble! Well, just wait!' And the door was closed. Mary came gliding over to Izzy.

'That dreadful Sharon Thompson of yours, Izzy – Tell me—' she dived conspiratorially into Izzy's shoulder and whispered so low Dick could not hear – 'what's wrong with Maria? She *does* look awful. I've never *seen* her so haggard. Some trouble at home? Her husband is *so charming.*'

'Excuse me, Mary,' Izzy gasped, 'but I've just remembered. I must make a phone call.' And she escaped to the payphone in the corner and dialled a very long number. It rang: a poised faraway purr.

'Mum? This is Izzy. Can I come next weekend?'

'Well, of course you can, love.'

'Oh, marvellous. I'll ring again later. I just wanted to know if it would be OK.'

'I'd better bake some shortbread, then, I suppose?'

'It doesn't matter about the shortbread, Mum – just let me come, that's all.'

'You're not in some sort of trouble, are you, dear?'

'No! Not at all! Everything's fine! I'll ring again later in the week. Must go – I'm at school – Bye!'

She sunk into a chair. Dick was still hovering. Oh Mum, Mum, Mum, thought Izzy. Mummy! Help me! I

114

don't like the nasty men! And I don't like the nasty ladies!

'Er – Izzy,' ventured Dick, 'I'm really sorry about that – stupid mistake – only I was thinking about Saturday morning.'

'Saturday morning?' What Saturday? What morning? What the hell was he talking about, at all?

'You know – you said your mother was coming.'

Oh, my God, *yes*. Way back at the beginning of time, Dick seemed somehow to have spent a night with her, and to have been prematurely ejaculated from the flat. Because someone was coming – *who*? Ah yes – *Michael*. Good Lord, she'd said she would phone him on Sunday, and she'd forgotten. *Forgotten Michael*.

'Mich – My mum was absolutely fine.'

'There's just one other thing.' His eyes were beginning to slither about and were not, for once, boring either into her head or body. 'Only I think I – I mislaid my – some underclothes at your place.'

'Oh, your *pants*! Don't worry about that, Dick. They're safe under my pillow.'

'Under your pillow – oh, Izzy!' Dick's face lit up with the awful neon of true love for a false god.

'Miss Comyn – Sharon Thompson wants to see you.'

The bell rang, though Izzy felt she had long ago been counted out. With such breaks, who needs lessons?'

9

A few days passed. Michael was filming in Lancashire. Gwyn did not ring. Maria started to go out every evening, to what she called 'groups'. She kept asking Izzy to come with her, but Izzy had a fear of groups and pleaded much marking. Dick tried to crowbar a few invites into the conversation, but Izzy told him she was very busy going to groups. Hideki, whose evening classes they now enthusiastically attended, initiated them into a splendid new exercise which involved sticking your tongue out as far as it would go. It was called the Lion. Izzy had a feeling it would come in useful one day. Life, by and large, settled down a bit. Even Sharon and Lynette were back on hugging-the-same-radiator terms. Izzy had given up trying to sort that one out. Perhaps giving up trying was the answer.

On Thursday night, with Maria out, and the marking done, Izzy was just embarking on washing her smalls, when the phone rang.

''Loa.'

'Oh – Gwyn.'

'Noa. 'Snot Gwyn. S'Hywel, darlin'.'

'Oh. You sound just the same on the phone.'

'Except 'e uses longer words, like. 'Ow are you anyway, girl?'

'All right now. Things have been a bit fraught, though, what with Gwyn and Maria splitting up.'

'I knoa. Gwyn's been doin' some serious drinkin'. An' I been 'elpin' 'im.'

'What sort of state's he in, Hywel?'

'Oa – very, very bad I should say, darlin'.'

'Are you still living there or have you moved to Streatham?'

'Noa. I'm stayin' with Gwyn, see, to keep 'im company.'

'Hey, Hywel – I'd really like to have a talk to you about it. A proper talk, I mean. Could you come over some time?'

'Noa time like the present, mon – I'll come over now.'

Izzy's mind was whirling with questions she didn't dare ask Maria, and other questions she'd never have the chance to ask Gwyn. How had it all blown up? What had Gwyn said? How did he feel, now? What did he think was the best plan? What did he expect Maria to do next? Had anything like this ever happened before? Did Gwyn think they'd get back together in the end? The more she thought about it, the more remarkable it seemed that they should ever have got it together in the first place.

Hywel arrived, installed himself on the softest part of the sofa, and took out a tiny plastic bag.

'Yere you are, darlin'. I brought a little treat for yew, like.' Izzy stared. He unfolded the bag, to reveal a little curling nest of greeny-brown fibre.

'Gosh,' exclaimed Izzy, 'drugs!'

'Grass. Best grass, mon. This'll blow your 'ead off, girl.'

'But, Hywel – I don't want to have my head blown off. I want to talk about Gwyn and Maria.'

'Yeah, yeah. I knoa.' He set about rolling a joint, with the slow, relaxed certainty of a man who could do it in his sleep. Hywel could do most things in his sleep. Izzy was dubious. She'd come across the odd Substance at college, but most of her contemporaries had regarded drugs as strictly for the geriatrics. Izzy would gladly have experimented if her peers had dictated it. As it was, she found white wine provided any necessary oblivion, and besides, it tasted so nice.

'What sort of state is Gwyn in?'

117

'Oa – orright. Pretty terrible, really, I s'pose, like. Drinkin' every night.'

'He came round and made a scene last weekend, but we haven't heard from him since.'

'I knoa. I think at first 'e thought it was just temp'ry. A big row, like. Only now it seems to be dawnin' a bit that she might be serious. Gis a bit o' cardboard darlin'.'

'Maria is really extraordinary. When she came here first she was beside herself with rage and hatred, and now she just ignores the subject. She won't see him, you know, Hywel, or even talk about him. Let alone *to* him.'

'Oa. Gotta light?'

'What do you think will happen? Do you think they've really split up for good? What does Gwyn say about it? Do you think he'll accept things as they are for a while, or will he try to force some kind of show-down?'

Hywel took a big drag, and held it in his lungs for ages. Eventually, he subsided with a great sigh. 'Grea' stuff, mon. Grea'! From Sri Lanka – a place called Adam's Peak.' He took another huge lungful.

'Do you think they'll sell the flat? I mean, they'll have to, won't they? Or will Gwyn refuse to admit what's happened and go on trying to delude himself that everything's all right?'

Hywel gazed blankly at his faraway navel. 'I dunnoa,' he decided, at length, and then handed the joint to Izzy.

'Maria's really strange. She seems determined to settle into a new life. She keeps going out all the time. It's odd. It's as if she's leapt straight into a new life even before she's properly out of the old one.'

'Maybe she's bin wantin' to get out for years, like.'

'Yes. That's a thought. Maybe she has. But, Hywel – I'm sure she really loves Gwyn still. I'm sure she really does love him.'

Hywel turned his head slowly towards her and gave a befuddled frown. 'Wha's *that* got to dew with it?'

Izzy found that Hideki's exercises enabled her to hold the magic smoke down for a very long time. She

118

imagined it blooming through the rosy branches of her lungs like a morning mist through trees. Rather like one of Hideki's songs. Does the mist go through the trees? Or do the trees go through the mist? The planet rolls through its vapours.

'Do you think they'll ever get back together again, Hywel?'

There was no answer. The room began to slant slightly. All its edges and lines sharpened. The colours boomed and whelmed. Hywel, sitting meditatively on the sofa, began to look very young and very different. Izzy's stomach, arms and legs buzzed. A curious radiance seemed to be filling the bathroom and spilling out into the hall. Izzy got up to investigate. She looked down on Hywel as it seemed from a great height.

'Hey!' she discovered. 'This is what it's like to be you!'

'Wha'? Wha'?'

'Up here. This is what it's like.'

In the bathroom, the light was bouncing off the bath, off the tiles, the mirror. Izzy watched it for a while.

'Hey, Hywel,' she called, 'I'd left the bathroom light on.' No answer. She left the light on again since it was enjoying itself so much, and made the trip back along the hall to Hywel – a long and mysterious journey, past cupboard doors slightly ajar. As she passed one, something within stirred. She suddenly realized there were little creatures living in her cupboard.

'It's a zoo!' she marvelled. 'My flat's a zoo. I throw 'em an apple core sometimes. They come out at night for exercise.'

'What yew talkin' about, darlin'?'

'The animals in my cupboards.'

Hywel stared at her with glassy eyes. 'I've turned to stone, mon,' he discovered.

Izzy suddenly thought of food.

'Food!' she cried, like Archimedes in the bath.

'Yeah – food!' echoed Hywel. 'Munchies!'

They ransacked the kitchen. Hywel prepared beans

on toast with basil sauce (out of a tin), anchovies, tinned asparagus and Emmental cheese.

'This is the most delicious thing I've ever tasted.'

'Noa, darlin'. Yew're wrong there. It's the most delicious thing *I've* ever tasted.' Then they ate half a pound of grapes, two tangerines, and a bowl of muesli with honey and yogurt. Still a desperate greed raged.

''Ave yew got any nuts, girl?'

'You're supposed to be the one with the nuts.'

'Well, I did 'ave some, like, but I buried 'em last winter, and now I can't find the buggers.'

A terrible tyrannical giggle kept bubbling up from their guts, leaving them gasping and weak, leaning on the furniture. Hywel began to thirst.

'The Chianti! The Fuckin' Chianti! We forgot the-fuckin' Chianti!'

'Do you *have* to use that word all the time, Hywel?'

'Oh, all right then, the fuckin' wine!'

'What wine?'

'Didn't I bring some? I'm sure I brought some. Didn't I?'

'When?'

'Now, like. Today, girl. Get a grip on yewerself.'

'Wine? Today? No. Not a drop. You tight-fisted sponger.'

'Praps I only dreamt it then.'

Izzy's doorbell rang. The squawkbox announced DXYZLK, Izzy translated *Dick*, and immediately invited him up.

'It's Dick! It's Dick!' she exulted.

'Watch yewer language, girl. I'm a well-brought-up boy. My mam warned me about dirty girls like you.'

Izzy's door opened, and there stood Dick, blinking anxiously in the light.

'I – I just happened to be passing, Izzy, so I thought – well, I wondered if you'd be in and – and I thought I might as well – um – drop by and – er – say hello – I hope I'm not – er – intruding.'

'Good God, mon!' said Hywel in awe. 'That was a fuckin' long speech. Oooo wrote it for yoa?'

'Come in, Dick, come in, it's marvellous to see you!'

Izzy pulled Dick, still resisting slightly, over the threshold. She looked rapturously pleased to see him. Dick doubted the evidence of his senses, but here was her smile, her eyes, her feather-soft, yielding hands. The Welsh hanger-on appeared to be drunk. Perhaps he'd been molesting Izzy, and that was why she was so pleased to see Dick. Dick would deal with him, somehow. Preferably not physically.

'Dick! We've been having a wonderful time! We had a great meal! Is there any of it left, Hywel?'

'Noa. But I'll make you somethin' new, mon. I wouldn't do this for just anybody, mind.'

'It's all right, thanks, I've had some t – some supper.'

'Oh, but Dick, you really should have something! Not in the sense of supper but in the sense of sheer greed.'

Dick was puzzled. 'You seem to be – enjoying yourself, Izzy.'

'Oh, Dick, I'm feeling absolutely wonderful! For the first time I can see how really handsome you are! Hey, Hywel!' She took Dick's glasses off. 'Isn't he handsome? Look – isn't he handsome?'

'Hey – don't—' Dick protested feebly, but Hywel stared at him with deepest concentration.

''E's very, very fuckin' 'andsome indeed, girl. I sea what you mean.'

'He's like that film star – what's his name?'

'Oa yes – that one that was in that film – what's it called – you knoa.'

'Yes – that's right. That's the one. You look just like him, Dick.'

'Er – can I have my glasses back?'

Dick was thoroughly alarmed. Were they taking the piss, or what? *Was* he handsome? What was going on? And, more important, were they lovers? And most important of all, were he and Izzy lovers? She seemed to

121

vanish out of his hand, like water.

'I tell you what, Dick, I'm goin' to give you a toaken of my esteem, like.'

Dick tensed every muscle. What was this? A prelude to a punch-up? Was the giant about to crack his skull in two with his mighty fist? But Hywel sat down at the table and brought out a little plastic bag. He opened it. Dick saw the greeny-brown jungle of stalks and leaves. Drugs!

A great spear of fear went through him. He'd always avoided them in the past, with a dogged working-class puritanism. He'd seen what happened when people took drugs. They lost all their inhibitions. Dick's inhibitions were so vital to him they felt like his skeleton. He was sure if he lost his inhibitions he'd unravel into a kind of amoeba.

'Er – thanks, actually, I – I – um – don't. Thanks all the same.'

But Hywel went on making the joint. Izzy snuggled up to Dick and turned her wildly exciting little stoat's face up to him.

'Come on, Dick, don't be so silly. We want you to join us on Adam's Peak.'

'On whose – what?'

'It's the mountain in the Garden of Eden where this stuff grew. Just relax, Dick. It'll do you a power of good.' And she began to stroke his chin, paralysing him.

Dick awaited his doom with a sickening sense of being trapped. Oh, Uncle Herbert, you were right after all! But it was too late. He had slipped too far down the slope. Below him lay ruin and dissolution.

'I – er – oh – well – all right.' He closed his eyes and awaited his doom.

They stood over him and supervised his inhalations, Izzy pinching his nose at times because he wasn't very good at it. Dick was sure he was going to feel sick. He was sure he'd feel sick at any moment. Any minute now.

122

He was bound to feel sick. Yes! There it was! He felt sick!

'I feel sick,' he complained to them.

'Tha's right,' encouraged Hywel. 'It'll soon pass off, like.'

It passed off. Now the backs of his knees were buzzing. He looked at his feet. *My feet!* he thought. *I've taken you for granted all these years.* Dick was away.

'Hywel and I were just talking about this Gwyn and Maria business, Dick,' said Izzy, unreasonably becoming very matter-of-fact now that he was deeply into his feet.

'Oh yes, terrible thing,' he mumbled, sneaking a look at his shoes.

'We were wondering whether they'll ever get together again. It seems unlikely, don't you think?'

'Yes. As unlikely as six toes.'

'That's it. That's it exactly. As unlikely as six toes.'

'Some people in the world do 'ave six toes, mon. I seen it in a magazine. Pterodactyls, they're called.'

'Well, there you are, Dick. Six toes are pretty unlikely – but you just might meet somebody who had them. And that's how I feel it is between Gwyn and Maria.'

Dick wondered how on earth Gwyn and Maria came into it all. For a while they sat and mused: on marriage, on toes, on words. What a funny word *ketchup* was, for example. Was it Arab, or Aztec, or what?

'Did the Aztecs use ketchup?'

'Noa, mon. They didn't need it, like. They 'ad real blood.'

Presently Dick stirred. He got up and walked along the carpet, one foot behind another, like a child on a kerb. He was walking along a pattern.

'I have something to say,' he announced at the other end, and turned and faced them. They looked up expectantly.

'I say this to you, Hywel, because I have a tremendous

123

respect for you. For one thing, you're a good deal bigger than me. And a lot handsomer, too. But I also respect you as a man, and an Unemployed Person.'

'You sound like the Mayor of Keighley, Dick!' Izzy squealed, clapping her hands.

'Kindly do not interrupt this speech, Madam,' warned Dick. 'It concerns you intimately, as you are about to find out.'

'Dirty bugger!' sniggered Hywel.

'Sir! I will not have any further interruptions.' It was true – he was the Mayor of Keighley. The sentences rolled off him: pompous, confident. Not a hesitation. Even the vocabulary was aldermanesque.

'I feel it is my duty to reveal to you a truth which may be unpalatable, Hywel. I am well aware that for a gentleman to divulge such things in public may not be – er – whatsit. But I feel we three all know each other so well that we are, in fact, in private.'

'That's *right*, Dick. We *are* in private!'

'Wha'? Wha's he on about, darlin'?'

'Hywel! It is to you I speak. I wish you to know that last Friday night, I was in that very bedroom, and I made love to Miss Comyn – *three times.*'

'Good goin', mon!' roared Hywel. 'Didyew put yewer back out, like?'

'Dick! You pig!' giggled Izzy. 'I'd never have slept with you if I'd realized you were the Mayor of Keighley.'

'I tell you this not as an idle boast, though God knows I am proud enough of it, but to let you know how the land lies. In case you yourself were intending to pay court to Miss Comyn.'

'Pay court to 'er, mon? I wouldn't dream of it, like! I'm a well-brought-up boy, don't talk dirty in front of me. She's my little sister.' And to illustrate the con-sanguinity, Hywel gave Izzy a great hug which would have hurt quite a lot in normal circumstances.

'Oh, well, then, that's all right,' said Dick. 'As long as

you realize that what happened on Friday, happened.'

'It happened,' affirmed Hywel.

'I can prove it if you like.' Dick was insatiable. 'Come with me.' The others got up and staggered after him to the bedroom. The bed was neatly made – Maria had, of course, been sleeping in it all week, at Izzy's insistence. Izzy had hardly been in the room at all.

'Under this pillow,' announced Dick with a conjuror's air, 'lie a pair of blue Y-fronts, which I bought in her honour in Tottenham last Thursday.' And he whipped away the pillow. There was nothing there. Just empty sheet. All three of them stared at the empty sheet.

'Well, that's a corker,' remarked Dick. 'Where the hell are they?' Izzy shrugged. Then Hywel spotted them.

'There they are, mon! On the wall!' They all looked. There, attached to the wall by a dart, were Dick's undies, looking very dismal and ashamed. Attached to them was a note which read EXHIBIT 'A' FOR THE PROSECUTION.

'It must be one of Maria's jokes,' suggested Izzy. Yes. This was definitely reassuring.

'Right then,' said Hywel, ''avin' 'eard your speech, which I admired greatly, I must now ask you to leave, as I wish to screw my little sister.'

'On the contrary,' boomed Dick. 'I must ask you to leave for the same reason.'

'Oh, do stop talking like that, Dick,' pleaded Izzy. 'You sound as if you'd got a paunch. Besides, I don't like the way you both assume I'm game. As a matter of fact, I don't want to sleep with either of you, thank you very much.'

Hywel fell into bed. 'Let's *all* sleep yere,' he suggested. 'There's plenty of room, an' I knoa yew're my trew comrade, Dick. We mus'n't let a mere woman come between us – excep' in bed.'

'You'll both have to go,' instead the mere woman, ''cos Maria's staying with me at the moment, and this is her room.'

'Oh grea', mon! Dick can 'ave 'er.'

'No, thanks. I bow to your superior – er – your superior – um – your superior thing, Hywel. Maria must be yours.'

'Tha's very kind of you, mon,' grinned Hywel. 'Noa one's ever told me my thing was superior, before. Well, not since Megan, any road.'

'Cocoa! That's it! That's what I really want!' Izzy made this discovery with glee. She felt she had stumbled on the secret of the universe: sex couldn't hold a candle to cocoa. They left the bedroom and, as they burst into the living room, suddenly beheld Maria standing there with a strange girl. The girl had short hair, was wearing baggy trousers, workmen's boots, and a donkey jacket. She was remarkably beautiful, pale, golden-haired, and wore not a scrap of make-up. A single blue stone glittered in her ear.

'Izzy,' said Maria, 'this is Charlotte.' Charlotte nodded in a wary way.

'Hey, we didn't hear you come in, at all,' cried Izzy. 'I was just going to make some cocoa. Charlotte, these are my friends Dick and Hywel.'

'Bon Gion – issimo,' said Hywel.

Charlotte did not even bother to nod to the men. She simply swept them with a glance and said, 'Shall I put the kettle on, Maria?'

Something about this simple phrase depressed Izzy. She felt the roundabouts begin to slow.

'Did you have a good group?'

'Yes. We had a very good talk. About social attitudes to menstruation.'

'Crumbs,' said Dick.

'My attitude to menstruation is, if it's all right by you, girl, it's all right by me, like.'

'Nobody asked you,' said Maria, and turned to the cooker. She put the kettle on. The others sat down, sobered by her tone.

'I want you to know, Maria,' ventured Dick, 'that I

126

admire you very much. Although you have always frightened the living daylights out of me.' Maria ignored this.

'Did you finish your marking, Izzy?'

'Er – yes,' Izzy faltered.

Maria turned to the silent Charlotte. 'When Izzy tells me she's got some marking to do, what that means is, she's going to get stoned with some men.' She said it not without affection, but not without spite, either. Hywel, meanwhile, was eyeing Charlotte up.

'Hey – harlot, or whatever your name is, girl – who the fuck are you, now? Why yew dressed up like a navvy? Yew got my uncle's boots on, look.'

'I like these clothes. They keep me warm.' Her voice was level. Not hostile, but only by a whisker.

'But, look, darlin', yewer a very very bewtiful girl, like. 'Scuse me if I'm speakin' out of turn an' that, but I'm not quite in command of my facilities this evenin'.'

'Do you want cocoa or coffee, Charlotte?' Maria asked.

'Coffee, please,' said Charlotte, as if on principle.

'Noa – I mean, what I was tryin' to say, was – '

'Oh, shut up!' snapped Maria, to whom the sound even of a blundering and honest Welsh voice was a trial.

'Now, listen, Maria, girl, I'm only tryin' to tell yewer friend that she's an incredibly attractive woman, an' I think she should stop tryin' to look like a site foreman.'

'I don't dress to please you,' Charlotte informed him. 'I dress to please myself. Have you got that book you said you'd lend me, Maria?'

Izzy was feeling bad. There didn't seem to be room in the world for all of her lives. She longed again for Yorkshire and her mother's scrubbed kitchen.

'I get it, darlin',' persisted Hywel, trying in vain to tear Charlotte's attention away from the book. 'I get it – listen to this – are yew one of thoase femininist girls, like?'

'Feminist, you berk,' corrected Dick.

Charlotte looked up briefly from her book. 'Of course,' she smiled. 'Aren't you?'

'Of course I am, like! I'm with yew girls all the way. I was sayin' to Gwyn only the other day, one o' those feminists right? One o' thoase 'd be worth ten ordinary women, right? An' 'e agreed with me. We both fancy you all somethin' rotten. All that short 'air an' stuff!'

'Shut up, Hywel,' ordered Izzy. 'Drink your cocoa up and go. And you, Dick. I'm tired.'

They obeyed. They simply drained Dick's mugs, got up, put on their coats, and went. If only Izzy could have that effect on 4C.

At the door Hywel paused. 'G'night, girls! Yew're all delicious!' He blew a general kiss, and was gone.

A very curious and strained atmosphere sprang up. Izzy felt deeply ashamed, and she didn't know why. And what's more, she didn't see why the hell she *should* feel so bloody ashamed. All the same, by Christ, did she feel ashamed! She pretended to do some washing-up in the kitchen, listening to Maria and Charlotte talking. They were discussing the next meeting. Someone called Anne was giving a paper.

'Then,' said Maria, 'the week after, I think we should all read *Patriarchal Attitudes*.'

'I wouldn't mind jotting down a few thoughts on that.' Charlotte's voice was so light, and yet it was the lightness of metal, somehow. Izzy went back, wondered whether to join them, hesitated.

'Do you want to come to the next meeting, Izzy?' asked Maria. 'We're all reading this book, and we're going to discuss it. I'm sure you'd find it really interesting.'

'When would that be?' panicked Izzy.

'Next Tuesday. We meet on Tuesdays and Thursdays.'

'Oh, gosh, no, I'm sorry,' lied Izzy, even more inexpertly than usual, 'Michael's coming back from Lancashire next week and I'm going to see him then.'

'When Michael calls, Izzy comes,' Maria observed to

Charlotte. Izzy went hot with resentment. Charlotte and Maria exchanged knowing smiles.

'Well, why not?' exploded Izzy.

'Why not, indeed, said the prisoner, shaking her chains.'

'And what's that supposed to mean?'

'Only joking. It's just that I think you're far too good for Michael.'

Izzy was mollified, but only slightly. She was also beginning to feel very tired and ratty. Should she go to bed? She would have to use the bedroom, then – and abandon her vigil on the sofa by the phone. Michael had managed to ring from Lancashire, once or twice, at about midnight. She wished Charlotte would go, but instead she picked up a book of Marvell's poetry and pretended to read.

Quite soon, Charlotte went. Maria said goodbye to her with evident tenderness, and they embraced fondly at the door. Izzy was amazed, but tried to contain her gawp within the book.

'Ah, well – good night, Izzy,' nodded Maria, and was instantly gone into her room.

Izzy lay on the sofa and looked at the grain on the cupboard doors. It swirled and whorled like a giant's fingerprint, or a secret map of some oceanic currents. The seas, the forests, the human tissue, it was all one. Down, down she felt herself falling, into an ocean full of mermaids. Their pale, coaxing arms drew her into the depths, and all their faces were Charlotte's. She followed the curving currents of her own cupboard door, her submarine map, and realized dimly that it was a map of sleep.

'Damn,' she thought, 'I'll have forgotten that by the morning.'

10

'Maria,' ventured Izzy, 'would you like to come up to Yorkshire with me this weekend? I'm going to see my mum.'

'Oh, Izzy, that'd be absolutely marvellous! Thank you so much. I'd love to.' Maria turned to her with such eagerness that it made Izzy jump.

'Mind that bike!' she shrieked. They were driving to school. She vowed she would never again spring things on Maria, en route.

'Yorkshire!' breathed Maria. 'Bliss!'

For a brief and very nasty moment, Izzy wished she hadn't invited her, for indeed she knew it would be bliss, and somehow also, most blissful alone. Then she banished the thought, thoroughly ashamed. If ever a woman deserved to get away from her torments and breathe a little fresh air, Izzy thought, that woman was Maria.

So, on Friday evening, after school, and in a dismal rainstorm, they battled up the motorway. Somehow Maria's driving seemed better on the motorway – there was more room for the other cars to escape into. Maria smoked. She had taken up smoking with a will, or rather, perhaps, a vengeance. Her thoughts were an enigma to Izzy, who dozed among the mysteries, like a cat on a newspaper. Maria was finding it a most exhilarating drive. The further she went, the better she felt. She wished the motorway would go right up to the North Pole and down the other side. Perhaps all those Polar explorers, she thought, were escaping from unhappy marriages.

As they passed Rotherham, the rain stopped. At Bradford, Exit 26, they left the motorway. Izzy woke up, refreshed by a most stimulating dream about Michael, in which he remembered it was all a mistake, he wasn't married after all. The familiar drystone walls leapt up in the headlights, and then – at the last moment it seemed, sometimes – smoothed away to the side. They reached Haworth with its precipitous cobbled streets. There was no one about.

'The whole of England seems to be empty,' remarked Izzy. 'Except London.'

'I don't know how your ma can live here all by herself,' wondered Maria. 'Stuck away in the country miles from anywhere. I'd go mad.'

'Oh, I don't know. She does live on the edge of a village,' retorted Izzy. 'Besides, all the neighbours have known her for years. She sees people every day. And the Smiths at the next farm would notice instantly if anything was wrong. It's her country. She loves it. She grew up here.'

Maria sighed, and her sigh came out of the heart of loss. Izzy wondered about Maria's parents. She had never been invited there.

'Don't your mum and dad feel the same about their place?'

'Oh, no,' Maria smiled sardonically to herself. 'Their place is just a sort of dormitory suburb of Oxford. Very lush, very wealthy. A sort of pastoral escape for the dons and their various hangers-on, where they can pretend to be leading a rural life. A rural life, my arse! You should see my mother's drawing-room. It's like something out of *House and Garden*.'

'This is it – this turning here.'

'Ah yes – I remember.' The car swung fiercely down a deep lane, then drew up in a farmyard. A modest stone farmhouse faced them. Maria switched off the engine and blackness and silence enveloped them for a second. And then the barking started. Not just the nearest dog, but far away up the valley, further and further, dog after distant dog.

'Every dog in the country knows we've come.'

The front door opened and there in the lamplight stood Izzy's mum: a dear little round woman, with Izzy's slanty eyes, Issy's plump cheeks, but instead of the sausagey lips some very pert little witty lips of her own. She wore an apron, and reached out to Izzy with plump paws covered in flour. They kissed, and stepped inside to the wonderful smell of baking.

Inside, a huge old kitchen range, black and shining, with a great fire blazing away right up the chimney. On each side of the range were old oak settles, high-backed and stern. Before the fire stood a great oak table laid for tea, with willow-patterend plates glittering in the firelight. Beyond, a huge dresser clothed a wall. More plates were ranged up there. There was a comfortable little parlour at the back, of course, overlooking the valley, with easy chairs and a TV. But Mrs Comyn had kept this room exactly as it had been when she walked into it as a bride in 1945. Izzy felt a deep sigh fold over her, sank down into the favourite corner of her favourite settle, and stared into the flames.

'How are you, Maria, love?' inquired Mrs Comyn. 'You're looking a bit peaky, dear. Sit down, take the weight off your feet. You must be tired out with all that driving.'

Cups of tea were brought. Cakes, in the back kitchen, were produced from the oven, a bowl of hyacinths bloomed on the dresser. Two old cats came padding in, to see what was what. Tabbies, both of them: once male, but neutered at the very last minute which made them absolutely enormous and probably quite indignant. They were called Bogie and Jack, after Izzy's dad's two favourite film stars. Izzy's dad had died six years ago: had been a restless, argumentative, noisy man, fond of laying down the law, and effortlessly dominating his buttery little wife. He'd adored his little Izzy, shouted at

132

his idle layabout of a son (now a research biochemist at Edinburgh University) and one day dropped down dead in the cowshed. The cats, Jack (after Jack Benny) and Bogie, had been two when he had died. Izzy could remember thinking how odd it was that the cats were still alive, but her dad was dead.

Jack was the larger, handsomer and infinitely more stupid of the felines. It had taken him a whole fortnight to learn to use the cat-flap. He used to stand and watch Bogie going busily in and out, flip-flap, flip-flap, for days on end, with a mystified expression on his furry chops. He was also useless at catching things. Bogie, an altogether slinkier specimen, snapped up anything that moved in the surrounding countryside: mice, voles, sheep, lost hikers – but Jack couldn't get the hang of it, and why the hell should he, with Fate sending him two great platefuls of Whiskas out of the sky every day?

Jack's other problem had been in the thorny area of affectional bonds. Whereas Bogie launched himself with promiscuous passion at all comers, rubbing himself ecstatically against every available inch of them and purring like the Queen Mum's Daimler, Jack watched from a blank world of feline anomie. He had a healthy appetite and he looked ravishingly beautiful. It was all he could do. Had he been born a woman, he'd have been a dazzling success.

Maria lost her cool when cats came on the scene.

'Miaucrepuss fiaucrepuss!' she drooled. 'Muesli Puesli! Pusscat Schlusscat!' Bogie launched himself recklessly into a full-blooded physical relationship with her, while Jack stared in amazement.

'Oh Jackpuss, don't you love me puss? Oh Bogie, Bogie, you are an abandoned old fogey.'

People often croon at animals in ways in which they would never address another human being: in voices full of rapturous, uncritical joy. Izzy thought this was especially noticeable in Maria's case.

There followed desultory talk, amongst the humans,

of school and the W1, the weather and the Japanese exercises. And the inevitable question finally came.

'How's Gwyn?'

'Oh, he's fine, thanks,' said Maria. Izzy sighed with relief. A log slipped in the fire. She could not have faced, at this moment, All That.

It was lovely to go to bed early, with baked faces, into cool bedrooms where the stiff sheets smelt of lavender. Izzy and Maria shared a twin-bedded room that overlooked the yard. Maria opened the window and listened to the staring silence.

'God, listen to that,' she marvelled. 'The sound of nothing.' Izzy, the country child, smiled to herself, knowing that it wasn't the sound of nothing, but of a quietly humming universe, with the whisper of foxes' tracks in the fields and the growl of trees against the wind.

'Cor! It's freezing!' Maria, having had her sniff, closed the country out. She found it faintly sinister but was very glad she had come.

'Oh, it's so nice to be home,' basked Izzy, snuggling deep into her bed. 'Have you told your parents yet, Maria – about you and Gwyn?'

Maria got undressed with a weary indifference. 'No. I can't face it yet. I've tried to write, but I can't put it into words that don't sound brutal and unforgiving.'

'Perhaps you are being brutal and unforgiving.'

'Perhaps I am.'

'Why don't you go home and tell them? I'm sure it would be easier.'

'I may have to. But – oh, it's so unlike this place, you can't imagine.'

'What is it like, then?'

'Well – it's a big old Tudor house, with a pear tree on the wall.'

'It sounds lovely.'

'It should be – it should be. But – well, it's all wrong, somehow. My father's often away – he goes off on long trips, ripping off innocent peasants in country districts – mind your mum doesn't ever let him into her house, he'd have that dresser out of her hands for a couple of greasy tenners if he could get away with it. And then sell it in Oxford for four hundred pounds.'

'My mum would never sell it.'

'Of course not. She's got more sense – Sense! I wonder if that's what's missing in my house. I don't know. Oooh, this hot water bottle is marvellous! All I know is, something's missing.'

'Like what?'

'Well, for one thing, my mother's never had an interest, except her house and her appearance. So she's always restlessly tarting up one or the other. Last time I went home she'd suddenly gone blonde. And then she showed me how she'd done up my father's study, like a Vermeer, she said.'

'What do you mean, like a Vermeer?'

'So it looked like a Vermeer painting. She'd covered the table with one of those cloths that look like Turkey carpets – you can get them in Amsterdam – and she'd imported a spinet.'

'A spinet!'

'Yes. My dad had just filched one from some poor old dear in the Lake District. And she'd put up a huge antique map on the wall, above the spinet. And she said, "There you are darling! Isn't it Vermeer?" I could've spat.'

'Why? It sounds rather a nice idea to me.'

'Oh, come on, Izzy! Bored women playing games. Re-arranging the tomb furniture. She might as well have a Caravaggio room, with a couple of under-age rent boys from Bologna getting stuck into the satsumas. Or a Francis Bacon room with a flayed carcass hanging from a hook and a Pope or two screaming in the corner.'

'It's probably just a harmless hobby.'

'I find the whole notion of hobbies extremely depressing. Work's one thing. A hobby's a little bland diversion to keep your mind off death.'

'Well, why not? Who wants to think about death all the time? It's bad enough when it happens.' Unlike Maria, Izzy had a real death to remember. 'Anyway, my mum has hobbies, too. She makes jam, and knits things for me and for Bob and his family. And she sings in the church choir.'

'But that's different.'

'Why? Why is it different?'

'I don't know. Hold on a minute. Let me think why it's different.'

There was a pause, in which Izzy heard an owl hoot across the parishes.

'I think it's partly the money. My parents have too much. And the roots. Your mum's always lived here. She seems part of the land, somehow. I don't know, my mother's life seems so meaningless – so wasted.'

'What does she do?'

'She farts about with the house, and the garden. But even there, you see, she pays other people to do it for her. There's this woman Mrs Davis who comes in three times a week to polish the balls and claws and defrost the chandeliers. And she's got a gardener, too, called Clive. A camp old man who used to be a don and had a nervous breakdown in the Sixties. So even that experience isn't really *hers* – she pays other people to scrub her floors and dig her soil.'

'Well, why, not, if she can afford it? She's creating jobs, isn't she? She probably couldn't manage on her own.'

'Oh, Izzy, you're so tolerant. I think you'd tolerate a bloody elephant if it came along and sat down on your face.'

'No I wouldn't! I'd stick a finger up its bum. I just can't understand why you've got it in for your mother so much, that's all.'

'Nor can I, really—'

Izzy switched out the light.

'—ever since I can remember, my mother's been obsessed with physical beauty. I've seen the way she looks at the Pembroke table, and the DeMorgan tiles, and the rosewood chiffonier, and I've seen the way she looks at me. And my God, she thinks I'm ugly.'

'Don't be daft. I don't know what any of those other things are but I bet you're a million times more beautiful than any of them. And I bet your mum thinks so too.'

'No, Izzy. I remember it all. I remember, when I was little, hearing her say to a neighbour, "It's a shame Maria's so plain – but she *is* a bright little thing." Being a bright little thing was definitely a consolation prize for being plain. I don't think she's ever really forgiven me for not being as beautiful as she is.'

'And have you forgiven her for it?'

There was a long pause, in which Maria wrestled womanfully with the truth.

'Of course I'd like to be beautiful. Of course I would. It's so stupid and successful. It just works – BOUM! You don't have to do a thing, you're just *there*: people fall about with admiration. It would be nice to look in the mirror without flinching. But since I'm actually very ordinary, in a way I'm glad. I'm glad. I've avoided a lot of the shit that men lay on beautiful women. And it's easier, when you've never benefited from a system, to fight it.'

'What about Hywel saying you've got great legs?'

'I hate that.'

'I don't believe you. And I'm going to sleep now, Maria, so please: do me a favour and *shutya face* as 4C would say.'

Even Maria did not lie awake long. The infamous country air came up behind her like a thug with a cosh.

The next morning revealed Yorkshire in all its pearly glory. The light came piling in off the moors like a coach-load of angels into Mrs Comyn's ambrosial caff. Outdoors, the air even tasted different. Hens fretted and crooned amongst the strawy stones. Izzy's mum still kept hens (and geese and ducks on the ponds) and an acre of garden: the rest of the land had been bought by Smith, the neighbouring farmer, who also used the barns and outbuildings. It seemed a good arrangement. The Smiths fancied they kept a careful eye on Izzy's mum, and she knew she kept a careful eye on them.

'Mornin'!' Mr Smith nodded in through the window as Izzy and Maria sat down to their breakfast. He had, of course, been up for hours. It was now 9 a.m. and Izzy and Maria were delightfully half-awake.

The breakfast was a no-nonsense Yorkshire salvo of heavy artillery: porridge, baconeggstomatomushroom-friedbreadfriedpotatoes and baked beans, and then toast and home-made marmalade, all washed down with gallons of brick-red tea. After this, the feeble townies sprawled groaning by the fire. But Izzy's ma was not standing for that.

'Come on, you girls! You can't lie by the fire all day. Your legs'll drop off. It's a lovely day out: off you go! A walk'll bring some colour to your cheeks, Maria, love.'

'A walk'll bring on apoplexy,' complained Maria, but she went. They climbed up the lane, then cut across the road and up a track that wound its way on to the moors, towards Top Withens.

'It's supposed to be Wuthering Heights,' panted Izzy. 'Or rather the site of Wuthering Heights.'

'Heathcliff! There's a typical female fetish-figure!' gasped Maria. 'What a load of old schlock, eh, Izzy? The burning eyes, the scowl – the manly way he'd hang about glowering, punching the walls and spitting at the servants.'

'Yum yum!'

'Izzy!'

'Only joking.'

'All this love business. "Begod, tha mus'na torture me like this, Izzy, tha she-devil, or I'll not be responsible for my actions".'

138

'It's only passion. People have always longed for it.'

'Why? More fools them. I mean, what do you get out of it, Izzy? As a fully-paid-up member of Masochists International, what's in it for you?'

'Well – it's exciting. I feel more alive.'

'Christ! What an indictment of life! You only feel alive in the back of somebody's husband's car parked down a side street somewhere. What about work? What about friends? Don't you get a charge from anything else?'

'Of course I do. You don't half categorize me, Maria. You want to watch it. You're way off-beam sometimes.'

'Well, what does make your heart beat faster?'

'Lots of things. Views like this.' They paused and looked down on the glimmering reservoir, and the patchwork of little green fields and settlements. 'Poetry, and some music. The kids I teach, sometimes. Passion's not just a grope in the back of a car, Maria.'

Maria was silent. That was the very point she'd have liked to make. She saved her breath for the last few hundred feet of climb.

Top Withens was a stone-built semi-ruin. A few sheep lurked behind its crumbling walls. 'Bah!' they said. 'Blah! Bleah!'

'You know, Izzy, when you look down on a view like this, and see human dwelling places spread out below you, and get a god's-eye view of things for a moment—'

'Bah! Bleah!'

'—don't you get this desperate feeling that somehow it's all gone terribly wrong, and that the history of the human race is an unmitigated disaster?'

'Bah! Blah! Beh!'

'Oh, I don't know. I think it's mitigated. What about Mozart and Shakespeare? And hot chocolate? Civilization can boast a few triumphs.'

'Our kids – the kids we teach. Those girls. What's waiting for them in the world? The same dreary domestic destiny: the madonna, the whore, the baker of cakes? They deserve better.'

Bah. Blah. Bleh. The light moved in great curtains across the land, which seemed sunk in sleep. Not a twitch of movement anywhere. Except for two walkers, with their fluorescent anoraks, like glowing ants far below.

'You're not going back to Gwyn, then?'

'Are you joking? I must have been mad to have put up with it for so long.'

'He is fun, though.'

'But should fun cost so much? The vanity, the irresponsibility, the deception, the arrogance? Does fun excuse all that?'

'Nobody's perfect,' ventured Izzy. 'And we have to live together.'

'Speaking of living together, Izzy, I'm really sorry I'm still cluttering up your flat. I'm looking for another place and I'm sure I'll find something soon. I'm really very grateful to you for putting up with it all.'

'Don't be silly.'

They fell silent, and romped down the hill and back to Mrs Comyn's kitchen where there was another vast meal waiting for them. They pounced on it like vultures.

'Mrs Comyn, you must stop feeding us like this!' croaked Maria. 'We will die!'

'Nonsense, Maria. You could do with an extra half stone on you, love. You look like a skeleton, you do really. Have some more apple crumble.'

'Ooooh, no, really, I'm sorry, I can't.'

'I will, Mum,' said Izzy.

That afternoon, as they fed the ducks, Maria said she though it would be nice if she and Izzy made the supper, or tomorrow's lunch, so that Izzy's mum could have a rest.

'Good God! Mum would never stand for that!'

'Why not? What's wrong with the idea? Here she is, slaving away cooking these enormous meals, waiting on us hand and foot – it's not right, Izzy.'

'But she enjoys it!'

'She can't enjoy it.'

'Yes, she does! Honestly, Maria! You might not enjoy it, but she does. It's her work, she believes in it and it makes her happy. I wish we could say the same about ours.'

Maria abandoned any further attempts to sort out her ideas about women. The phenomena seemed to defy her. Instead she let Izzy's mum lay before her a steaming mountain of roast beef, Yorkshire pudding, parsnips, carrots, potatoes, cabbage and gooseberry tart. She and Izzy had peeled the vegetables but this was very much a token concession. Mrs Comyn believed that there was only really room for one woman in a kitchen.

'Do you really enjoy cooking for people, Mrs Comyn?'

'What a question, love! Of course I do! If folks are all right wi' their food, other things generally follow.'

Her kitchen was obviously a delight to her, with its rows of gleaming jars, its cupboards full of jams, preserves, bottled fruit, its own freckled eggs, home-grown herbs, its scrubbed wood and bright china, its snowdrops in a tiny glass vase on the windowsill, catching the sun. If there had been a man on the scene, Maria would have seen it all as the cultivation of meaningless rituals by a woman in chains. As it was, Mrs Comyn lived alone, and did it for herself. Trapped in the trivial treadmills of an earlier life?

'I've been reading that *Persuasion* book you told me about, Izzy,' remarked her mother as they washed up, 'and it was so sad, and so happy both together, that I were laughing and crying all at once over it.' And she polished her wine glasses for an extra few seconds, to give them a special shine.

11

'Oh Michael – stop! Stop a minute! I'm getting cramp!'

'Christ! All right – where?'

'Ow! Ow! In my right instep – owowowowOW! Massage it, can't you? Oh! Please! OW!'

'How can I massage it? I can hardly bloody move.'

There they were, sandwiched together in the back of his ludicrously low-slung car. Izzy's instep was a terrifying journey away. To get to it he'd have to wriggle out of his own car door, backwards, with his trousers down. And even then the offending instep was tightly encased in patent leather.

Yes, the mating season had once again descended. The sanities of a Yorkshire kitchen had given way to the trysts in the mews. And Michael was worried, for his sensitive antennae detected spring in the air, bringing with it not only all that wretched blossom and sap but also the 'sodding light evenings'.

'It's all right,' soothed Izzy. 'By then Maria'll have moved out.'

'She'd bloody well better have. Can't you find her somewhere else?'

'I don't know anyone who's looking for a lodger. Except you. Of course! The perfect solution! Maria moves in with you.'

'Over my dead body.'

But until Maria found somewhere, the trysts in the mews, with their attendant cramps, were unavoidable. Izzy could have asked Maria to stay away from the flat for a couple of hours, and indeed Maria was often out, but somehow Izzy couldn't face it. She found it easier to deceive.

'Oh, thank God, it's eased off now. I'm sorry, Michael, but cramp is terrible.'

Michael grunted and adjusted his clothing. The mood had passed. 'I'm getting to old for this,' he grumbled.

Izzy's heart leapt in panic. Did he mean this messing around in cars? Or this messing around, period?

'I heard of a terribly funny story about some people in our position.'

'And a bloody uncomfortable position it is, too.'

'Yes. Well, anyway, there they were in the back of her car, having a merry old time, when he slipped a disc. He couldn't move. And he was on top of her – they were trapped. She had to attract help by honking the horn with her foot. The fire brigade had to be called and they had to cut a hole in the back of the car to get him out. Then as he was being lifted into the ambulance, a kindly passer-by comforted the girl and said. "Don't worry, love, they'll take good care of him in hospital." And the girl said, "Bugger him! I'm trying to work out how I explain to my husband what's happened to his car."'

'What terrible stories you tell, Izzy.'

'Isn't it funny, though,' sniggered Izzy. 'Think of it!'

'I am,' groaned Michael, and ran his fingers through his hair.

'Michael—' They were driving to Earl's Court. 'Michael – how would you feel if you didn't have to tell lies to Louise any more?'

'What? What do you mean?' He gave her a suspicious glance. What was this? The lead up to the Chop? How dare she? Wasn't he worth all the cramp in the world? Had she found another guy? Someone with *more hair*, for Christ's sake?

'Well, wouldn't it be nice if you could say to Louise, "I'll be a bit late home tonight, darling, because I'm going to drop in on Izzy for an hour or two."?'

'Come now, my dear, what world are these people

living in? Is this the trendy open marriage I've heard so much about? Have you been talking to someone from Hampstead?'

'Well, what about it – as an idea? Doesn't it appeal to you?'

'Good God, Izzy, the idea of eating caviar and roast beef every day appeals to me, but I can't for a moment contemplate it.'

'Why not?'

'My dear, it's simply out of the question. How could I say that to Louise? She has no idea who you are.'

'Well, why not tell her?'

'What? Tell her I'm having an affair with you? Are you mad? Have you any idea how she'd react?'

'Have *you* any idea how she'd react?'

Of course he hadn't. His previous adulteries had all been conducted without Freedom of Information. The only one which Louise had rumbled had already been Ancient History when she'd discovered it, had only been a ship-in-the-night anyway, and Louise had been on the point of going off to the States where Michael suspected she'd gone in for a bit of hanky panky herself to pay him back. So it all blew over without Louise revealing very much in terms of reaction, at all. Come to think of it, how *would* Louise react? Her ways were all still so mysterious to him, even after eight years of marriage. Maybe this was one of the sources of her potent attraction. He never really knew what was going on in her head. Whereas Izzy – darling creature – was utterly transparent of course, like a little jelly.

'Of course I know how she'd react, my dear. She'd break a bottle of scotch over my head. And scratch your eyes out into the bargain. She once said to me, "If you sleep with anyone else, so help me, I'll kill you."'

Had Louise really said such a thing, ever? He wasn't sure, actually. He was pretty certain he could remember her saying something like it, though. And if she hadn't, well, she jolly well should have.

Izzy was terrified at the sound of this jealous tyrant. All the same, she persisted.

'I've become so fed up with all this deception, Michael. It's since Maria's marriage broke up, really. The harm it does.'

'Well, your friend Maria over-reacted.'

'Maybe she did, but I can understand it. Being deceived for years on end! That's enough to make any woman go over the top. Or any man, either. But it's nothing like your case. If you made a clean breast of it with Louise, you'd only have to tell her about that girl Caroline three years ago, and me.'

Michael was silent, thinking ruefully of Sally, and Diane, and Sue, and Theresa, and Maggie, and what's-her-name.

'In fact you wouldn't really have to tell her about Caroline, would you? Just about me.'

'And what would I say?' Michael was now parking more carelessly than usual outside Izzy's flat.

'Well, you might say that you'd met somebody who was very important to you, and you'd like to spend a bit of time with her now and again.'

'In order to screw the living daylights out of her?'

'Michael!'

'Well, honestly, Izzy, that's what she'd think, wouldn't she? Even though of course we spend all our time in flower arranging and yoga.'

'But what would her reaction be?' persisted Izzy. What would my reaction be, in the same position? Izzy was fascinated by the question, and tried to imagine it. But she had never been married, nor lived with anyone for more than a few months. Her twinkling life offered her no clue of the rigours of the relationship that goes on for year after year, its head bent beneath the weather.

'It's no use, my dear – attractive though the idea is in some ways, it's simply out of the question. Dear Izzy! You're quite right to want a better world, but the fact is we've got to make do with the one we've got. And a

145

wicked old world it is.' He bent to kiss her, and she gathered up her things. 'Believe me, darling,' he added portentously, 'I know.'

Izzy skipped up the steps and vanished into her house. But all the same, she panted at the second landing, I don't *altogether* believe him. And I'm not completely convinced he knows. Still, so far she was a prisoner of his will.

Inside the flat Maria, Charlotte and another girl called Ally were hard at work, surrounded by papers. They looked up as Izzy came in, and she instantly felt, though she hadn't been aware of it before, the sheerness of her stockings, the dizzying height of her heels, and deafening twang of her suspender belt. They greeted her in a thoroughly friendly way, but as if from the other side of a glass screen. She twanged and teetered past them into the bedroom, where she changed into her jeans, sweater and plimsolls. She didn't have to remove her make-up, though. Michael's jacket had already done the job.

She put the kettle on, and offered them coffee. They accepted. They were all smoking, and the place smelt like a French railway station. Izzy coughed a few times, not so much to provoke a reaction as to convince herself that she'd registered a token protest. Suspender belts don't give you cancer, she thought, with a brief, silly rebelliousness. She carried their coffee to them.

'What are you busy with?' she asked, looking over their heads at the mass of paper.

'It's a revue we're putting together,' explained Maria. 'You ought to be in it, Izzy. Izzy teaches English and drama at the same school as me.'

'Well – I don't know – I'm not much use on stage,' mumbled Izzy slyly. 'I'm more a behind-the-scenes sort of person. What's it about?'

'Menstruation.'

What menstruation *again*? Didn't they think about anything else?

'How can you do a revue about menstruation?'

146

'Well, it's a collection of songs and sketches, based on the life of a girl called June. It's called *The Moon and June*.'

'Hey, it sounds like a Noël Coward piece! Won't you get lots of old ladies turning up from Worthing expecting a bit of high camp romance?'

'I hope so,' grinned Maria venomously.

'But – why menstruation?' Even as she asked the question Izzy realized she'd made the biggest mistake of the evening.

'It's symptomatic,' announced Ally, 'of the oppression to which women have been subjected over the centuries. In many cultures a menstruating woman is considered as taboo – it's not just the industrialized West which wants to pretend it doesn't exist. The conspiracy to deny its existence is a sign of men's fear of women's power, and their hostility towards us as the mysterious, crazed, unpredictable, intuitive creatures they want us to be.'

'Blimey,' exclaimed Izzy, thinking she wouldn't mind being thought of as crazed, intuitive and mysterious. 'But – is it worse than people not having enough to eat, or the vote, or things?'

'It *is* an impoverishment,' insisted Ally. 'And it *is* a tyranny. The greatest impoverishment, and the greatest tyranny, that a whole section of the human race has ever been subjected to.'

Izzy felt the rising panic she always suffered in the presence of The Political. They marshalled their phalanxes of language and marched at her, and yet she felt as if they were marching through her, a ghost on the battlefield. She could not engage with them, but she could not be trampled into the mud, either.

'I look forward to seeing it,' she said. 'I'll bring my mum.'

'*Will* you?' pounced Maria. 'Really, Izzy? Bring your mum? Do you think she'll come?'

'Of course,' said Izzy. 'Why not?'

'Will you tell her what it's about before she comes?'

'Oh yes. I wouldn't want her to think it was a Noëly

Coward sort of thing.'

'Do you and your mum talk freely about periods, then?'

'Oh yes, when it's necessary, of course. But most of the time we talk about much more interesting things.' Whoops. She hadn't been able to resist it, and the glass screen instantly snapped down again, between them and her.

'The trouble with you, Izzy,' smiled Maria with loving condescension, 'is that you still co-operate with the patriarchy, and reflect their views and prejudices.'

'I know, I know. I'm a woman in chains. But one day, Maria, I shall see the light, and then I shall talk about menstruation till it's coming out of my ears. As it were.' Izzy gave her broadest grin. This flat was too small to quarrel in. 'And now please excuse me. I must read some Shakespeare. Queen Lear.'

They didn't laugh. But then, it was a very cheap joke. Izzy took Shakespeare into the bedroom with her, but found it hard to concentrate. Instead, her ears were straining to catch what was being said in the next room. Alas, the door was thick, and their voices were low. Presently Izzy's eye fell on a book Maria must be reading – it was beside the bed. Dorothy Wordsworth's *Journal*. What would Maria's account of Dorothy be? A gifted woman who had wasted her time washing the Great Poet's shirts and making him pies? Izzy opened the book at random.

'Saturday 27th March 1802. A divine morning. At Breakfast Wm wrote part of an ode. Mr Oliff sent the dung and Wm went to work in the garden. We sate all day in the orchard . . . Wm and I walked together in the evening towards Dalemain. The moon and stars.' Izzy read on and on, led by Dorothy into their world of glow-worms, nightingales and rain. Of female headaches and a noise of boys in the rocks. When she finally closed the book, she felt that a flood of joy had gathered about her heart. So much better than anything Wordsworth had written – so much more lively, direct and humane.

Izzy went into the next room to tell Maria what she'd discovered, but Maria had gone to sleep on the sofa, her friends having left long ago. She'd obviously not wanted to disturb Izzy. Izzy tiptoed over to her. In the moonlight Maria looked like a little boy, her cropped hair glistening, her tiny round ear like a baby's, the relaxed tendrils of her hand on the pillow. The quilt had slipped. Very gently, Izzy drew it up around her shoulders. Then she went over to the window, opened it and looked out. 'At 11 o'clock Coleridge came when I was walking in the still clear moonshine of the garden.' What was to become of them all? Would men and women lose each other in this weed-strewn wilderness? Or would they walk together under the moon and stars?

As the days passed Izzy felt Maria slipping away. Even in her presence, sometimes, there was an absence. In the old days of Maria's marriage there had been no thought too ghastly or daft to be shared, but in her new life Maria seemed to have bitten into something, like the man who bites into the branch of a tree and swings there in the air, held by his teeth. And if someone else should come along, stand underneath and ask him a question, what could he do? The teeth must stay sunk in. It was all or nothing. Izzy felt like the man below, on the forest floor, who looks up and thinks, how extraordinary! What strength! And yet is lonely for an answer.

And yet they slept within a few feet of each other in a tiny flat. At night Izzy felt the dreams billowing between them, but by day they were considerate and polite as they had never been before. Occasionally, Maria would give her a brief, passing hug, like a bridge across an abyss. Hugs had not been part of it before. But then, their souls had been cheerfully and effortlessly together, like a couple of daffodils in the same jar. The longer Maria spent away from Gwyn, the better she slept. But now Izzy was finding it harder. She felt something was leaving her: she could not say what. It was like a draught that fretted away at her back, and would not let her rest.

With Michael, she saw herself more and more as a caricature. She watched herself getting ready to meet him: watched the complex rituals with puzzlement. She began to neglect little details: wear flatter shoes, not bother with blusher, not always wash her hair. The self-consciousness which was setting in surprised her at moments of greatest passion. She would suddenly think, My feet are on the dashboard! I hope I don't touch the horn, like that other girl! Often there seemed to be another Izzy in mid-air, looking down and sniggering at the silly Izzy who clip-clopped along the pavements or sat vamping across the candles in restaurants. And now the gilt was off the gingerbread, it did not seem so very nourishing, either. She saw someone twice a week, at best, and left him feeling starved.

Izzy would lie awake and wonder what to do about this, and about the deadly devotion of Dick, who pad-padded around after her like some horrible Nemesis in Hush Puppies. She juggled and lied as she'd never juggled and lied before in order to see Dick for lunch instead of at night, and at night resorted to a series of fictitious ailments in order to pack him off back to Tottenham. She had cystitis, twice; headaches, often; and vast endless periods that lasted for three weeks in a row. Dick was mystified, but his not to question the workings of Dame Nature. And since that other old slag Fortune had been bountiful enough to give him a night with Izzy once, he *would* keep trying. In vain did Patric Walker warn *Taurus . . .. you will achieve nothing by initiating things now*. Dick's skin could be very thick when he chose and Izzy's hints dropped off him as quietly as his own dandruff.

So. Izzy would lie awake, whilst Maria plunged easily to sleep. The consolations of philosophy, perhaps.

One night the phone rang, but Izzy caught it at the

first preliminary click, as she was wide awake.

'Hulloa, darlin'!'

'Gwyn!'

''Loa! How are yew? 'Ow's your bewtiful self? Still knockin' about with that fuckin' effete layabout from the BBC? Lucky bastard.'

'Well – sort of. How are you, Gwyn?'

'Oa – terrible, mon. I'm so drunk I think I've drowned.'

'Well, maybe you should go to bed, then. It *is* nearly two.'

'Noa! Lissen, I gotta talk to Maria, right? I seen it all the other night. Everythin' looks very, very different to me now, like. So it'll be all right, darlin'. Tell 'er to get 'er arse over to the phoane.'

'Don't start that again, Gwyn. I won't disturb her. She's very tired and run down at the moment.'

Actually, this was another lie. It was Izzy who was tired and run down. Maria seemed to get stronger every day.

'Well, lissen now, look, I *got* to talk to 'er, right? I knoa I reacted very very badly at first but I was bein' very defensive and irresponsible, like, right? Soa I feel that I've reelly got somethin' new to say now, darlin'. Be ower arbitration service. Tell 'er the money's on the table and we want 'er back on the shop floor.'

'Gwyn – I suggest you write her a letter. Or ring tomorrow at a reasonable hour.'

'Reasonable hower! Reasonable hower! Lissen, darlin', the workin's of the human heart do not necessarily clock on at 9 a.m. y'knoa. Don't give me any of that fuckin' bourgeois shit, now. I gotto see Maria tonight and I'm *goin'* to see 'er tonight. I'm goin' to drive over there now, like. Orright? Tell 'er I'm comin'.'

'Don't be silly, Gwyn! Besides, you're surely too drunk to drive.'

'I'm always at my best when I'm too drunk to drive, girl! I drive best from the pits of my unconscious, like.

151

I'll be right over.'

'No – Gwyn.'

But the phone had gone dead. Izzy hoped that he might immediately have fallen asleep, but her deepest forebodings told her otherwise. She got up, got dressed and went downstairs to hang about in the hall. The moon was bright, an Eastern moon, as befitted Earl's Court. The hall was cold, and Izzy hoped no one would come in and find her hanging suspiciously about. But she wanted to intercept Gwyn before he started ringing her doorbell – a horrible device that did murder sleep. And Maria needed her sleep.

She heard someone fall up the steps outside, followed by some gruff curses. She opened the door and joined him in the moonlight.

'Gwyn!'

'Darlin'! 'Elp me up! Every time I come to yewer god-forsaken flat I do myself an injury.'

'What's the matter?'

'I slipped on a bit of ice, like. 'Old me up, darlin'!' He leaned heavily against her, and his breath foamed round her face like a brewery.

'How much have you drunk tonight, Gwyn?'

'Oa – nothin' much, like. Sixteen pints or soa.'

'Rubbish! Why do you men have to boast so much?'

'To impress yew women. Now, 'elp me upstairs, girl. I gotto see that wayward wife of mine.'

'Not a chance.'

'Wha'? What you mean?'

'I said no. And I mean no. You can't see her.'

'Oh, noa, noa, noa!' He set up a wail which sailed through the naked twigs of Nevern Square. 'C'mon now, darlin', take pity on me, like. Doan't be nasty. I'm a poor chastened 'usband come to make my reparation. C'mon now, sweetheart, 'elp me up these stairs for fuck's sake – I'm not so young as I was earlier in the evenin'.'

'You're not going up there.' Izzy's finality impressed

Gwyn. She propped him against the railings for a moment.

'Where we goin' then?' He was dumb and inert as a sack of lentils, but not nearly so wholesome.

'I'm going to get you a room in one of these sordid little hotels, and put you to bed for the night.'

'Oh, noa, noa! I'm not a great baby, for fuck's sake! I'm still compos mentis! I can drive 'ome as easy as fall off a log!' he protested, and fell heavily on to the pavement.

'Come on, you terrible old disaster,' grumbled Izzy, heaving him up and draping him round her. She managed to stagger with him the twenty yards to the Eros Hotel, in whose lobby a light dimly burned.

'Now, look, for God's sake, Gwyn, behave yourself in here, or you'll blow it. Keep a low profile. Let's pretend we're going in there for a night of passion, OK?' She wanted to make the idea as attractive as possible.

'Never mind pretendin' – let's fuckin' *ave* a night of passion in there!' he boomed, lurching alarmingly up the steps. In the hall, a superior Asiatic porter sat behind a greasy desk, reading *The Sun*. He looked up without surprise: the advantage, Izzy thought, of the Oriental.

'My friend has just turned up from a holiday in America,' explained Izzy, 'and there isn't room in my flat to put him up for the night. So could we book him a room here, please?'

With the greatest disdain and suspicion the porter consulted his ledgers.

'She's lyin' to you, Jimmy,' warned Gwyn with a massive belch. 'We're contemplatin' a night of wild passion, like, within the purlieus of this Erotic Establishment.' And he leaned heavily against the desk, till it creaked.

'My friend is a little the worse for wear,' explained Izzy. 'He needs to sleep it off. Have you got a room?'

'Woom Twev. Doubuw woom. Twenty poun'.'

The porter wasn't hedging his bets. He wanted the

money now. Gwyn had less than three pounds on him, so Izzy wrote a cheque.

'Sign book pwis.'

Gwyn took the pen and drew a knot of snakes in the right column.

'Tha' you Mr – Wobinson,' the porter consulted the ledger. 'Woom twev, seco' floor.'

There was no lift, so Izzy dragged Gwyn up the stairs.

'Doan't these 'otels stink, like!' he observed in stentorian tones. 'An' look at this fuckin' wallpaper! It's got views of 'onolulu on it! It's the death of art, darlin'. We're in the Mausoleum of the Modern Era.'

Room Twelve was the usual cardboard-walled tomb, with the soft creaking bed, the neon strip above the bedhead, and the smell of economy soap. Gwyn fell on the bed, taking Izzy with him.

'C'mon now, darlin', let me get to grips with yewer scrumptious body!' he roared. 'And not before time in my view, like!' He rolled over on top of her and fell deeply asleep. What should Izzy do? His sleep was good, and not before time either, in her view, like. But could she stay in this posture for more than two minutes, say, without getting a hernia? Probably not. She rolled his dead weight over and started to take his shoes off for him.

''Ulloa, darlin'! Sorry about that, I nodded off, like. Nothin' personal. Let's get this shoa on the road.' He made a grab for her, but she skipped away and he ended up face down on the pillow. 'Oa,' he droned into it. 'Where yew gone? Yew're a slippery little thing, now, aren't yew? Tell you wha', darlin', I think I'm a bit beyond, like. You'll 'ave to give me a platin'.'

'A *what?*'

'A platin'. You lick me all over, startin' – well, startin' where you like, reelly.'

'Get away with you!' rebuked Izzy gently, undoing his belt and removing it.

'Wha' – wha' you goin' to do?' he croaked into the

154

pillow. 'Thrash me with my own belt? Well, if that's yewer thing, girl, far be it from me to stand in the way of yewer pleasure. Only go easy – I gotta bum as soft as a baby's.'

Izzy pulled the sheets and blankets from under him and snuggled him down among them.

'Good night,' she whispered, but he flung his arm out and locked her to his side with considerable strength.

'Doan't leave me, darlin',' he whinged. 'I'm very, very sorry that alcohol prevents me from payin' the tribute dew to yewer bewty. Doan't go, though!' And he held on like a leech.

'Don't be silly, Gwyn. I must go. Let go!'

But he held on tight, crooning to himself. 'Yew're my mam. Don't leave me in the dark, Mam! The bogey man will get me, Mam! Please, Mam!'

Finally Izzy slipped off her shoes and got into bed beside him. There they lay, fully dressed, till break of day: Gwyn's thunderous snores raking into her brain. At first she tried to stop him, but he only muttered, 'Noa! I don' snore, mon! Never!' and plunged back to sleep. Izzy did not even manage to doze. At dawn she crept out. He stirred as she left, whispered, 'No offence, right?' in his sleep, and then slumped again.

Back at the ranch, Maria was up and making coffee as Izzy pushed her bleary way in.

'A night on the tiles, eh, Izzy?' she grinned freshly, 'I must say, these men get their money's worth out of you.' She hadn't meant it to sound so awful, and half regretted it immediately. Izzy picked up one of the non-Dick cups off the draining board, and hurled it at the wall, where it shattered. Then she walked away to the bathroom.

When she emerged, Maria had gone, leaving the fragments of cup where they were. Izzy had to go to work by tube; was late, got in a spin, had a cover lesson in her free period, was cornered by Mary Greenfield at break, was on duty at lunchtime, and only fainted at 3 p.m. in the Lower Sixth lesson. Jennifer Jackson brought her round. She'd got one of her Guide Badges for First Aid.

12

St Valentine's Day came. Izzy received three Valentines: one with a muddy thumb-print, one with a witty rhyme, and one with two spelling mistakes in her name. A vast bunch of red roses arrived for Maria. She tossed them on the floor, their little envelope unopened. Izzy rescued them, put them in water, and left the little envelope by the vase. As she looked out across the rooftops that evening she felt a great weight gathering in her chest. Was she sickening for a cold? Or was it just the approach of spring, for which such desperate courage is needed? She looked at Maria's roses and had a brief snivel. She was surprised at herself. Was it pre-menstrual tension? She couldn't for the life of her remember.

Maria was out, as usual, rehearsing *The Moon and June*. It was a night for cleaning up, Izzy decided. Maria was much tidier than herself, but all the same, an extra person in her flat and instantly the place seemed to sink under piles of knickers, marking, used cups and abused books. She pulled on her rubber gloves. The doorbell rang.

'DXYCZTK,' it announced.

'Come up, Dick.' But she kept her rubber gloves on. And there he stood in the doorway, beaming and shuffling, his glasses steamed up even more than usual. Let us hope it was the stairs, not the spring.

'Izzy!' he announced, with none of the apology of the earlier, more tentative Dick, 'I've brought you a casserole!' And he produced a cardboard carton.

'Good God, Dick, this is very kind,' she exclaimed,

unwrapping the glorious brown mottled thing.

'It's called a Leopard Glaze,' he explained, 'because it's sort of spotty.'

'Then it'll suit me down to the ground!' beamed Izzy, and plonked a most unromantic thank you kiss on his cheek. He tried to grab her, but she was away and filling a kettle before any how's-your-father could develop. 'I expect you'd like a cup of tea, since you've come so far and been so extremely generous?' she beamed: a deadly beam.

'Oh, yes, please,' panicked Dick. Mere tea? That had not been the idea, at all. Still, there was his Valentine card on the mantelpiece. There were two others there, to be sure. Bastards. Who were they? He'd strangle them with his bare hands, if he ever found out.

'Excuse me if I carry on with the washing-up,' said Izzy brightly. 'It's the Day of Reckoning in this kitchen. A moment's hesitation and they'll be sending the Public Health Inspector in.'

'It looks very nice to me,' offered Dick, gallantly, but then he was looking more at Izzy's bum than anything else. There she stood at the sink, her hands deep in suds, her buttocks presenting a most monkeyish appeal. Dick often felt a bit Neanderthal, and today was worse than usual, what with its being February 14th and all the sparrows wooing in the gutters and his sap rising so fast that he could almost hear his corduroys creak.

'Spring's in the air – then, Izzy?' he panted.

Izzy rinsed a few soapy plates, and then bent down to pick the odd piece of superannuated spaghetti off the rush matting. 'Oh, God, I hope not. Not yet,' she groaned, and looked at him for a moment between her legs. 'Hello Dick. You're upside down.'

Dick sprang decisively to his feet, but she had returned to the washing-up, so he strolled over to the window with his hands deep in his pockets. But having his hands in his pockets was not enough. Even now Izzy was scrubbing away at a charred saucepan with such *brio* that it made her bum positively blur. In Dick's present mood, handcuffs would not have been enough.

He walked up behind her and placed his hands on her buttocks, then moved them round to her equally-baroque façade, and boldly squeezed. Izzy froze. Nothing is worse than the feeling that your rubber glove has a hole in it. Except, perhaps, being goosed at the sink by a colleague when you were relying on his behaving like a Perfect Gentleman. Alas, that is all too often how Perfect Gentlemen behave.

'Ooooh, Izzy,' he moaned into her neck, 'there's something so irresistible about a woman at the sink!' Izzy stood apparently still, but in the privacy of the washing-up bowl she was removing one glove and filling it with water. 'You've no idea how I – go for you, Izzy. Oooh, you're *lovely*!'

SPLAT! She hit him squarely on the chops with the water-filled glove. OUAGH! Dick reeled away to the other end of the kitchen. Some water was trickling down Izzy's neck, but what the hell? It was a sort of baptism, after all. Dick hovered by the fridge, making inarticulate choking sounds and cradling the outraged part of his face.

'Get some milk out of the fridge, whilst you're there, will you, Dick? And there's some of my mum's short-bread in that tin.' Dumbly Dick reached for the tin, arranged the shortbread on a plate, got the milk out of the fridge. Would he ever be able to speak again? His larynx had turned to concrete. 'Make the tea, will you, love?' Love? *Love?* He made the tea and then turned his newly-steamed-up face to Izzy, who was watching him with arms folded and a patronizing smile. 'There's something so irresistible about a man making the tea.'

'What – what do you want me to do now, Izzy?' he squeaked at last. He would have licked the street for her. Izzy, in attempting to deflect his attentions, had inadver-tently stumbled on the formula that would make him her own for ever: punishment and rubber.

'Sit down and have some tea.' Oh, and submission. Dick slunk to the sofa, not daring to look up from his shortbread. Izzy talked gaily of school, of Mary Greenfield's ghastly teeth, of the Deputy Head's appalling paunch: he'd need a wheelbarrow soon to trundle it about in. Then, when ten minutes had passed in the most carefree cruelties on her part and the most craven acquiescence on his, she jumped to her feet. Dick cringed, in delicious expectation of more brutality.

'Well, Dick, you must push off now, I'm afraid. I've got masses left to clean. Unless you'd like me to hose and scrub you down, too, like an elephant in the zoo?' He was speechless with longing. But she waltzed to the door, threw it open, blew him a kiss, and with a 'Thank you for a *lovely* casserole,' kicked him downstairs.

Izzy had scrubbed half the kitchen floor when the phone rang.

''Loa, darlin'. It's Hywel. I got a present for you, like, only I wanted to make sure Maria was out before comin' round.'

'A present for me? How kind. Bring it over right away! How long will you be?'

'Oh, noa time at all, like, girl – I'm jus' around the corner.'

Izzy scrubbed the rest of the floor. This housework was really quite exhilarating. The bell rang, she opened the door, and not one but two ebullient Welshmen fell inside.

''Ulloa, darlin'!' 'Appy Valentine's Day, like! Dew! Yew're lookin' bewtiful in that apron, isn't she, Hywel?'

'You didn't say Gwyn was with you,' objected Izzy. 'And you said you'd got a present for me. Where is it?'

'I'm it!' giggled Gwyn. 'I'm the present! We was goin' to tie me up with pink ribbon but we couldn't find a bit big enough, like!'

'We thought we'd come round and 'ave a little surprise party, like – just you, me and Gwyn,' leered Hywel.

'Maria out at one of 'er fuckin' feminist meetin's, is she? Won't be 'oame for owers and owers, like?'

'No – she's usually back late.'

'Right! Perfect, mon. Gis a kiss, Izzy, girl, you're lookin' mind-bendin'ly scrumptious tonight. Get the dope out, Hywel, doan't mess about, now.'

'What's the plan, then?' asked Izzy, pushing Gwyn away.

'Oh, nothin', sweetheart. Just a bit of drugs and rock'n'roll, like.'

'An' sex – don't forget the sex, mon!' warned Hywel.

'What sex was this you had in mind, exactly?'

'Well, we were goin' to spring it on yew, like, but I think it's more chivalrous to lay it on the line before 'and, like – we're not animals, after all, are we, Hywel?'

'Noa!' declared Hywel proudly, with a great fart.

'Well, sweetheart, we wondered if yew might dew us the honour of comin' to bed with boath of us, like – a St Valentine's Day massacre, sorta.'

'Good God! *Both* of you? Do you do this sort of thing often? How does it work?'

'Well, I'm not sayin' it's exactly a test-run, like. 'Ow did we swing it with Megan, now, Hywel?'

'First you 'ad a goa while I watched *Match of the Day*, then I 'ad a goa while yew took photographs. I doan't knoa what 'appened after that, 'cos I fell asleep.'

'How interesting. Well, I'm sorry to pour cold water on this delightful little scheme, but I'm afraid it's my night for spring cleaning.'

'Oa, come on now, darlin'. Noa girl's ever declined ower kind offer in favour of scrubbin' the floor, for fuck's sake.'

'Well, I'm doing just that. Sorry. Out!' Izzy pointed to the door as if they were bad dogs. Ah, but they were *very* bad dogs. Gwyn winked at her. Hywel licked his lips. There were two of them.

'C'mon darlin',' urged Hywel, caressing her arm.

'C'mon sweetheart, now, doan't let us down,' cajoled

Gwyn, toying with her ears.

'No. Sorry. Absolutely impossible. I don't want to. Some other time, perhaps. Now please go away: I've got work to do.'

But what was this? She was being lifted up: Gwyn had her shoulders; Hywel had her feet, and she was flown into the bedroom and on to the bed, where she bounced like a cork, and with her bounced Dorothy Wordsworth.

'Let go, you pigs! I'll scream! Mind that book!'

'Never mind the old book, sweetheart,' Gwyn was ripping off her shoes. 'You jus' relax now an' we'll give you the best time yew ever 'ad.'

'Let me go!' Izzy was furious, thrusting and thrashing to escape, but they were so strong that she was immobilized in two seconds, and silenced by Hywel's great mouth. In mid-kiss, suddenly, she found wisdom.

'OK, OK,' she gasped. 'You've convinced me. Let me go, for Christ's sake.' They did, grinning. They did not believe they were resistible. 'Only you must let me just have a quick pee and a shower. And – tell you what – why don't you two get undressed and wait for me in bed, and then I'll come in and get undressed in here.'

'It's too excitin'! I can't stand it!' moaned Hywel. It was a deal. Izzy ran to the bathroom, and sat down on the edge of the bath for a minute, her mind racing. She turned the shower on, and it streamed and steamed beside her, but she just sat and watched it until she judged it was time. Then she turned it off and went back into the bedroom with a triumphant gleam in her eye.

There they were, undressed in bed: side by side, sitting up and ready to go. Their brown skin glowed, and a joint leer was spread from ear to ear. Their clothes were in a heap on the floor.

'OK,' exhorted Gwyn, 'get this shoa on the road, girl.' Izzy went over and opened the window. 'Hey! Whassat for?'

'It's quite mild,' she reassured them. 'And anyway – you know what cold air does to the female anatomy.'

161

'Noa? What does it dew, for Chris' sake?'

'Pull yewerself together, Hywel, mon, an' stop lettin' me down in public, now.'

'But what does it dew?' wailed Hywel, in an agony of anticipation. Izzy paused before them in a provocative pose and twanged her apron strings, then bent, scooped up all their clothes and flung them out of the window.

'Jesus Christ!' Gwyn leapt from the bed and raced to the window. 'She's throan our fuckin' cloathes out the windoa!'

'Wha'?' Hywel struggled to understand what was going on.

'She's throan our bloody cloathes out of the windoa, mon! Look, they've landed on a sorta garage roof down there.'

Hywel lumbered from the bed, and stared down to where his best shirt was spreadeagled on the garage roof and his scanty HOMs dangled from a sycamore twig. Both furry backsides bristled with indignation.

'Wha' the hell do we do, now?'

'Goa down there an' get them, Isabelle, you stupid bitch!'

But Izzy started to giggle. 'It's *Planet of the Apes*, Gwyn! You look terrific!'

'Don't give me that, girl. This is serious. Goa down and get them cloathes back!'

Izzy screamed with laughter. 'Oh, Gwyn, you look so funny, for God's sake don't try to look dignified, or I'll die!'

'For Chris' sake!' Gwyn turned his attention to her clothes cupboard. 'There must be *somethin'* yere that'll fit me.' But no. All her baggy trousers were at the launderette. There were only her tightest jeans, and Gwyn pulled them up as far as his knees and then crashed to the floor with a roar.

'These jeans is like a fuckin' tourniquet!'

Meanwhile Hywel had tried on a pink stretch leotard. 'Hey, Gwyn, look! Dew I look like Rudolf Newreyev?'

'You look like a fuckin' great pixie, mon – take it off for Christ's sake.'

In the end Gwyn had to wear Izzy's fragile and holey Chinese dressing gown, and Hywel had to adopt the leotard after all – nothing else would fit. Izzy lay on the bed crying into mouthfuls of duvet.

''Urry up, mon, for Christ's sake,' urged Gwyn, 'there's some fuckin' Arab down there stealin' my trowsis. Oy, you! Put that back! It's mine!'

They fled to the rescue. Izzy locked the door after them, and watched from the window weeping and gasping as they climbed the garage walls, Hywel like a great glistening pink gnome, Gwyn's dressing gown snaking round his shoulders in the breeze and revealing his bare arse to the several amused bystanders. He paused, having regained his trousers, looked up at Izzy's window, and shook his fist.

'You'll suffer for this one day, girl!' he roared.

Izzy washed her eyes and finished cleaning the flat. Then she made herself a cup of cocoa. 'Three down,' she murmured. 'One to go.' Right on cue the phone rang.

'Hello.'

'Izzy, this is Michael.'

'Hello! How are you?'

'Averagely ghastly. Happy St Valentine's Day, darling. Thanks for your Valentine.'

'I didn't send you one.'

'Didn't you? How intriguing. I wonder who the third one was from, then?'

'Who were the first two from?'

'Oh, only Louise and my PA – are you *sure* you didn't send me one?'

'I may have done. And forgot about it, I suppose.'

'Yes, I bet you did, artful puss. I bet it went straight out of your furry little head.'

'Yes, well, Michael, what do you want?'

'What do I – well, darling, don't flip your lid, but I could come and see you tomorrow afternoon – and

163

Sunday afternoon. Louise is showing prospective tenants around the house, and she's told me to keep out of the way. So I could be with you for two whole afternoons – how about that?'

'I'm sorry, Michael, but I'm busy this weekend.'

'You're what?'

'Busy.'

'But, darling – couldn't you put it off? What is it?'

'I'm doing the spring cleaning.'

'You're doing the WHAT?'

'The spring cleaning. I'm halfway through it now. You know. Sweeping away the cobwebs.'

'But surely – can't you – couldn't you take a couple of hours off tomorrow afternoon? Won't you need a rest by then?'

'Is it a rest you were contemplating?'

'My dear, anything. Anything you like. Your wish is my command.'

'Well, what a shame – because I really can't spare the time.'

'Well, bugger me.' Michael was flabbergasted. 'I appear to be less attractive than a dirty floor.'

'Oh, I wouldn't say that,' Izzy reassured him.

'Good God, Izzy, are you angry with me about something?'

'Not in the least. You are quite delightful.'

'But look here – what am I supposed to do without you, all weekend?'

'You could play squash for once. Now you really must excuse me, Michael. I'm halfway through something which is demanding my total attention.'

'What's that – have you got another man there?'

'Certainly not. How dare you!' And she slammed the phone down and went back to sipping her cocoa. Then she watched telly for a bit, had a bath, and was reading Dorothy Wordsworth on the sofa when Maria came in.

'My God!' Maria threw her bag down and fetched up a sigh from her very heart. 'I'm completely shattered.'

'Never mind,' consoled Izzy. 'Saturday tomorrow. How was *Period Piece*?'

'Oh, God, Izzy, absolutely awful!' Maria's dam suddenly burst and Izzy was swept away on a tide of weary rage.

'Tonight was a fiasco. I have to admit it – some of those women really drive me round the bend. Jennie was supposed to have duplicated the scripts, but she'd done the wrong bundles so we had about five thousand copies of pages one to fifteen, and no copies at all of fifteen onwards. Then we started the rehearsal, and Rachel stops in the middle of her piece to say she feels it's not quite *right*. She won't say exactly what she means by *right*. But we all know what she really means – this sketch was written by Ally and she's got it in for Ally for some reason.

'Then we had to sit through yet another of Jennie's horrendous autobiographical *I have suffered* trips. OK, she's suffered, and we've all heard the gory details about fifteen times now, so maybe it's time to listen to something else for a change. When she first came out with it all we all thought, wonderful, great, she's really letting her anger out, but now we look round desperately for a sock.'

'I will make you a cup of tea – you obviously need it.'

'Oh, thanks, that's lovely. Anyway, at last we got cracking again, and we've got this girl called Joanne who plays the saxophone wonderfully, it's an absolute treat. Then Charlotte does her Moon monologue. It's a scream, she's really funny in a deadpan way, like a Lancashire half-wit.

'But then we got on to Rachel and Jennie's scene in which June's mum tells her the facts of life, and the whole thing fell apart again. Rachel kept saying the writing was *peculiar*. Then Ally lost her temper and said it was only a document for discussion anyway, and she couldn't write dialogue, she'd never claimed to be able to, she'd only done it because no one else would, and why didn't Rachel write it herself if she thought it was so bloody peculiar.'

'Are you feeling weak enough to have honey in your tea?'

'I'm feeling weak enough to have honey straight into the jugular. Oh, God, Izzy – I was on the point of storming out two or three times but I've committed myself to it and I suppose I must do my best to help. The trouble is that some people want to use the sessions for personal therapy and others want to organize a show that'll make people think. My God, Izzy, I'm glad I didn't drag you into it. I'd have felt dreadful.'

'But you're getting a lot out of it, though?'

'I don't know. Charlotte is absolutely great – a wonderful, wonderful woman. You must get to know her better, Izzy.'

'I must.'

'And Ally's very clever, and very committed. But in a way she's been too committed from too early an age, so life hasn't managed to get through to her somehow. She seems a bit untouched and theoretical. The girl who plays the saxophone is great – but then, she never opens her mouth except to blow.'

Izzy smiled.

'Hey – here I am blasting away non-stop at you and boring you out of your mind and there you sit looking as fresh as a daisy. What did you do this evening? Did you go out on the town? Or a quiet evening with Dear Dorothy and Our William? C'mon, tell me, tell me, tell me!'

'I cleaned up,' Izzy beamed.

After her tea Maria felt refreshed enough to get out a battered copy of *The Times* and go through its Accommodation column.

'I must find a place somewhere,' she apologized. 'Now you've cleaned up I can see what a mess I'd made.'

'Don't be silly – it was my mess mainly.'

166

'But I must find somewhere anyway. There's all my stuff back at Notting Hill – my books and everything. I've got to be able to get at them again. Where shall I live, Izzy? Would Streatham be too far south?'

'Oh, I don't know – Amundsen managed to get there all right, didn't he? And Hywel's got a friend down there.'

'If Hywel's got a friend down there, let's leave Streatham to its doom. What about Shoreditch? Oh no, it says vegetarians only. Here's one in Camden – whoops, no, it costs a bomb. I don't want to be *too* near school do I? It's awful when the little buggers are under your feet day and night. Hmmmm – Muswell Hill. This sounds nice. "Two rooms in family house, big garden, twenty-five pounds per week".'

Izzy's heart gave a skip. 'I bet I know what the phone number is – 883 1328.'

'How the HELL did you know that, Izzy?' Maria gawped at her with the veneration of the primitive for the witch doctor.

'It's Michael's place. They're renting out the top of the house.'

'What a shame – it sounded nice.'

'Well, why not go, anyway?'

'Don't be daft, Izzy, I couldn't possibly go. Anyway he hates me. No, no – out of the question. What about Stoke Newington? Now, that's very near school, but not *too* near, and it's cheap. Where's the *A to Z*?'

After three unsuccessful phone calls Maria gave up and went to bed. Izzy sat up in the night for a while. A red rose twitched in its jar, as if something invisible had touched it. Maria's *Times* still lay on the sofa. Izzy picked it up and looked at Michael's ad crouching so innocently among the others. Behind every ad there lay a forest of tangled lives, too. Maybe people answering the ads would be drawn into the maze of desire, guilt and recrimination. Izzy sometimes thought she would love to be a telephone operator in an old-fashioned exchange where she could listen to all the calls, learn the whispered secrets, lies, declarations, flattery, insults and ingratiations buzzing their way through the knots of wires.

Next morning the paper was till there, lying in a pool of sun, as if some divine finger prodded Issy into action. Issy looked at the phone, then the paper, then the phone again, and finally lifted it, with a pounding heart. She dialled. What would she do if the wrong voice answered? She would hope and pray for the right one.

'Hello?' A light, pleasant woman's voice. The right one, this time.

'I'm ringing about the ad in *The Times*,' began Izzy. 'Has the room been taken yet?'

'No. Various people are coming to see it over the weekend. Would you like to come?'

'Oh, yes please. When would be convenient?'

'Well, what about tomorrow afternoon, say, at about three?'

'Yes. That'd be fine.'

Louise – for it was she – gave Izzy the address, which she already knew, and asked her a few questions in return. What was her name?

'Diane Clifton,' said Izzy, at last, commemorating her primary school pal.

'What do you do, Diane?'

'I'm an English teacher.'

'Oh, really? Where?'

Beware now. What if Louise and Michael were discussing the details of the people who phoned?

'At Holland Park.'

It wasn't quite a lie. Izzy had taught there a few years ago as a probationer. She prayed Louise would know no one there now.

'That sounds interesting. You must tell me all about it when you come. I'm an illustrator.'

Izzy waited for her to say that her husband worked for Schools TV, but she didn't.

'You're lucky, Diane,' Louise concluded. 'I'd just decided to put the phone off the hook, so you're the last caller to get through! See you tomorrow.'

'Yes, thank you very much. Tomorrow, then, at three.'

'Yes. I look forward to that.'

13

What should she wear? It seemed extra-indecent to turn up in any of her Michael gear, much of which was indecent anyhow. Nor did she want to wear her tight jeans, which would reveal all too clearly the romping cellulite to which this innocent woman's husband had so often hastened. Eventually, Izzy borrowed some baggy cream trousers of Maria's, and a brown silk blouse – the sort of expensive, tasteful things she might get around to buying herself in her mid-thirties. Or mid-fifties, more like. Maria wanted to know what it was all in aid of, but Izzy couldn't dredge up any more stories. For the moment, the treacle well had run dry.

'I'll tell you when I get back,' was all she could manage.

The house was more or less as she'd expected: not quite so grand perhaps. Three storeys and a basement, and a wild rambling garden full of evergreens and bursting with the earliest bulbs, over which the spring sunshine tremulously tip-toed. Izzy looked around for Michael's car, the scenario for so many worse-than-parking offences, but it was not around. Thank God. Perhaps he was at the squash courts, venting that energy which would have been hers for the asking. She climbed the three steps to the front door, and never had three steps seemed so high or hard to climb. Oh, for an oxygen cylinder, or failing that, at least a large lump of Kendal Mint Cake. Izzy pressed the bell, her heart leaping in her throat. Someone, singing, came to answer it.

'Hello – Diane?'

170

Izzy nodded dumbly. Words were impossible for a moment as she stood sledge-hammered by Michael's wife's beauty. The bright, red-gold curls, the green eyes and wonderful curved bone structure, the long, straight legs, the tiny waist, the flashing smile, the delicate mist of freckles. Izzy's fur coat lumbered in over the threshold, and Izzy co-operated with it like a rag doll. What on earth was wrong with Michael, for Christ's sake? Forsaking this angel, this extraordinary, luminous creature, to consort with a waddling oaf like herself. Was he not quite right in the head? Had he eyes, senses, judgment? Had he been smacked enough as a child?

'Would you like to come through to the kitchen and have a cup of tea? Then we can go up and have a look at the rooms afterwards.'

The kitchen was one of those billowing London kitchens that sail out over a garden. Sunlight streamed in and though there were a good many space-age units there was also a big old dresser covered with toy cars and moon buggies. Under a table was the washing basket, and Izzy's heart gave a lurch as she noticed the arm of one of Michael's shirts dangling over the edge, as if waving to her. How often had that sleeve embraced her!

'Will Earl Grey be all right?'

'Yes – lovely, thanks.'

So here she was, seated at Michael's table, about to drink his tea. His very bum had rubbed around on the seat of this Windsor chair. But such poignancies soon faded away in the face of Louise's smile, which could have melted granite. It seemed to go straight through Izzy's old fur coat, through the silk blouse and the silken skin and wind itself round her heart.

'So you found us all right, Diane.'

'I found you all right. It was kind of you to let me come.'

'Not at all. I like teachers.'

'You like teachers? You *like teachers*?'

There was obviously some kind of pervert lurking

171

beneath this dazzling beauty. Louise gave a merry laugh.

'Yes, I actually like them. Admittedly, the ones I know are mostly art teachers.'

'Ah – that's different. Art and drama are the only lessons that the kids run towards.'

'And you teach drama, don't you? Oh, that must be a laugh. Is it all *be a tree* stuff? Don't they beat the hell out of each other, though?' Her eyes were all a-glint. Izzy had never seen anybody who looked so alive.

'Well, they certainly beat the hell out of me!'

'Tell me, what do you do if they get out of control? I mean – *do* they get out of control, ever?'

'Do they ever get out of control – oh, boy, do they ever! I'll never forget the first lesson I ever had with 2V.'

'What's the V stand for? Volts?'

'No – two volts wouldn't be nearly enough for this mob. V is for Vickers, their form master. They're a very unfortunate little crew. Remedial, really. There's a little girl called Debbie who doesn't know when next Tuesday is.'

'I get like that sometimes! But what did happen in the first lesson you had with them?'

'Well, I was so green. I thought I'd get them to Express Themselves. You know, Drama as Therapy sort of thing. Explore the Boundaries of the Imagination. I'd heard it all at Education lectures and I thought it sounded wonderful. So I waltzed in there and said to them, "Be Wild Animals." What I hadn't realized was that they *were* wild animals.'

'Oh, no! What happened?'

'They broke six windows, three chairs and pulled down the stage curtains on to the Headmaster's lectern.'

'How marvellous!' Louise laughed like a tornado. 'But you poor thing, not a very good start, was it?'

'No. I ended up hiding behind the kettle drums and the Deputy Head came bursting in. He went purple in the face and the minute he came in they all stood stock-still and he said in this voice that sounded like God, "ARE

YOU WILD ANIMALS OR CHILDREN?" And then Wayne Staskiew piped up, "Miss told us to be Wild Animals, Sir." Anyway, there I was still behind the kettle drums and I just didn't dare move, I didn't know which was more frightening – them or him. Then he said, "WHO ARE YOU WAITING FOR?" and Sheila Sage said, "We ent waitin' for anybody, Sir, Miss Comyn's behind them drums." So I had to come out. I pretended I'd dropped a contact lens behind there. And ever since I've had to go through this charade with him of pretending I wear contact lenses. He'll say, "How are the contact lenses today, Miss Comyn?" and I'll say, "All present and correct, Mr King!" Honestly, I'm always getting into situations like that.'

'I told you I loved teachers!' laughed Louise. 'They tell such fantastic stories! But did you say your name was Comyn? I'm sorry, I got it wrong then, I thought you said Carter on the phone.'

'Oh yes, that's right.' Izzy seemed to have swallowed her tonsils all of a sudden. My God, they tasted vile. 'Carter is my – my – married name. I was married for a while, once. Er – but I'm using my maiden name again most of the time. Only I forget sometimes.'

'Oh, I see. Sorry – I didn't mean to pry.'

'Not at all, not at all – you said you were an illustrator?' gabbled Izzy, smarting from her stupidity. 'What are you working on at the moment?'

'Some children's books. They're about a Vegetarian Vampire called Vincent. He's a bit of a social misfit, you see, because he hasn't got any teeth, so he has to live on blood oranges.'

'That's a nice idea. Have you got any children to try your work out on?' Ah, cunning, cunning, now, Izzy: much better.

'I've got a little boy called Jack. He's six. But he thinks the stories I illustrate are soppy. Ever since he's been at school, all he's interested in is gore. I suppose all boys are the same, really. I wish I'd had a girl.'

173

Questions crowded into Izzy's mind. Are you going to have any more children? Are you having a secret affair, by any chance? What's your attitude to open marriages and husband sharing? How's your sex life? Does Michael also tell you that you're the sexiest woman in the universe? (Well, he *should*.) Would you scratch out the Other Woman's eyes if there was such a person? Would you break a bottle of scotch over your husband's head if he Strayed?

'Have you got a – a—' Izzy was fluttering vainly towards the word 'husband', but her courage – or bare-faced cheek, call it what you will – failed at the last moment, and she substituted, miserably, randomly, '—cat?'

'A cat? Why no, we haven't. Why?'

'It's just that I'm – er – allergic to them.'

'Oh, you poor thing. What happens?'

'Nothing special. I mean, coughing, that sort of thing. Coughing, sneezing.'

'Oh dear. Can you take anything for it?'

Oh hell. Oh help. If only Izzy had listened more carefully when allergies were being discussed in the staff room.

'No – I don't – I don't really know much about it. I've never really gone into cures very much. It was my up-bringing, you see.'

'What, were your parents Christian Scientists, or something?'

'Crumbs, no. Not Christians or Scientists. Just – well, they believed in Nature.'

'Gosh, no! Naturists are nudists! Imagine your parents as nudists!'

They giggled companionably, on safe ground, at last, for a moment. Wonderful, the cosy feel of women's laughter. Then, suddenly, 'Haven't I seen you somewhere before, Diane?'

'Seen me? Oh no. Impossible. Couldn't have.' Izzy felt an enormous menstrual blush spread across her face.

174

'Really? I just, somehow – your face seems so familiar.'

'No, it doesn't! I mean, it couldn't be. Familiar.'

'Couldn't I have seen you around somewhere?'

What sort of question was this? An innocent one? Surely not. So far Louise had been spinning a welcoming web, now Izzy was all lined up, paralysed, the victim. The breadknife lay glinting not three feet away. Couldn't I have seen you – *hanging around my husband's body*? SCHNAK!! What did a breadknife feel like as it plunged through your breastbone? How far would her blood spurt? As far as the spotless freezer? Christ! Was that *where she'd end up*? 'How about a touch more of the stew, darling?' 'Yes, please, Louise – it's delicious, what is it?' 'Oh, only some of that *Cuisse de Maîtresse* out of the freezer.' 'My favourite!' Izzy had to make a vital decision: had Louise, perhaps, seen her around somewhere?

'Well – I suppose you might have seen me on TV,' she mumbled recklessly. Louise can't kill somebody who's been on TV, for God's sake.

'Really? Have you been on TV? When?'

'Oh, nothing much – just a few ads.'

'Fantastic! Ads are my favourite thing on TV! Let me try and remember which one you're in – is it that Jamaican rum one on the beach?' Izzy shook her head. 'The shampoo one with the horse?' No. 'The baked beans one in the rain?' Far wide. 'All right then, I give up. Which one is it?'

Yes. Which one *was* it, Izzy? Just which one of those TV ads includes a glimpse of your jolly little face, eh? For a moment Izzy contemplated seizing the breadknife and plunging it through her own breastbone herself.

'Well – there are several—' *Several*, Izzy? Have you gone stark staring Bonkers? No, listen, safety in numbers, thus: 'There was a lager one, and a – an insurance one, and – let me see, I think there was a lawn-mower one—'

'But wait a minute – what's a teacher doing appearing

175

in all these TV ads?'

What indeed. You have, my dear Louise, hit the nail so firmly on the head that we are deafened by its howling. Or at least, Izzy was. Only the howling seemed to come from somewhere inside her own reeling consciousness.

'Oh, it's the – drama connection, you see – I trained at Drama School, and lots of my friends are in the business, and so I get a bit of work now and then. Comedy, mainly,'

'But what about the union position?'

But what about the running-away-right-now position? What about the getting-up-without-another-word and racing-to-the door position? What about the hurtling-away-into-the-sunset scene? What indeed. Alas, Izzy's shoes appeared to have been welded to the floor-boards.

'Oh – the union position's OK – I belong to both.'

'Which ones?'

Which *ones*? Look here, Mrs Tristram, beauty is not always enough. We are beginning to understand why Michael may have fled from your exquisite presence now and then. This is not breakfast TV, dear lady: you are not the fearless probing reporter. Can't we just get back to that jolly laughing-together bit we were doing awhile back there? It was difficult enough for Izzy to remember the name of her own union, let alone other people's.

'Oh, just the usual ones. The NUT and – um – er, Equus. I mean, Equity.'

'What's it like making a TV Commercial? It always sounds so glamorous. Have you ever been whisked away to some exotic setting?'

'Oh, once or twice.'

Izzy was now flying kamikaze, her eyes glazed, the Earl Grey storming in her blood.

'Oh, really? Where?'

'Well, I went to Tenerife once.'

'Did you? You lucky thing! Tell me – where exactly *is*

176

Tenerife? I've always wondered.'

'Oh,' said Izzy, casually waving her arms in the direction of Louise's back garden, 'somewhere down *there*, you know. In the middle of the sea. One of those hot seas. To tell you the truth, I can't quite remember. They kept us so juiced up with cocaine that the whole thing's sort of vague in my memory—'

Louise's eyes grew large, as well they might, for it was no longer Izzy talking, but Janis Joplin, dead druggie and rock star, whose serialized life story Izzy half remembered reading once in an ancient magazine.

'Tell you what, though,' said Izzy, or rather Diane, or rather Janis, for without Janis, Izzy and Diane would've sat there like a stuffed toy, with more of the stuffing spilling out with every wretched word. 'Why don't we have a look at those rooms. I've wasted so much of your time rambling on – I'm sorry.'

Louise led the way upstairs, and at every step Izzy's heart grew heavier and heavier. Here was this enchanting woman whose smile had encircled her heart, and Izzy had driven her further and further away and made a nonsense of it all with her absurd farragos of lies, mocking their time together, humiliating Louise, corrupting herself, condemning them both to rotten planks on which to face the gathering storm.

'This is it.' Louise walked into the most magical room Izzy had ever seen. It was long and white, and at the far end were French windows that issued on to a balcony. It was full of colour: shell pink, sand, cream, rose, cork, pale brown. Rugs, cushions, curtains, tapestries.

'Oh,' groaned Izzy with pleasure, the sound of truth at last. On the wall hung a painting of a child rushing into a field of poppies. Izzy knew without asking that it was Louise's work. Louise went to the window and drew the curtains back a little. The low spring sun flew in and roosted in her hair until it seemed all ablaze. Then she turned. She seemed hesitant.

'Do you like it?'

Izzy's heart was lead, was ice. This glorious creature, her wildly beautiful room: Izzy was shut off from it for ever by her tawdry nature, by the black lies that buzzed around her, smelling her most filthy bargain. She was carrion. Louise was blazing gold: a lion. The lion who deserved its share.

'You don't like it, do you? I can tell.'

'No! I – I – love it.'

'Well, come and see the bedroom.'

Next door, a little room. A green bed, a green blind, and white dried flowers in a green jar. Somewhere, a musky, smoky scent, as of old houses. Outside, a windowful of twigs, on which a thrush sat and would sing.

'Do you like it, Diane? Only – only I really like you, and I'd so much like you to have it. Would you? Would you like to come?'

Louise's eyes looked into hers so direct and true that Izzy flinched, feeling herself turn to cardboard.

'Never mind if you don't think it's what you're looking for. It doesn't matter. I can see it's not quite what you're looking for.' She sounded jarred: hurt.

'It's not that!' cried Izzy, seizing Louise's gaze again. 'It's just that – it's just that I must talk to you about – about Michael.'

She sat down on the bed; she had to: her cardboard legs would not do their work. She dared not look at Louise's face. Instead, she looked at the carpet – pale green, it was, and looked like a field, only paler. As if a meadow had suddenly heard something terrible. Izzy noticed a little feather lying down there: the sort of tiny downy feather that escapes from pillows sometimes and gets blown about the world, hapless and helpless, and then comes to rest somewhere and is noticed by somebody at a moment like this. And is remembered for ever.

But no, it was Louise's face, when she finally looked up, which she'd remember for ever. No longer the lion

178

or the angel, but a vulnerable woman well over thirty whose delicate fair skin was fretted with lines and who now looked down at her with defeated pleasure and reluctant suspicion.

'Why didn't you say so in the first place, Diane?'

'It would have been different. I'm sorry – I shouldn't have – the whole point of coming here was to stop the lying – but I did so want to get to know you a little bit, before you knew who I really was, and it's been so hard, and I've longed to tell you so much, and you're so – so – so – marvellous.' Izzy's face buckled, her nose filled with tears, the sausagey lips shook, and she dissolved into her shame.

'Oh, poor Diane!'

Louise swooped down in an instant, and Izzy was in her arms.

'Don't cry, Diane, please – don't be upset. It's all right. He isn't worth it.'

'I'm not even Dur – Dur – Dur—' sobbed Izzy.

'Hush now, it's all right, really, Diane.'

'I'm not even Dur – Dur – *Diane*. I even lied to you about my name. I'm Iz – Iz – *Isabelle*.' The nicer Louise was, of course, the more Izzy cried, and my goodness, she cried and cried: such glad floods of tears, that had Louise had any commercial sense she could have set up a hydro-electric scheme. At length, however, the tears were done, and Izzy took to a little dry shuddering, with Louise's arm still warm around her shoulders.

'Well—' smiled Louise at length, 'the sun's going down – how about a drink?'

They descended into the kitchen, and Louise poured out two good whacks of gin. They sat face to face across the table.

'OK, then, Izzy – what do you want to talk about?'

'I don't know, really. I think I just wanted you to know. I've got so sick of lying. But Michael wouldn't agree to the idea of telling you. He said you'd – he said you'd scratch my eyes out.'

'Oh, I'll get around to that eventually. But first I have to grow my nails. So you've got two weeks' grace— Now, Michael doesn't know anything about this today?'

'Good God, no: I just came – I had to come. He'll kill me when he finds out. It'll be the end of everything.'

'No it won't. Don't worry. Michael can't end anything. He hasn't got the heart.'

'Yes – he is very tender-hearted.'

'No – he's cowardly. He has no faith in people. Fancy telling you I'd scratch your eyes out! Stupid git. As if any self-respecting woman would scratch another woman's eyes out, when she could sit around and have a gin with her.'

'But, Louise – you don't seem to mind. Or you don't seem surprised, or something.'

'I'm not surprised. I knew something was going on. Something nearly always is.'

Izzy's heart leapt in shock.

'Really? I know there was Caroline, three years ago, but—'

'Caroline? That's a new one on me. There was a Sue and a Theresa and a Maggie, I think. Though I never had the pleasure of meeting any of them, of course. Sue used to ring us up and pretend to be a wrong number if I answered. Silly cow. She must've thought I was as daft as a brush. Maggie used to leave little love notes in his pockets. I think he never even saw some of them, they just came straight through to me when it was time for the dry cleaners. And Theresa kept asking us to dinner. She'd wheel out some awful wally with goofy teeth and fat white hands and pretend he was the man of her dreams, and all the time she was shooting Michael such hot looks I'm surprised the poor old goat didn't burst into flame.'

'But you never said anything?'

'I did once. But afterwards I decided it was counter-productive. Better to let sleeping dogs lie. Let him lead his life and get on with my own.'

'And now I've come along and forced you to take account of it all. I'm so sorry.'

'Don't apologize for coming, Izzy – please! I really mean it. It's been such a pleasure meeting you. I'm just rather sorry—' Louise looked troubled, and stared beyond Izzy, out of the window.

'—sorry that I have to be who I am?' asked Izzy.

'Oh no, no. I'm just sorry that you weren't really interested in the room – that seeing the room was just a pretext for coming here. It was, wasn't it?'

'Oh yes – I've got my own little flat in Earl's Court. It suits me very well.'

'Do you share?'

'Well, I didn't use to, but—' And Izzy embarked on the whole Maria saga, to which Louise listened with flaring eyes. Her eyes were like Dorothy Wordsworth's – those *shooting lights*. Suddenly the light in them kindled and grew to an idea. She seized Izzy's hand across the table.

'Come here anyway, Izzy! Let Maria have your flat and come and live on our top floor! Oh, please do!'

Izzy was amazed. 'You mean you'd – you'd consider having me living under the same roof as – as you both?'

'Consider it? I'd *love* it!'

'But – but what—'

Izzy could not find the words. They were all too naughty.

'Listen, Izzy, if Michael's going to go goating round after other women, I'd rather it was going on in my own attic. It would be so much better than him being lured off to some mysterious siren Out There, with all the Lies and Excuses that he'd resort to. Besides, if I was still jealous of him, which I really don't think I am any more – but *if* I was, it would be so consoling to know that it was you up there and that he'd already done it all with you. Imagine a new unknown girl moving in and all the uncertainty and anguish that would cause. What's he thinking? What does he feel about her? What'll they do?

181

But with you, it's all safely done, and there's no crying over spilt milk, is there?'

Izzy was astonished.

'Anyway, Izzy, this is all really irrelevant. I didn't offer you the flat in the first place because I thought it would be a good strategic move with Michael's mistress – I didn't even know you were his mistress – I offered it to you because I liked you very much, and thought it would be fascinating to get to know you and lovely to have you in the house. And I still think so.'

'But surely – you wouldn't want me here, really?'

Louise laughed. 'You must believe me, Izzy – I want you to have the room. I really do. Please do come and live here. And you and Michael can do your goating whenever you want. He *is* a good lover, isn't he?'

Izzy blushed and nodded.

'Yes,' sighed Louise, 'he's great in bed. That's what he does best. Just keep him there. Don't ever get involved in the wretched business of trying to run a house with him, or organize a shopping trip, or buy a new bedroom suite.'

'Is he – is he difficult to live with, then?'

'Oh, he's all right, I suppose. He's a weak, vain and rather silly man. But he has plenty of compensating virtues.'

Izzy's ears seemed to expand. Weak, silly and vain? Her Michael? At one level she was amazed, but deeper down, not entirely surprised, somehow.

'But why, if you think he's weak, silly and vain, and he's so often unfaithful – why stick with him?'

Louise shrugged. 'Well, there's little Jack, and here we all are in this rather nice house, and Michael's jolly useful at putting up shelves and heaving things about. And he's not smelly, and he does his share of housework – oh, he's all right, and after all, what can one expect from men?'

Izzy was silent. She had been in the habit of expecting everything.

182

'But all the same, we've got to live with the buggers and bear their children, haven't we? And if to err is human, well, men are certainly human.'

And to forgive's divine, thought Izzy, gazing at Louise through a growing mist of adulation.

'Don't get me wrong, Izzy. I know which side my bread's buttered. Michael makes good money – he certainly subsidises my painting – I'd starve on my own unless I could do commercial graphics all the time. We've hammered out a sort of *modus vivendi*. We can read together in the same room. We laugh at the same things. We like the same people – including you, obviously.'

'Well, what do you think Michael would say to the idea of my moving into your attic?'

Louise looked mischievous. 'I don't think it would do a lot for his libido. I think he thrives on secrecy. Having an exciting mistress stashed away somewhere is one thing, but we used to keep old skateboards up there – I say, Izzy, I'm terribly sorry, I didn't mean—' But they were both laughing uncontrollably, like a couple of old drains in a gale.

'Imagine the subterfuges he'd have to resort to, to visit you in secret! He'd get up in the middle of the night and say, "My dear – go back to sleep, it's all right, but I simply must go and prod my prize marrow".'

Izzy cackled and joined in with a will. 'We'd have to have a special place in the house somewhere – a trysting place. Where could it be?'

'The broom cupboard?' Louise leapt up and opened its door. A mop fell out. 'God, no, it wouldn't do much for you having those horrible broom handles sticking into your back! And the smell of polish – ugh!'

'Oh, but wait – the polish, now – the polish could be great – all slippery and shiny!'

'Yes, but terribly *incriminating, Izzy*. I mean, if you both started hanging around with bits of old broken broomhandle dangling from your belts and your hands and faces covered with polish, I think I'd smell a rat – no, the airing cupboard is the place.'

'Is it big enough?'

'Not really, no – you'd both have to be kneeling all the time. Still, that would be convenient, wouldn't it – you could pray at the same time and ask the Almighty forgiveness. The trouble is, you'd get so terribly cramped in there, you'd probably have to stay kneeling for ever! What a penance!'

For a moment Izzy was tempted to tell the story of the cramp in the car, but she wisely desisted. Fantasy was one thing, anecdote another. Since when did Izzy have so much sense? Since very recently. Not that sense was a great help in her present most remarkable situation. Here they sat in a darkening kitchen, getting just a bit tipsy, crying a bit from having laughed so much: Izzy and Louise. And laughing a bit from having cried so much – not just today, but back in history.

For Izzy felt the reality of Louise's tears. She knew there had been tears and pain. She saw them around her eyes, heard them in her voice. But she felt that there was new tissue and that the new tissue would not tear as the old had done. And here they sat – smiling in delight into each other's eyes, Izzy and Louise. It *did* make sense. And it was also, of course, nonsense. It was so preposterously unlikely that it was bound to work.

'I'll come,' said Izzy on an impulse, 'I'll come, what the hell – Maria can have my flat, and if it's all awful, well – I can always move out again, can't I?'

At this very moment they heard a key in the door. They fell silent, looking at each other, listening to the man and boy coming in. The boy ran in, telling Louise eagerly about the gorilla, Mum, and the chimp, Mum, it peed in the other chimp's face and he'd got a book, Mum – then he registered the stranger's presence and went off shyly to read in his own room. Still his father had not come near the kitchen: he was out in the downstairs loo. Having had a pee, he washed his hands and blew his nose

184

loudly. Izzy heard it with surprise. He had never made such a noise in her flat. It was the trumpeting of the banal Michael, the New Man she was about to meet.

He came into the kitchen, stopped stock-still, and stared. His mouth dropped slightly open and for several seconds he was bereft of speech. Finally he reached right back to his prep school stockpile, so portentous was the moment, so great his need.

'Sacred Norah!' he exclaimed. He had pulled out the big one. 'How long has this been going on?'

The women burst out laughing.

14

March, which maddens hares, brought 4C to a rolling boil. The end of term shimmered, mirage-like, a couple of weeks away. The kids were fractious and the teachers jaded. Or the teachers were fractious and the kids jaded. They took it in turns. The mock exams – those wonderful things which keep them quiet and hypnotized for days on end (educationally abhorrent as they are, of course) were over. Their *Ship of Fools* now lay in the grey and greasy seas of extempore teaching. They were too tired to plan lessons, and the restless children demanded unusual liberties. The smart-ass little first years played droll word games, smuggling in rude words wherever possible; the unspeakable 2V performed a whole series of plays featuring dogs peeing against trees. Izzy prayed no one Important would come in during these execrable rituals.

As for 4C, they wanted to talk about sex. Officially in class, instead of just the whole of the rest of the time.

'G'on, Miss, g'on please, Miss, please c'n we 'ave a discussion please, Miss, please it's too 'ot t'work Shrup Gary Gerroff Wayne. Miss, tell 'im NOT TO 'e ent arf rude, Miss, dyer know what 'e jus' said. Please, Miss, please a discussion, Miss, ay.'

At length Izzy decided to bow to the inevitable.

'All right. I'd like you to think about The Family.'

'Ugh no, Miss, no it's borin', Miss, SNOT FAIR we wanna talk about abortion, Miss, Garry wants to talk about rape, Miss, 'e don't just wanna talk about it either

Shrup don' be rude don' spoil it Gerroff Newman OUCH.'

'All right, if you don't want to talk about The Family we can always do writing.'

'Ugh WRITIN'! Ugh no, Miss. Ssssh Shrup shush shush.'

Silence, punctuated only by the faint smack of bursting bubblegum.

'All right then. I want you to consider whether a family unit is the best possible way to live and bring up children.'

'Yeah course it is, Miss, course.'

'Why's that, Andy?'

'Well, the mum does the cookin' and the dad fumps 'em if they get out of line.'

Chorus of protests.

'No, Miss, no that's stupid, Miss, 'e's stupid, Miss.'

'My dad does the cookin' in our 'ouse anyway,' boasted Sharon.

'Only 'cos your mum's always out on the game.'

'Shrup Gary! Miss didyer hear that, Miss, send 'im out, send 'im to old King Kong, Miss, let him frash 'im.'

'I'm sure Mr King has got better things to do than thrash Gary.' (Though, come to think of it, perhaps *not*.) 'Anyway, nobody gets thrashed in school any more as you very well know. Gary, any more remarks like that and you'll find yourself with a lot of most interesting extra work to do. Now – how many of you know a family that's not a simple unit of mother, father and child?'

Every hand in the room went up.

'My cousin, Miss, my cousin Darren down Deptford 'e lives with 'is Uncle Joe.'

'Why's that?'

''Is mum run off, Miss, run off with a long distance lorry driver. Went to live in Newcastle, Miss. And Darren's dad's mental so 'e lives with 'is Uncle Joe.'

'Is his Uncle Joe married?'

'No, Miss, no 'e ent married 'e's a brickie.'

'An', Miss – Yvonne Davies in 4K, she lives wiv 'er grandma 'cos 'er mum and dad died in a car crash, Miss.'

Izzy was beginning to regret the subject she'd chosen.

'An' my mate Pauline lives wiv 'er grandma an' all – she ent never 'ad a dad never.'

'She must've done.'

'I know, *stupid*, but 'er mum never let on oo it was.'

'Miss?'

'Yes, Roger?'

'Miss, whatdjer think about Jesus Christ, Miss? I mean djer reckon he was really the Son of God or djer fink 'is old lady 'ad been messin' about wiv some ole geezer?'

'She messed about wiv the angel.'

'Nah she didn't, angels ent got nuffink to mess about wiv, berk!'

'Nah it's all just fin air ent it?'

'I don't believe in angels anyway 's a loader bollocks. All religion's a loader bollocks it don't stop people killin' each uvver does it? What about Norvern Ireland ay what a mob call 'em Christians?'

'Angels, Miss, angels,' gabbled Stephen Masters, 'angels – there's this bloke, Miss, I seen 'im on telly 'e says angels are really aliens, Miss, they come down in a spaceship and there's this bit in the Bible where it describes it, Miss, and it's just like a UFO it was on Nationwide.'

'Shrup Masters.'

'We're straying a bit far from our subject of The Family aren't we? Do you think a woman or man living on their own could bring up a child just as well as a couple could?'

'No, Miss, no course not yes, Miss, yes corse they could. My mum brung me up on 'er own and me and me, Miss, and my dad brung me up on 'is own. Our gran brung my cousin Mark up, Miss.'

'So really it's not necessary to be a couple to bring a child up happily?'

'Nah, Miss, nah not reelly. Yes it is, Miss, Shrup Masters.'

'And what about the couple itself? Do you think that's the best living arrangement, one man, one woman?'

'Nah – free or four women to each bloke,' said JJ, looking sly.

'They 'ave four wives in Muhammad Ali countries, don't they, Miss?'

'Sometimes. And I've heard of an island in the Pacific where the women can have more than one husband if they like.'

'Wha'? Where? Nah! Reelly, Miss, where is it, Miss, we wanna go there.' Bursts of giggling. 'Be a bit crowded in bed wouldn't it, Miss, eh?'

'Miss, my Auntie Sissie she's got two blokes, Miss.'

'Really? How does that work?'

'Well, she's got Uncle Roy, Miss, and Mike.'

'Bet 'e's a lodger.'

'No, Miss, 'e ent just a lodger I know 'e ent. 'E did start off as a lodger but 'e's a proper uncle now.'

'Owdjer know?'

''Cos I 'eard my Gran and Grampy arguin' about it. Gran said it was disgustin' and my Grampy said live and let live, Miss.'

'Does the idea appeal to the rest of you?'

'Cor yeah, Miss, yeah! No, Miss, I don't fancy it too much like 'ard work ay!'

'Miss?'

'Yes, Roger?'

'The best way to bring up kids I reckon, Miss, is like what they do in Israel it's called a Kidbutz. The kids aren't brung up by their own mum and dad – they're brung up in a big kind of gang.'

'It's called a crash, Miss, ennit ay a crash.'

'Yeah – an' then they can be looked after by people what really knows about kids you know, Miss, experts and that.'

'What might be the disadvantages of that system?'

'Be a bit noisy, Miss, ay.'

'Any other disadvantages?'

'It wouldn't be very nice 'avin to give your kid up and never seein' it.'

'You do see it, you stupid slag! You see it in the evenin's and on Sundays.'

'Nah – not Sundays, you berk. They don't 'ave Sundays over there, do they, Miss, they 'ave Saturdays instead. Saturday's the Passover ennit?'

'It ent the Passover, pill! It's the Sabbath ennit, Miss, ay.'

'Well – we've seen there are lots of different ways of organising life – there's no reason why families should consist of a mother, a father and children. So what about you? What are your aims? Do you still think conventional marriage is the best thing?'

'Oh yeah, Miss, yeah No Miss no 'srubbish, Miss, 's a fing of the past ennit? Don't talk outa yer bum Shrup Masters Shrup yerself.'

The bell rescued Izzy from the consequences of this *sacra conversazione*. They raced out, desperate for their Player's No 6 behind the Science Block. Lynette, Tracey and Diane stayed behind however and hung around Izzy's desk as she packed her books.

'Miss, I never said it in the lesson 'cos Razors was there.'

'What, Tracey?'

'Well, Miss, well 'e doesn't 'ave a mum or dad neither, Miss, does 'e?'

'Where does he live, then?'

Izzy knew that each member of her class had a file but for certain nearly-baked political reasons she'd never consulted them.

''E lives down Newington Green, Miss – wiv Big Eileen.'

'And who,' marvelled Izzy, 'is Big Eileen?'

'She's 'is auntie, Miss.'

'No she ent! She's on the game.'

'She's a pro, Miss.'

'No she ent.'

'She's still 'is auntie.'

'No she ent! She's his – you know.'

'She ent, is she?'

'No, not that! She's his – whadjer call – guarder?'

'Guardian?'

'Yeah, Miss, yeah that's it. Guardian.'

Izzy wandered off to the staff room, trying to remember when the next Parents' Evening would be. Alas, the characters one really wishes to meet never show up. No doubt Big Eileen would be Otherwise Engaged.

In the staff room Dick was waiting with her coffee all stirred and ready. Dick had gradually given up all claims to her bed and was busy instead carving out a role for himself as her devoted slave. Izzy treated him with increasing cruelty, sensing that this was what he wanted. She was a kind-hearted soul.

'Thanks, Dick. I hope it's not bloody cold like it was yesterday.'

'No – I think it's all right this time.'

'How's tricks then? How's life in dreary old Totten-ham?'

'All right. It's been much better since Hywel moved in.'

Yes, Hywel and Dick were becoming a very odd couple. Gwyn and Maria had agreed to sell their flat, so Hywel had flown and Dick needed a tenant. What was even more astonishing was that Hywel had taken to pottery and even got out of bed at about noon in order to make mugs all afternoon. Dick reported dolefully that he thought Hywel would eventually be a much better potter than himself. This was a self-deluding view. Hywel was already a much better potter than himself. He'd done a bit before, at his Welsh comprehensive, and he used to go and do extra work in the lunch hour because the pottery teacher was so pretty. Hywel had seduced her years later on the night he'd got his HGV licence. So in a way he'd kept his hand in.

'Do you enjoy living with Hywel, then?'

'Oh yes, he's – well, he's quite domesticated really.' And of course there was Hywel's job as a barman in the evenings. Dick often went along there and they used to chat up women together. Or at least, Hywel would chat them up, two at a time, and there was usually a slightly fatter or frumpier one for Dick. Dick discovered that hanging around with Hywel had its attractions. Women often assumed that since Hywel had the looks, Dick must have the brains.

'I knew you was brainy when I saw yer glasses,' one semi-beauty confessed. And Dick cultivated this impression by saying as little as possible. Still, today he had something on what passed for his mind.

'Have you ever been to San Francisco, Izzy?'

'No. Why?'

'Well, there's a notice on the board about how some teachers there are organizing an exchange with London teachers. I thought I might – well, I might – er – apply.'

'You'd have to be gay to be accepted.' Maria had joined the party.

'Oh, Maria – have you been there, then?'

'Yes. Gwyn and I went a few years ago. An Oxford mate of mine had a fellowship thing at Stanford, so we stayed with them.'

'What was it like?'

'Not your sort of place at all, I should think, Dick. You have to be gay or Chinese to be really somebody.'

'Oh, I don't want to be really somebody.' Dick's modesty remained unimpaired. 'I just thought I'd like to – take a look, sort of thing.'

'Oh, come on, Dick, don't be such a wimp,' grinned Izzy. 'You can't do anything about not being Chinese, I grant you, but you could make a bit more of an effort on the gay front.'

'I don't know, Izzy.' Maria seized the challenge.

'After all, Dick is sharing a house with Hywel. And Hywel *is* very beautiful. Go on, admit it, Dick, you're one of those artistic Yorkshire queens. London's full of them. You can't switch on the telly without—'

'Wait a minute, Dick – why don't you take Hywel with you? You'd be accepted everywhere then, and you could keep your hetero whatsits a dark secret.'

'But—' Dick was troubled. 'Wait a mo – do you mean – there aren't any women out there?'

'Oh yes, masses,' grinned Maria mischievously. 'And it's incredibly frustrating for them of course. All the men are gay. So it's a straight man's paradise. Lots of spare women.'

'What – really?'

'Yes. Trouble is, a lot of the women are gay, too. And they all do self-defence courses. So you'll have to be very careful about who you chat up, Dick – or you could end up in the gutter.'

'Oh. Um. It all sounds a bit – dangerous.'

'Oh yes, it is. Somebody gets killed every five seconds or whatever it is.'

'Yes, well – it was only an idea.'

'But then, of course, there are the drugs.'

'Drugs?'

Maria was the Compleat Angler.

'Oh, lots of drugs, Dick. God, yes. Especially cocaine. Ever had cocaine?'

Since Hywel had moved in, the gates of Dick's consciousness had swung open with a deafening creak.

'Cocaine? No. What's it like? Is it nice?'

'Nice? NICE? Really, Dick, I said cocaine, not cocoa.'

'When I was young there was a rumour that Coca-Cola had cocaine in it,' mused Izzy. 'I went behind the barn once with John Wilson and drank six bottles of it. And had two aspirins. It was supposed to get us high.'

'Did it?'

'No. I peed a lot, though. And John had a pain.'

Just then a whining child came to the staff room door

to warn Dick that a pack of wild Remedials had broken into his pottery room and were running amok. Dick fled. Maria smiled at his disappearing back.

'I really like Dick a lot more, now I know him a bit.'

'Yes. You're mellowing, Maria.'

'Mellowing? I think I'm disintegrating. How's life with Michael and Louise shaping up?'

'Well – er, it's a bit hard to say, really, after only three days. I do like Louise, though. She's marvellous.'

'I don't know what sort of game they're playing, Izzy, but you'll be cracked between them, like a nut.'

'Oh, don't go into all that again, Maria – please.'

'All right. Sorry. I don't half miss you, though. I get vilely depressed living on my own. The trouble is – I do miss Gwyn horribly, the bastard. Horribly. And it's completely against my principles, too.'

Her eyes filled with tears and she rummaged in her bag for a tissue. Then she seized *The Economist* and buried her head in it. Though nowadays, of course, that sort of thing is only likely to result in many more tears: saltier, rounder and more universal.

15

There are times when one's continued presence on the planet does cause a measure of dismay. Michael had felt a lot like that recently. Take the immortal moment when he'd arrived home, only slightly pickled and looking forward to his dinner, to find Louise and Izzy together in the kitchen. Louise and Izzy. Together. The sense of obscene harmony was unnerving. One moment he occupied his familiar, pleasantly-disordered universe: impossible, chaotic, one woman here, another there, can't help himself poor bugger, dreadful the scrapes he gets into, can't imagine where he finds the energy – and then, suddenly – WHAM! It was like coming back home in the old adolescent days to find that your mum's tidied up your bedroom, and all your dirty secrets are ironed and folded in view.

Izzy and Louise, both, he couldn't help noticing, looking nauseatingly agreeable, faced him across the remains of what had clearly been several gins. He had the unpleasant sensation not merely of egg on his face but also seasoned flour and possibly even breadcrumbs. He was, there was no doubt, poised above the frying pan. And for a brief moment he thought, Christ, why didn't God make me a Wiener Schnitzel? It can't be so bad. All right, so you're castrated, kept in the dark, butchered, fried and finally devoured, but what's that compared to the subtle kindnesses human beings inflict on one another?'

And say he'd managed to dodge the dark stable and

the frying pan: there was even a fighting chance that, as a bull calf, he might have ended up as a bull. And then he could have swaggered about the field glowering complacently at his fifty or so wives – and everybody would think it was quite all right, for God's sake. And instead here he was on his own hearthstone, confronted by a mere pair of the fair sex, and expected to writhe in humiliation.

Well, he writhed. But at least he made a dignified exit. He shot them a dismissive glance, spat out some sardonic quip or other, and on a sudden impulse walked out of the back door. This, like all his sudden impulses, turned out to be catastrophic. The Arctic wind corkscrewed up his corduroys and he realized anew just what a gutsy geezer old Oates must have been. Michael made for the shed which he dimly remembered to be at the bottom of the garden, turned the rusty key and ensconsed himself there. At least the cold stood still in there. It didn't come rushing at you with bared teeth from all directions. So one could as it were writhe in humiliation in peace.

At first Michael messed about with a chisel and wondered, Which is the artery that really counts? He couldn't bear the thought of cutting his throat, of course – too near home, somehow. But if there was a vital and out-of-the-way sort of artery somewhere down around the little toe, and if you knew that with one deft slash oblivion would be yours— Or there were those mouldy old seed packets – surely by now they must be pulsating with lethal bacteria? A gobful of 1979's Webb's Wonders maybe and one could be sailing up through the stratosphere in a white nightie. On the other hand, he was tempted to wait a couple of days and throw himself under a municipal lawnmower in one of the public parks. He had the distinct impression that the more pieces he ended up in, the better his chance of escaping ridicule. A hamburger, perhaps, rather than a Wiener Schnitzel. Presently it got dark, and he cut himself with the wretched chisel. Accidentally, of course, and only on the finger, and what's more he was so cold by then that he could hardly even bleed. So he went in.

He let Louise know what he thought of her by behaving with chilly good manners for the next few days. A public school education can have its advantages. When she asked if he minded if Izzy had such and such a chair from the study, or such and such a lamp, he waved his arms about in a genial, Gallic, shrugging sort of way and was effortlessly good-tempered. Well, when I say effortlessly, I have to admit it was all he could do at times not to strangle the cow. But he knew that they only get the better of you if they can see you're rattled. What's more he wasn't exactly clear about the amount of indignation he was entitled to, as it were.

In fact, he found his thoughts were altogether about as far from being clear as they had ever been, and that was saying something. His feelings were unmistakable enough: though whether murder or suicide were the more alluring prospect varied from moment to moment. But as to thoughts, he seemed paralysed, unable to manoeuvre his defences. Counter-attack was impossible.

Louise boxed very clever indeed. She accepted Michael's frozen acquiescence at face value and cheerily went about organizing Izzy's arrival as if she had been some benign great aunt about to pay a visit. Never for a moment did Louise confront her spouse or attempt to open any serious topics of conversation. And when he turned his back on her every night she only went straight to sleep with a sigh of satisfaction – deeper, he was sure (though this may have been paranoia) than he'd ever heard her utter at his hands. She was always asleep long before his toiling soul could find friendly unconsciousness.

Then Izzy moved in. Michael watched from an upper window. She was helped by two unpleasant looking men, one of whom possessed a terminal van. Doug and Howell they seemed to be called, though Michael trusted he had got their names wrong. One was about seven feet tall, with the sort of moronic good looks that went out of fashion in the Sixties; evidently a third-rate Lothario. The other appeared to be a door wearing glasses. They carried Izzy's inevitably shabby boxes and bags upstairs: Michael gaily excused himself from helping on account of having put his back out at squash.

'Well, mon, that's yewer story an' you're stickin' to it,' leered the Lothario. What it meant Michael knew not. He assumed it was some primitive form of sexual badinage. Michael had of course realized that Izzy must have some friends tucked away somewhere, but he was shocked that they did not seem to possess between them a vocabulary of more than twenty-eight words. A rogue thought entered his head: that either of these troglodytes might at some time or other have been Izzy's lover. The thought stung like orange juice on the retina.

Bumping into Izzy on the landing, Michael seized the initiative and set the new *modus vivendi* going in tones of faintly parental snarling.

'Was either of those two pituitary cases ever a lover of yours, my dear?'

'Wouldn't you like to know!' she retorted, with, God help him, a bolshy grin, and bounced into the bathroom. Just as he was contemplating a leisurely enthronement there himself. He became haunted by the feeling that he had somehow lost a mistress and gained a loathsome teenage daughter.

You can imagine the living hell that then became his lot. He hardly ever saw Izzy. In fact, he would rather not have seen the assortment of clapped-out vans and cars which carried her off to unknown trysts; or the letters that arrived for her; or heard the urgent male voices asking for her on the telephone; or the thuds, bellows and obscene laughter from her quarters upstairs. Nor did he particularly want her to see him at the breakfast table, in that cruel early morning light in which his wrinkles were most apparent. Not so much crows' feet as Where Eagles Dare. Once Izzy had been the apple of his eye: now he was left with the core and the pips.

As for Louise, she was unbearably cheerful. She sang a lot around the house, was indecently considerate towards him in an entirely superficial way, and seemed quite infuriatingly taken with Izzy. They were forever dashing off together to some secret feminine soirée or other. Izzy initiated her into Hideki's Oriental aerobics, and Michael would occasionally wander into the bedroom to be confronted by his wife's face scowling strenuously at him from between her buttocks.

What's more, she and Izzy were always staying up together, talking in the kitchen and drinking more than was good for them until late – too late for him to cruise about serenely ignoring them any longer. (At twelve Michael's eyelids crashed and his knees buckled.) As soon as he'd gone up to bed he could hear them shrieking with laughter down there. What were they laughing at? His scarcity of hair? The smell of his feet? His clumsy British attempts to give the Female Creature pleasure? Not that either of them was ever going to experience that again. Oh no. They were both definitely untouchables as far as he was concerned. Not that the wretched women seemed to care, or even notice.

Michael thought of revenge. Every man of sense enjoys it. He would leave them – both. But no, it was partly his home, and jolly comfortable, too. Why should he abandon it? Let the hoydens abandon it. Let them run off together. It would be something to say, in the BBC Club, 'My wife left me, you know – ran off with my mistress.' Yes, that would be really something. But then again, nowadays, perhaps not.

Finally the best of revenges struck him. He would be unfaithful to them – both. He would seduce his PA. Michael had often entertained foul thoughts about his hazel-eyed ingenue. Little did he dream that she was fully equipped with a Turkish boyfriend, a black belt in self defence, and a rather unreasonably rooted hatred of

199

himself. He had several interesting bruises after that little débâcle, but of course it didn't matter, because no one was looking.

One night the hoydens had gone off together to their Oriental session. Michael put Jack to bed and dawdled downstairs to the kitchen. In the middle of the table stood a jar of daffodils, looking strong and optimistic, blast them. For a moment he wondered what life might be like as a daffodil. There you are, your massively developed sexual organs uplifted to the air, penetrated by a succession of tickly brown creatures of another species, and the more the merrier. No wonder they looked so bloody cheerful.

The doorbell rang. It rang quite often these days. Michael answered it. A scruffy looking cove stood before him: wall-eyed, with a slightly Gippo face, greasy curls and a disreputably handsome air. Was he perhaps looking for gardening work?

"Ulloa, there, mon, yew must be Michael, right? I'm Gwyn Jenkins.' Michael was subjected to a frighteningly robust handshake. 'Sometime 'usband of Maria Shadwell, the sometime flatmate of Izzy Comyn, 'oo now adorns this establishment.'

'Ah, yes, Gwyn! Come in! I've heard a lot about you.' Michael wished he'd been concentrating a bit harder when it had all been said. But that was back in the good old days when Izzy had been safe in her Earl's Court eyrie and all had been well with the world. And when she'd started to talk about Maria and Gwyn it had usually been his cue to murmur: 'Come, that's enough talking for now, don't you think?' Not a very classy manoeuvre, he had to admit, in the cold light of day. What's more, it had certainly left him very ill informed.

Though Izzy was out, Gwyn consented to step in for a moment and strolled about a bit. Michael was faintly intrigued by him, and wondered if he, too – but that way madness lies. Gwyn noticed some old grocer's scales and an African drum which Louise had placed artfully on the hall table.

'What the fuck's this, now, Michael?'

'Oh, it's just some Victorian grocer's scales and a tedious old drum from the Cameroun which Louise gave me for Christmas one year.'

'Well – I could make a few pointed remarks about the cultural parasitism of the bourgeoisie, like, but instead I'll just say it's a nice place you got here, mon.'

'Sorry, but I'm fed up of apologizing for being middle class.'

'Quite right, mon! Quite right! The middle classes can teach us sly old peasants a thing or two. I well remember first arrivin' in London and realizin' that I was goin' to the wrong places for my 'olidays and I 'adn't got nearly enough fuckin' plants in my 'ouse.'

'So now you're a fully paid-up member of the bourgeoisie. You lecture in a Poly, I believe?'

'Sright. I tell you what, mon, I'm fuckin' thirsty at the moment. You 'aven't got the odd can of Pils in the fridge by any chance?'

As a matter of fact, he had.

'But most of all, Michael, the things which yew middle classes 'ave got down to a fine art, is the cultivation of delicious women.'

'I'm not so sure about that.'

Michael was extremely jaundiced about middle class women at the time, and was thinking with increasing longing of Woolworth's till girls.

'They're fuckin' magic, mon – thoase middle class girls! All that education and them violin lessons an' things, and the fantastic silk boilersuits they wear, and the way they can argue the hind leg off a donkey, and their magnificence in bed, and the sheer style with which they leave you – well, they've left me a shattered hulk, a mere shadow of the man I was, as you can probably see.'

'You look all right to me.'

'Orright? Oh, I'm, orright, mon.' A crafty wink. 'But not nearly so fuckin' orright as yew are, by the sound of things. 'Ow the fuck d'yew pull it, for Christ's sake? Two of the moast bewtiful women in the universe under your roof.'

'Oh, I didn't do anything,' Michael shrugged, not without a certain frisson of undeserved pleasure (always the best sort).

'Don' give me that, mon – it's a fuckin' *'arem*, right?' Michael felt a silly grin developing.

'Well, isn't it? I knoa for a fact that the supremely desirable Isabelle 'as been mad about yew for months, an' yewer glorious wife, 'oo I 'ad the pleasure of meetin' a few days ago, told me you've got a *modus vivendi*. I thought at first it was a kind of Fiat, mon! Anyway, I wouldn't mind a bit of fuckin' *modus vivendi* with thoase two bewties!'

Michael shrugged again, but it was a bigger, beefier shrug than he could have managed even three minutes ago.

'Tell me – 'ow d'you keep them satisfied, mon? Takin' iron pills or somethin', are yew? 'Ow d'you swing the physical side of it, if you doan't mind my askin'?'

'Oh, sex isn't terribly important in this house,' Michael sighed, with a note of regret.

'Doan't give me that, mon – I knoa that Izzy Comyn an' she's a reelly reelly dirty girl – in the nicest possible way, of course. An' she used to tell me about you and 'er and she made out yew was some kind of satyr, like. An insatiable beast.'

'Oh, nonsense.'

The man was preposterous. Michael handed him another can of Pils.

'Well, I tell yew something'. I take my 'at off to you. You've exploded the deadly newclear family which 'ad its iron grip on 'uman passion for soa long; you've chucked out the model of bourgeois respectability, and you've put in its place a fuckin' *'arem* for Christ's sake.'

202

Gwyn choked on his lager. Michael laughed, too, long and loud. There was a sensation as of Dynorod bursting through much damned-up muck in his soul.

'The truth of the matter is, Gwyn,' Michael grew expansive, 'I'm hag-ridden!'

'C'mon Michael, now, doan't give me that. If them two girls is hags they can ride me any hower of the day or night. Doan't be soa modest, mon: yew've won the jackpot, and the rest of us poor miserable buggers can only say more power to your elboa, right?'

Half an hour later, Gwyn had to go to 'a pressin' engagement'. He left Michael in high good humour, his world somehow magically transformed.

Dear Izzy. Beautiful Louise. They'd be back soon from their Japanese torture session, and this would be a great homecoming. For not only were they coming home: Michael was, too. Tonight he would join the ladies. He got a bottle of Louise's favourite Sancerre and put it in the fridge. He found some trout and prawns and prepared a fishy feast. And when he put his mind to it, nobody could conjure up a marine marvel in the same class. He even scoured the house for the stumps of last Christmas's candles to create the right atmosphere of blurred edges and blooming complexions. None of them was getting any younger, though the bloody women were making a heroic stand.

Then, just as the scene was set to perfection, they arrived, humming with fiendish Oriental energy and ravenous as usual. Their eyes lit up. They fell on him like kids on candy. Oooooohs and aaaaaaahs. Kisses all round. The last perfect touch was that they'd brought him back a bottle of his favourite Chablis.

'Girls,' Michael announced gaily. 'I mean, of course, Ladies—'

'Women,' asserted Louise.

'There's no need to be political, my dear wife, but on this most happy of occasions, we'll let that pass. Mesdames – I have a highly important announcement to make. I'm giving up smoking. This is positively the last Gauloise that will ever droop from my lips.'

'All right then,' grinned Louise, 'if renunciation is in the air, I will stop biting my nails.'

'I thought we were halfway through Lent already,' claimed Izzy. 'Anyway, I'm game. I'll give up chocolate cake – after tonight.' They could afford to give up their consoling little vices. True happiness was perched on their roof, and his long blue glistening wings tickled every window. Or so it seemed.

16

That night Michael stood and watched while Louise got
undressed. On a clear day you could see Oxfordshire.
When she was down to her leotard, he stepped forward
and fell on his knees before her. It seemed the least he
could do.

'Dear Louise!' he exclaimed to her exquisite navel.
'You are the most beautiful woman in the world, and the
most forgiving, and the most patient, and the most
imaginative.'

'Good God,' smiled Louise, tenderly caressing his bald
spot. 'I sound almost perfect.'

'Almost – if only you'd stop wearing these terrible
bloody leotards.'

He held her tight, his cheek to her belly.

'Forgive me, Louise. You are centuries ahead of me, I
flounder after you in the dark. Bear with me. I am but
Neanderthal.'

'Dear Michael, you are sweet.'

'I just want you to know that – Jesus Christ! I can't get
up. My knee's gone out of whack – sort of seized up.
Give me a hand, love – ouch! Jesus!'

Louise helped him into bed. His knees did tend to seize
up at moments of abject apology. But in bed he soon
recovered all his faculties. Afterwards, she whispered
into the warm whorls of his ear, 'Michael – do make it up
with Izzy, too, please. She's been so worried about you.'

'Whermmmm?'

'Izzy. She's been so unhappy whilst you've been – well – you know – absent in spirit. So do be nice to her and make it all right with her.'

'Wha' – not now, surely.' His hormones gave a lurch of protest.

'No, no, not now, of course not.' Louise giggled and snuggled more deeply into his armpit.

Next day Louise took Jack to the Spurs match. Michael sat alone in the kitchen, listening to the quiet hums and clicks of the machines which had cost him so much and went wrong with venomous accuracy on Christmas Eves and Good Fridays. Izzy was upstairs. Not a sound came from her room. No male guffaws. No heavy thuds. A ringing silence up there. He could hear her reading.

Eventually he got up and walked slowly upstairs, pausing at the first landing. It was odd – he felt little flickers of excitement and nerves, like his first night in the prep school panto. He crept to Izzy's door, and, unaccountably, almost went away again. Then, at last, he tapped a lascivious tattoo.

Izzy looked up from the windowseat where she sat, drawing. 'Oh, Michael! I thought it was the cat.' A deep blush of pleasure filled her face.

There is nothing more attractive than a woman blushing at the sight of you, thought Michael. *It's chemistry, you know. They can't help it.*

'You're drawing?' This time he would do it right and take an interest in her work.

'Yes. Louise got me hooked on drawing. She lent me this book all about drawing with the right side of the brain. Have you heard of it?'

'Oh yes. Louise raved about it all last summer. I never listened, though.'

'Well, you should have. It's fascinating. It's all about how the left side of your brain is normally in control – it's the verbal, logical side that conceptualizes and

206

argues, all that sort of thing. The right side is to do with spaces and shapes and what things look like. And when you start to draw, the right side takes over. And that's why it feels so nice. It's bliss!'

'What, do you mean you actually feel different?' More relaxed, receptive: might one say – turned on?

'Yes, totally different. You lose all track of time, you start to feel deeply relaxed, and you feel your – well, your Unconscious slowly rising to the surface.'

A satirical guffaw escaped him. It sounded so like *Jaws*.

'That's the left side of your brain laughing, Michael.'

'I was violently sick once in Paris because I ate some calves' brains.'

'Serve you right. You shouldn't mess about with the insides of animals' heads. It's bad enough eating their bodies, but when you start eating their dreams – well!'

Michael sat down on an old beechwood rocking chair and rocked gently to and fro. He seemed to want to take his time – a new sensation with Izzy. There she was, framed in the window; surrounded by Louise's colours. Her eyes seemed bigger, somehow; her cheekbones more pronounced. Less bust, though. What you lose on the swings, you also lose on the roundabouts.

'You've lost a bit of weight, Izzy.'

'Have I? Well, I've been, I suppose, excited, and well, anxious. Anyway, I've plenty to lose.'

A little silence broke out, during which they could hear sparrows seething, lecherously he hoped, in the gutters. Their eyes seemed shy of meeting for longer than a few seconds: it was charming.

'Michael – I'd like to try and draw you.'

'All right.'

He was happy for an excuse to go on sitting there without having to talk. And, of course, he was used to being drawn, having been Louise's model for years. And being not a little vain, Michael liked having his image made.

207

He could see Izzy roughing out an outline. His head became a tilted sphere; his pelvis, an axis; his arms and legs, poised and dynamic lines; his joints, circles. She did it surprisingly well. But then, her eyes did look better. Perhaps she could see better, too.

'I'm sorry if I've made you feel anxious in the past couple of weeks, Izzy.'

'Hrrrrrrrrrm?'

The verbal side of Izzy's brain appeared to be already half asleep.

'It's just that the surprise of it all – and, well, I suppose I'm deeply reactionary despite my—'

'Shut up for a minute,' commanded Izzy. 'I want to do your mouth.'

Michael talked no more. It was strange to see her so totally absorbed in his mere geography, and so totally disengaged from his sense of himself. Her serious concentration, her oblivion, and her lack of make-up gave her a momentarily boyish air. A weird frisson travelled through his system. This boy who ignored him was even more exciting than his plump little mistress had been. She reminded him of a certain Plunkett who had disturbed his peace of mind at Sherborne.

'Right.' Izzy swam to the surface of her concentration and broke into the air. She blinked, filled her lungs. She looked critically at her sketch. 'The hands are hopeless.'

'Can I see?'

He climbed eagerly out of his chair, but was not a little dashed at the sight which met his eyes. There before him was the secret Michael who lived in the mirror: tired, balding, anxious. What a bore he was.

'Hmmmmm. Is that how you see me?'

'Oh no!' Izzy smiled up into his face. 'It's just how you look. How I see you is different.'

Thank God for that.

'How do you see me, then?'

'Well, you know, it's curious – it seems to change from moment to moment.'

208

They were close now. Michael could feel her flower-soft breath on his face. He was near enough to hear her smile. He placed his right hand on her cheek. His heart beat wildly. Would it all end in a coronary, or something more delicious?'

'You hand feels like the sun, Michael.'

'The sun?'

'Yes. When I was camping in Greece, I used to get up before sunrise, and then when the sun came up, it felt just like that – your hand against my cheek.'

'That's funny. I didn't know you'd been to Greece. But then – in a way I suppose – I don't know much about you, Izzy.' He bent down and kissed her lightly on the other cheek. Izzy hesitated a moment and then moved away. God, how exciting. She'd never done that before. His libido was lapping this up, the dirty beast.

'Tell me about Greece,' he smiled. 'Where did you go?' He would play this new game. He liked it.

And what a game it was! Villiers House in Ealing (where Michael attempted to make television programmes for Schools), is a glass-sided tower, and when the sun shines you're trapped like flies in amber: hot, stunned, paralysed, incapable of any sort of activity. Ideal pre-conditions for fantasy. He spent hours daydreaming about Izzy – egged on by the delightful ebb and flow of faintly undulating secretaries, by the trees outside all freckling up with leaves sprung from spring sap, and by the excruciating boredom of his daily task, any departure from which was bound to be erotic: even eating sandwiches or going to the dentist.

Michael's PA had obtained an attachment elsewhere since his attempt on her virtue, and was now secreted away in the bowels of Bush House in the Strand, making worthy programmes for Eastern Europe. Serve her right. In her place he had received Deborah, whose coltish grace was somewhat marred by adenoids, vacancy and continual gum-chewing. What's more, she always wore those terrible baggy trousers that girls like so much

209

nowadays: the ones that make them look as though they've got a brace of pheasants stuffed down inside.

Come to think of it, Izzy had changed the way she dressed. Though Michael knew that for her to have appeared in her Earl's Court gear amidst the brown rice and stone-washed denim of Muswell Hill would have been reckless brinkmanship. But it went beyond that. She didn't seem to wear skirts at all any more – not even decent tweedy flared ones, thank God. And her high heels had disappeared. she must had palmed them off on some Oxfam shop or other. Michael hoped they wouldn't cripple the poor bloody Biafrans. Nowadays Izzy wore rough cotton shirts and rough cotton poachers' trousers, and flat shoes that were made in China and only cost £3.00, and Michael reckoned must be one of the more popular forms of birth control over there.

And yet – the magical Izzy managed to transcend all this, for she had discovered what was as far as he was concerned an even more erotic accessory: self-possession. She gave him secret coquettish smiles and then disappeared. She breathed up his nostrils like an elf-child taming a raunchy old stallion, and then skipped away. What a tease! What a tickler! Who had taught her these gossamer ways? *I hate to boast*, thought Michael, *but the inevitable conclusion must be – yours truly*. She had picked up the throbbing laser-like glares of his reviving passion and was sporting in them like a mote in a sunbeam. She was going to make it even more exciting by making him wait. She had saved Eros from suburban blight. She was surely a genius of sensuality. And he was just as surely her schoolmaster.

All this had, of course, an electrifying effect on Michael and Louise. *I hate to boast*, mused Michael, *and God knows I've never thought of myself as His gift to women, but I must say that since Izzy's arrival Louise and I have enjoyed a sort of second honeymoon* . . . He had never before seen her eyes open quite so wide, or her teeth go quite so surely through the duvet as if it was a tatty old omelette.

He often had to lean back in his chair at Villiers House to give the old ticker room to expand at the thought of Louise. (I refer, to scotch conjecture, to his heart.)

Being alone with Louise was so much more of a treat than before. They hugged their history to them. Michael thought they were rather like a medlar: the most delicious moment coming when they were so ripe, they were half rotten. He pinched the back of his hand. The skin sank slowly back like an old dinosaur's dewlap. He noticed his secretary Deobrah was watching, her jaw suspended in mid-chew.

'Heard it on the radio this morning,' he explained. 'As you get older, the skin doesn't snap back like it did when you were young.'

Deborah pinched the skin up from the back of her hand, and it snapped back like nobody's business. He let her think she'd won. The very young have so little to console themselves with, apart from youth.

That night, after a positively Wagnerian episode, Michael and Louise lay in bed, enfolded in concentric rings of light, her slightly salty shoulder jammed against his tonsils. She breathed warmly across his scalp and he began to drift dimly down and out.

'Darling,' murmured Louise. 'It's been so good recently.' He grunted consent without committing himself to further discourse. Morpheus already had his fingernails into Michael and the God of Sleep could be such a bitch if his victims escaped back into wakefulness at the critical moment. But Louise said something which jolted Michael's dozing cerebellum into overdrive. He felt sure a few braincells actually fell out of his ear and on to the pillow.

'Is it OK with Izzy, too, Michael?'

He spat her shoulder out and mentally zoomed through a few possible clichés. What a question! Since they'd pulled down the barriers of social whatsit he'd been completely at sea. What the hell did she want to hear? And in Michael's view, that was the only thing that counted. Honesty was no policy at all, for him. Scouts had no honour, he knew: he'd been one. And when did you ever like anyone *more* for telling you that you looked *tired*? So: was it OK with Izzy? Well, was it?

'Oh, yes, erm – it's very nice – not as – well, not as wonderful as with you, of course, but, well, really OK.'

Dull but diplomatic, he thought, so he was a bit non-plussed when Louise cackled like an old hen, 'Michael you are funny!'

She rubbed his bald spot. She was always doing it. It was her other imperfection. Christ! Michael suddenly thought, *maybe it's all her fault. I was never bald as a kid, before I met her.*

'What do you mean, I'm funny?'

'Nothing. It's all right. I'm glad it's all right with you and Izzy.'

And hey presto! She was off down the darkening lanes of sleep without even waving goodbye. Michael lay awake for longer: he knew he would. Morpheus had flounced off, but Michael didn't care. He savoured the morrow. Louise was going to take Jack off to see his granny in the country, Izzy and he would be alone for the weekend, and it was quite clear to him that this was the crystalline moment up to which all these suppressed quiverings had been leading. It was time for Izzy and him to come clean. Or preferably, dirty.

17

At lunchtime next day Izzy promised to feed the gerbils, and Michael to defrost the fridge, and then off went Louise and Jack: she driving and he scowling. (It was Louise's dogged 50 mph on the motorway which really irked him. Michael was scared of speed, but he put the old foot down a bit occasionally so Jack wouldn't think him a sissy.) At last Izzy and Michael were alone. A light, seed-stirring rain tiptoed about in the garden. Perfect. He could have done without the Radio One disc jockey jabbering away and Izzy was engrossed in reading a cornflake packet, but this domestic dross only heightened the buried excitement.

'Izzy?'

'Yes?'

'Got anything planned for tonight?'

'No, thank God.'

'Good. Let's stay in – I'll cook you something nice.'

'Ooooh – lovely. You're such a good cook, Michael.'

Michael washed up singing bits from *The Marriage of Figaro*. If only Mozart had written an aria around the promising phrase of *Let's Stay In*. Izzy was looking particularly charming. Her journey towards androgyny intrigued him more and more. Her newly-slim form was arrayed today in rough green cotton shirt and baggy black trousers: the colours of Nature and of Night. And tonight she would be Queen of the Night and they would be Children of Nature. He did wish she'd look up from the bloody cornflake packet just once, though.

Her increasingly-beautiful boy's head rested elegantly on her newly-slim wrist. His heart ached at her self-possession. When, oh when would she set her plimsoll on his neck? Suddenly she looked up. Their eyes met, and the electric shock must have curdled the yogurt. She faltered slightly.

'I'm not – in your way, am I, Michael?'

'In my way? God, no!'

'Oh – I thought you might be wanting to – wipe the table, or something.'

She leapt lightly to her feet and – you've guessed it – moved away.

'I'm terribly impressed by all this domestic stuff, Michael.' Michael was indeed wiping the table now; so caressingly, it might well have burst into leaf. 'I had no idea you had it in you. I thought you were just a boring old demon lover.'

And the grin she flashed him then was followed by a dreadful roaring in his ears, as of thunder. He clutched the edge of the table. Was he getting a bit long in the tooth for such voltages? Were the old aortas going on the blink? As the roaring cleared, Izzy disappeared, like a fiend hid in a cloud. But ah, that last look – he actually tore the tea towel in half in his excitement. It was no mean feat. These National Trust tea towels are tough cookies: best quality linen.

Michael tossed the halves remorselessly into the rubbish bin. Who cared about the Lapwing and Shoveller Duck anyway? Let them wait till he was seventy. No, perhaps even then – perhaps Izzy's daughter – he raced off to Safeway's and laid about him like a Viking. Anyone would have thought he was planning to fatten Izzy up for the pot, not sweep her off her trainers.

When he got back she was – out. Of course. How perfect. Absence. How erotic. Tantalizing. Mysterious. What a good job she hadn't been this clever before, in the old Earl's Court days. She'd have driven him completely off his trolley. He unpacked the Safeway's goodies, ripping the bag in his haste. There it all lay, naked on the table: the turgid grooves of celery, the swelling curve of cantaloup, the quiet ooze of Brie. For a moment Michael didn't know whether to cook it or join it. He flung the Sancerre in the fridge, threw the watercress under a sluicing tap (his ma-in-law swore that if you didn't wash watercress seven times you'd get liver fluke), and he was releasing the olives from their plastic tomb when the front door slammed, fit to shake the foundations, as usual. Izzy was home. A couple of seconds and she was in the kitchen.

'Oh, Michael, it all looks smashing. Let me give you a hand – oh, but I absolutely must have a bath first. Don't do any more, Michael, just wait till I've had a bath, and I'll come down and help you. Have a rest. Have a drink.' And she ran off.

I absolutely must have a bath. Bless her! Curse Her! Both! He heard the bath water throbbing through the arteries of the house. The emotion heater, as his ma-in-law called it, had good cause to boil and bubble. Michael began to lay the foundations for a disgracefully rich pudding made with bananas, cream and brandy. The knives and forks flashed at the speed of light, and a delectable cloud of pud grew under his flying fingers. Nothing could cramp his style, tonight.

Upstairs, Izzy turned off the taps and was no doubt lowering herself with lascivious delay into the fragrant steam. Yes, Izzy! Lean back and let go! Anoint your dark gleaming head with the spiciest shampoos, massage your floating breasts and the white sweep of your thigh – at this point Michael simply had to run out into the garden. You know how it is. One absolutely must have a bit of parsley for the most delicious salad in the world. The trouble was, he couldn't remember where the hell Louise had sown it.

As he came out, so did the sun. The garden breathed at him and opened its arms. He floated into its embrace, whilst in the apple trees around his head a thousand tiny diamond points of rain water flashed amongst the opening buds of pink and white. By his right knee, the strong musky whiff of Crown Imperials, like the track of a fox. To his left, the soft cascades of broom. Beyond it all, the overpowering surge of leaves and grass.

His fingers trailed gently against bark and bud and fluttering leaf, and he wandered in a trance towards the parsley, smelling Eve with every earthy exhalation. It seemed there was the distant ringing of bells, as in a world beyond a dream. On towards the parsley. It was by the shed, of course – as far as possible from the kitchen. He remembered now. It was to keep him fit, she'd said. He smiled. The parsley smiled. There was again the distant ringing of bells, as if – bloody hell! It was the front doorbell!

He thundered back up the garden, but a low orchard isn't the easiest thing for a tall man to run through without the risk of a do-it-yourself lobotomy, so by the time he got to the house Izzy was already at the front door, dripping and wrapped only in a towel, and, not much of one at that. She opened the door, there was a sound as of wardrobes falling downstairs, and a brace of Wild Welshmen lurched in.

''Ulloa, bewtiful! Christ, mon! Doan't look, Hywel! 'E's loaded, see darlin', and the sight of a naked woman might make 'im goa off pop!'

They devoured Izzy with great slobbering kisses, and when she managed to extricate herself, she turned to Michael dripping, steaming, wet, gleaming, and – curse her – even beaming, and cried, 'Oh look who's come, Michael! Isn't that just perfect!'

'Michael! 'Ulloa, mon! 'Ow's the 'eroic alternative to bourgeois marriage shapin' up, like? Terrific apron you're wearin', mon – can we get Izzy to put it on later?'

Michael braced himself for the inevitable physical assault – this time it was a megaton thump on the shoulders, so violent that for a moment he feared, or perhaps hoped, that his heart had been dislodged.

'It's so fantastic to see you both, Gwyn,' grinned Izzy. 'And you couldn't have come at a better time – Michael's cooking the most delicious dinner and we couldn't possibly have eaten it all by ourselves, could we, Michael? Do have a drink and I'll be right down.'

'Doan't get dressed for us, now, darlin'. It would in my view be an entirely retrograde step. Tell her, Hywel, mon – doan't get dressed at all, darlin', ever again. I'll pay the central 'eatin' bills, won't I, Hywel?'

Hywel was propped against a wall. Whether his intoxication was due to alcohol or acute lust remained in doubt. But as Izzy flashed up the stairs Michael knew his duties as a host. He would take the boys into the kitchen and decapitate the bastards with his electric carving knife.

'Care for a drink?'

He tried to make the words *before you go* hang in to the air after the invitation, a kind of invisible echo, but the lads flung themselves on to the kitchen chairs with the air of men who have reached their journey's end. Michael knew he was beat. His heart sank right through the cork, composition floor, rubble topsoil and subsoil and went plummeting through the boiling earth towards Australia.

'Grea', mon, I'll say this for yew, Michael, you hand's never off the fuckin' corkscrew. Gis a bottle of Pils first, though – my throat's like the back end of a Juggernaut.'

They began pouring alcohol down their necks as if on the eve of Apocalypse. Which, with Michael in his present mood, was not entirely off the cards. While his real self was otherwise engaged in being rolled in earth's diurnal round with rocks and stones etc., a polite fictional fellow took over his body and listened with an amused and empty leer to Gwyn's monologue.

'I see you been to Safeway's, Michael. Grea' place, mon, isna? Christ though, I had a fuckin' turn in there the other day. I'd been writin' this paper on the early unionization of agricultural labour, see, an' it 'ad given me a thirst like a fuckin' camel. So I went off there, loaded up with six packs, and then went over to that delicatessen bit, right? Well, I was just celebratin' the triumphs of capitalism and middle class values, not without a few pangs o'guilt, o'course – I'm not an animal through and through, despite all this fuckin' fur on my

217

chest, an' I couldn't help reflectin' on the emptiness of our comrades' food cupboards in Poland – still, I'd just about conquered me qualms an' was reachin' for the Camembert, when – guess what?'

'Whaaaaaarf?' What Hywel supplied was half belch, half interrogative.

'I 'eard this female voice sayin' my name: *Gwyn,* she said. Well, I turned round and stared at her, and y'knoa – my mind went a fuckin' blank. I 'ad *noa idea* 'oo in the world she was. She wasn't bad lookin', an' she'd got this babe in arms – it put the bloody wind up me, mon, I can tell you. I thought it might be a singin' paternity suit or somethin'. Anyway, I still couldn't bloody place 'er – mindyew, I been so *definitely* drunk a few times, that recognition might well 'ave been out of the question. Anyway 'oo the 'ell d'ye think she was?'

'Ooooa?'

'Bonnie.'

'Bonnie?'

The polite fellow standing in for Michael felt himself at a loss. 'Bonnie? Who's she?'

'Oh, Christ, mon – I forgot – yew doan't knowa 'er – course – yew never met 'er – sorry – well, she was the wife o' one of the more 'omicidal of my colleagues, nice enough bloake, called Dave. They came to dinner once. Izzy might remember. Well, get this – apparently 'e'd gone and left 'er when she was actually *in labour.* Well! The sexual politics of it is unmistakable, see.'

'Huuuargh?'

'Not yew, Hywel! Anyway, 'e'd left 'er with one kid and another new baby, 'e'd run off with one of 'is stewdents, and taken the car, an' Bonnie can't drive anyway, and their central eatin' 'ad broken down and she was in a right ol' state about it all. It gave me a nasty turn, I can tell you. In fact I got stuck into a can o' Pils right there an' then, even thoa I 'adn't paid for it.'

'I trust you did the decent thing by her?'

'Tew bloody right I did the decent thing.'

'An' the indecent one an' all!' Hywel gave a great

foghorn whoop of laborious wit.

'Well, never min' that – does nobody any harm to couch up to another lonely human creature for fuck's sake, Hywel – wipe that smirk off yewer face – but the trouble is, see, Michael, I'm landed. Nothin' deadly like cohabitation, mind (no offence, mon, as you knoa my admiration for yewer *modus vivendi* knoas noa bounds) – but I 'ave to keep goin' round to see the poor kid, and mendin' all the bits of the 'ouse that are fallin' round 'er years.'

'Quite right. One must rally round.'

'Right. But what I doan't understand is, 'ow could he bear to leave 'er? Orright, soa she could be a fuckin' bore if left to drift on on automatic pilot, but 'e needn't 'ave listened, surely? And anyway, 'ow can anybody leave someone like that – at the very moament she's givin' birth to yewer fuckin' child, for Christ's sake? I mean, I couldn't leave anybody – I couldn't 'ave left Maria, even if she'd done twice the number of terrible things to me that I done to 'er – Oh, noa noa noa.'

Here he was ambushed by tears, and tried to beat them off.

'Get a grip on yourself, mon! Noa more fuckin' cryin', for Christ's sake. Doan't dilute the Pils, now!'

But it was no use. He threw his head back and howled. For a moment Michael was sorely tempted to join in. Hywel picked his teeth with a bus ticket and belched in a sorrowful, comradely sort of way. Then Izzy came in.

And of course, Izzy organized them. Within a few minutes Gwyn was washing the lettuce. ('If you're going to cry, Gwyn, you may as well be standing over the sink.') Hywel was given some carrots to chop up. ('Do you think you can manage that, Hywel?' – the mixture of satire and fondness was so deft.) And as for Michael, he had to wrestle with the crab. ('You're the only one of us with the education to tackle these buggers, Michael.') She did lots of other things; laid the foundations for a soufflé, set the table, and went out and picked primroses to decorate the salad.

219

Izzy had learned that Michael considered primroses in the salad absolutely essential. It worried him slightly sometimes that the only other guys he knew who would even begin to understand that were gay.

But then, what with Izzy's boyish transformation, as she flitted around the kitchen in her – wait for it – *playsuit* (not nearly as exciting as it sounds, actually – just a kind of boilersuit without the boils) one could hardly escape the fleeting impression of certain members of the Lower School about whom one had trembled, during those evenings in the nets all those years ago. Thinking back to cricket matches lit with heroic light, coaxing the crab out of its rosy carapace, watching Izzy flaming amazement at the cooker, and above all drinking fairly deep for so early in the evening, Michael was soon surprised by a total sense of recovery. So the boys had come. Excellent. So much the better. Dear fellows. How brightly the shared light of being in love shines in a crowded room! Their presence would only sharpen the secret appetites. And in the end they would slip away to their beds: Izzy to Michael's. Hywel and Gwyn could sleep in Jack's room. There were two beds in there.

Ah, the empty bed in Jack's room! How often had the poor chap pleaded with his father for a sibling! How oft had the longed-for conception slipped away with the tides of the moon.

'Dad,' Jack had said once when he was watching Michael shave (about the only male activity in which Michael surpassed him), 'Dad – a boy said something, today, at school.'

'What, sweetheart?'

'He told me about it and I thought I'd better tell you in case you'd forgot.'

'What?'

'About fertolization and things. How the Daddy plants a seed in the Mummy's tummy and then the baby grows.'

'But I thought we'd told you about that ages ago.'

'Oh, yes, but what this boy said, Dad, is, that Mums

can get too old to have the fertolization. So I thought I'd remind you, Dad.'

'I see.'

'In case you'd forgot. Mummy keeps telling me I might get a little brother or sister, but I keep waiting and waiting and every morning I look in your sock drawer and there isn't one there.'

'In my *sock drawer?*'

'Mum said I might find one there.'

'Did she indeed?' What medieval fairytales was she dishing out, now?

'Yes, Dad – anyway I do want to have a baby brother or a sister 'cos I could muck about much better then.'

'I see.'

'So I thought I'd remind you, Dad, in case you keep forgetting about the fertolizing thing and in case Mum gets too old. Don't forget, Dad, please.'

'All right.'

'And Dad – when you're going to do it, don't lock yourselves in the bathroom or anything like that, will you? That wouldn't be fair. I want to watch.'

Healthy, this boy. Undeniably. Sociable, venal, curious, loved travelling fast, insisted on a complete briefing every day. Michael could just see him in thirty years – the tight-lipped colonel coming to visit him in his Sunset Home. But wait! No! His darling daughter was supposed to take care of him in old age. And where was she? *What's keeping you?* Michael used to say sometimes to the black spaces in the sky. *Come in Miss Tristram your time has come.* But her time hadn't come. And they were beginning to fear it never would. The empty bed (one of a couple of bunks) haunted them. What presumption on their parts to buy it! Would it remain for ever the terrain over which Jack conducted his NATO manoeuvres? Or would a softer influence arrive, and the killing give way to the kissing games? What hope for them all if it did not?

The feast was prepared. The crab was dressed so immaculately that they seemed to be feeding off a

221

member of the ruling class. Well, that would suit Gwyn. The salad lay all before them, its colours tumbling as landscape. The walnut and cheese soufflé which Izzy and Michael had prepared, soared – a triumphant affirmation of their love. They were halfway through it when Gwyn roared confidentially, 'Well, darlin', tell us, 'cos we dirty ol' buggers is dyin' to knoa – 'ow's the *ménage à trois* comin' along, now? 'Ave you achieved trew common-welth of Eros? Plurality of Loves, like?'

'Oh!' Izzy gave a great sigh and threw her head back with the most intoxicating freedom. She looked at Michael, her eyes dancing. 'It's so incredibly marvellous, Gwyn – shall I tell them, Michael?'

'Of course.'

'Yeah, tell us, now! An' give us a few filthy details, girl, for Christ's sake – we boys is livin' blameless lives. The ordure of respectability is on our souls. Wash us clean, give us the goods babe.'

'Oh, it's not like that at all, Gwyn.'

Michael's heart gave an exultant kick at the lovely generosity of her face.

'It's not at all filthy. I mean – it's all over between Michael and me, for ever. We've got way beyond sexual infatuation.'

'Wha'?' The monosyllable was Hywel's. Michael could not have said half so much. His mouthful of walnut and cheese soufflé turned instantly to pickled lizards, leprous blisters and wet cardboard, and yet – and here is the true heroism which will go for ever unrecognized – *he went on chewing it*. What is more, he even swallowed it.

'It's so strange, isn't it, Michael?' Her eyes shone across at him. Strange? Strange? She had no idea of the meaning of the word. 'But ever since I moved in, all that sexual business has just slipped away.'

'Well, stroll on fuckin' down, like!'

'And something far, far more precious has come in its place. Hasn't it Michael?'

He made a strangled, retching noise which was interpreted as consent.

'You see, it was as if once I'd started to live with him, I actually saw Michael for the first time. I began to get to know him, little by little. We would sit for hours and talk together. Sometimes I'd draw him. And he'd tell me all sorts of things about his past – didn't you? Like the cricket matches at school, and how he'd first got drunk at The Green Dragon at Andoversford, and had to lie down in a ploughed field on the way home, and saw the Plough up overhead.'

'The wha'? Was 'e run over, like?'

'No – I mean, the *stars*, Hywel. And I told Michael all about my past, too: my holidays, my boyfriends, my mum and her cats, my dad dying. And I can't explain it but all the time I was getting to know Michael like this – it was, well, more exciting by far than falling in love ever was. And yet it was precisely because we knew that sex was out of the question, and we'd left it far behind, wasn't it, Michael?'

Michael nodded. Not too boisterously. He didn't want his head to roll off and plummet into the salad. He seemed to be composed of spent ash, smoked right through like a cigarette. Oh, for a friendly ashtray in which to spill his few remaining atoms. Or would he perhaps spontaneously combust, leaving only a few shreds of scorched corduroy on the floor? Unfortunately not. He had to sit through the rest.

'And, oh, you can't imagine how exciting—'

'Hoald on a second, darlin'! Let me get this right, now.' Gwyn was evidently struggling to comprehend her. Michael knew the feeling. 'D'ye mean that you an' Michael, now – you – you doan't make love any more, like?'

'Oh no!' she twinkled remotely, like some chaste star. 'But there's so much more to it than that, Gwyn. Ever since I've moved in with Michael and Louise I've felt myself changing in all kinds of subtle ways. Like tidiness, for instance. Somehow, Louise's house was so lovely that I actually started taking pride in being tidy myself. Folding my clothes up became a – well, a kind of

223

graceful ritual—'

"Ang on a minute, babe, only I reelly – I'm reelly 'avin' trouble gettin' to grips wi' the propositional substructure of yewer argument, like. Did yew say that you an' Michael doan't – well – meddle with each other any more, is it?'

'That's right, Gwyn – but I must tell you about the eating. I simply stopped gorging myself as soon as I moved in here. All that greedy stuffing must have been a substitute for something, I must have been really unhappy, because it stopped as soon as I got here. And I lost weight – *and* my skin cleared up. And then there was the drawing—'

'Stop! Lissen! I'm havin' extreame difficulty with this major concept, Isabelle, now. Are you tellin' me that yew and Michael *doan't 'ave a sexual relationship any more*?'

'No.'

'Well – well – knock me down with a fuckin' feather, girl! That's the moast erotic thing I ever heard in my life.'

By this time, of course, they were all extremely drunk. But not yet catastrophically so. The evening still held some promise.

'Well, well, well – I 'ave to 'and it tew yew. It really is the moast erotic thing – unimaginably erotic, like.'

'But 'ow can it be erotic, mòn, if they doan't, like, *dew* anything?'

The mystery had driven Hywel to a whole sentence, and it seemed to Michael the first sensible thing anyone had said for hours. Gwyn gave him a contemptuous look.

'Noa, noa, Hywel, you got it all wrong, mon. Yewer sexual attitudes is still locked in yewer primitive social structurin', see?'

'Bu' – I doan't see 'ow it can be erotic if there's nothing' goin' on, at all, mon.'

He shot Michael a pitying, mystified glance which nearly broke his heart.

'Well, tha's just *it*, see? The fact that nothin's goin' on, except talkin' and drawin' an' all those delicious middle class indulgences – that's precisely what makes it soa fuckin' erotic, right?'

Hywel turned to Michael with an appealing frown.

'I nearly went to Art School once, y'knoa, Michael. D'yew think I'd understand all this better if I'd 'ad some more education, like?'

'My dear fellow—' Michael did wish he didn't sound so patronizing but it leapt out of his mouth before he could stop it— 'you mustn't feel inadequate. Your attitudes, if I may say so, are entirely natural and totally admirable.'

''Sright, Hywel, you're all right, mon. Doan't take it to heart, now. These esoteric mysteries is not everybody's cup o'tea, see? 'Ave another drink.'

So they drank on. And on. The moon rose and passed over the roof. Hywel engaged Izzy in something that would have passed for conversation on a dark night. Which it was. Never darker. She appeared to be explaining to him the idea of Mind over Matter, but he couldn't get the hang of which was which. At the other end of the table Gwyn entered a fantasy about a Utopian Republic where free love, free beer and free lancing was the norm. Michael hardly listened. His delicious pud sank into a brown and disappointed skin at the bottom of his dish. He couldn't face it. It was, after all, Just Dessert. Untouched. Untouched for ever. His blood had become black rivers, and a great abyss of mist and poisons hung where his guts used to be.

'Y'knoa, though, Michael, tell yew what, mon—' Michael hauled his senses reluctantly towards the garrulous Celt. 'There's a sense in which yewer abandonment of the sexual role does reflect a genuine weariness, like, which has crept into social intercourse since the soa-called sexual revolution – which in my view was never more than the toy of the intelligentsia an' fuckin' bourgeoisie, anyhow.'

'What? What are you on about, Gwyn? You're too bloody clever by three-quarters. Explain it in nice little monosyllables for me, there's a good chap.'

'Well, sexual freedom has dissipated the revolutionary energies of young people, see? So a in some ways it can be seen as a cynical concession by an extremely fuckin' cunnin' Establishment, like. An' your withdrawin' from this tedious charade makes yew a genuine revolutionary again, see?'

'What do you mean, again? I was never one in the first place.'

'Even better, mon! A convert in the ripeness of yewer mature judgement. Ignore the crude demands of the sexual revolution and build yourself a Platonic world of conversation an' the arts, right? Magic!'

'Well, as for the sexual revolution – I must admit there have been times when it's palled. I mean – I sometimes long for the days when a glimpse of someone's ankle could keep you going for years.'

''Sright, mon! An' I've lived through so many bloody awful cynical evenin's, in the knowledge that at the end of it I'd got to take some little darlin' back to her place afterwards.'

'Yes, the dreary sense of obligation—'

''Sright, mon! No use sayin' yew've got a headache if you want to sustain yewer bloody reputation, Noa—'

'The terrible moment when you catch someone's eye and then – POW! You know you're committed at least to a full-blooded flirtation—'

'When all yew reelly want to do is go out wi' the boys and sing hymns in the coach on the way back from Internationals.'

· 'The awful expense of it, too – the intimate little lunches in those horrible restaurants—'

'An' the brainwork, mon. Tryin' to work out what to say an' what not to say—'

'That's right! The deceptions – oh, my God, the deceptions.'

'Doan't start on that, now, Michael, for Christ's sake, or yew'll set me off—'

And he burst into tears again.

'Yes! Now I come to think of it, Gwyn, I really yearn

for those good old medieval days when you worshipped someone else's wife from afar and wrote her poems while he was away on crusades—'

'Or even better, mon, you went off on the fuckin' crusades yourself.'

'Oh yes! Cutting the Saracen hordes to pieces, collecting a few old relics, dying of cholera in Jerusalem—'

'Noa doubt about it, Michael, you're absolutely right; noa doubt about it at all: thoase were the days!'

The evening lurched, stalled and went cold at about 3 a.m. Michael then had to witness a sight which put his already heroic endurance to a new test.

'C'mon, now, Isabelle, babe.' Gwyn seized her hand across the table and began to gnaw at her finger ends. Michael got up and escaped into the washing-up. 'Since yew an' Michael are just good friends these days – take me off to bed, there's a good girl. I'm wasted – wasted and blasted. I need female succour. 'Ave pity on me, darlin', now.'

'Get off, Gwyn! You can sleep in Jack's room.'

'Wha'? Yewer not goin' to shack up wi' Hywel, surely, babe? It's coals to Newcastle in 'is case. Only last night 'e was shamefully ensconsed with twin eighteen-year-old sisters from 'Ounslow, as God's my witness.'

'Noa! 'Snot trew. Don't believe 'im, darlin'. We're goin' to couch up, like – you an' me – aren't we, now? Just like oald times!'

A dinner plate somehow came to pieces in Michael's hands.

'Sorry, but I'm not interested, boys. Let's help Michael to wash up. Come on! Let me go!'

'Oh noa noa noa! Tell you what, babe. Do us a favour an' let's all crash out together, like. You knoa – like we was goin' to do on St Valentine's Day before you 'ad an attack of premenstrual tension and threw our fuckin' cloathes out of the windoa.'

Deep in the washing-up water a vile strand of discarded pud wound its way round Michael's finger.

'Come on, now, darlin'. Just you an' me an' Hywel, now. Nothin' fancy. No funny business. Just want to couch up wi' yew, like.'

'Let go, Gwyn! And shut up about all that. I'm not interested, and that's final.'

'Wha' – wha' – you ent gone dykey, 'ave yew, babe? Only I noticed yew've started lookin' a bit boyish recently. You're not deep in some unspeakable scene with the luscious Louise, I 'ope – or rather, wait a minute, now – now that *would* be the moast erotic thing I ever heard in my life.'

Eventually the Welsh were helped upstairs and into the bunk beds, where they lay roaring feebly at each other for a few minutes. They had to fold Hywel up to get him into his.

'I'm thinkin' of havin' my legs off,' he apologized into the pillow, 'an' replaced with wheels, like.'

Then Izzy placed a dry little kiss on Michael's cheek and flitted away into the dark. He stumbled off to his familiar but strangely empty bed, feeling like a dinosaur sensing its last hours on the planet. Lying down made him feel even drunker. He was sure the bed reared up a couple of times in the night and tipped him out on to the floor. Was it registering a symbolic protest? Maybe he would report it to the Society for Psychical Research. As for the morrow – no, let us take no thought for the morrow. Nor indeed several morrows after that.

18

It wasn't for ages that the thought struck Michael that
things might have been even worse. He was in a
crowded tube train at the time. Supposing he'd made it
clear to Izzy that – and suppose she'd handed out an
unequivocal – Crumbs! The thought struck him in mid-
leg. His knees buckled and he sat down emphatically on
the lap of a rather fat, jolly woman who seemed not at all
put out. Michael apologized fulsomely about the tendency
of the District Line to lurch, but he had to admit he was
tempted to curl up on the matriarch's ample knee, shove
the old thumb in the mouth, and stay there for ever.

Sexual rejection was not something he'd experienced,
you see. Sheer luck, of course, no reflection on his
meagre seductional powers at all. There had been the
odd entanglement in which some unfortunate girl had as
it were given him his marching orders, but then when
things were getting impossible he liked to give the girls
the chance to perform the old heave-ho themselves. This
was usually achieved by his behaving so badly that the
aforementioned damsel's patience would crack and she
would hurl him out on his ear. Then she would go away
with her self respect and pride intact, and he had the
consolation of knowing that he had done the right thing
by her at the last, as it were. Even if up till then he'd led
her a right old dance and made her life merry hell.

But sexual rejection was quite another ball game. The
thought that Izzy could cheerfully contemplate a future
without any resort to his manly arms was such an
outrage that at fleeting moments Michael was tempted
to seize her and administer a sound spanking. He could

only assume that she'd come under the influence of some feminist mumbo-jumbo and that her finer (and indeed coarser) feelings were at that moment strangled by some kind of half-baked principle. Thank God she had remained unaware of his boiling breast. A tribute in a way to the elegance and poise of his demeanour.

Yes. He must have behaved impeccably for her to have missed his drift. He thanked all the Gods fervently for her blindness and found some consolation in treating her with a lofty, disinterested friendliness. Further consolations rapidly crowded in. Izzy's recent boyishness began to strike him as a rather unfortunate departure from Nature's plan. Yes, the more he thought of it, the more Michael became convinced that Izzy was meant to be a plump little trollop, teetering about on high heels, not a slender Ganymede palely loitering around the house in Hamletian black. She began to look a little like a transvestite: something gone wrong.

It was just as well she'd been duped by this feminist ideology which required her to beat her swords into ploughshares and her lover into Platonic pulp. Just as well. Because the fact was – he'd probably have gone off her anyway. Short hair and baggy trousers, indeed. It would have been more appropriate to buy her a catapult than cast a sheep's eye in her direction. And anyway – the fact was, whenever Izzy and Louise appeared together in Michael's appraising gaze, he could not escape the fact that Louise was in quite a different class. She was the queen bee. Not only captivatingly lovely, with clouds of glowing hair and a skin as fine and pale as parchment – and such Pre-Raphaelite prerequisites were to Michael the true form of feminine beauty – but she was also an undoubted creative genius.

The house was so beautiful and so comfortable that even had Louise been a crew-cut hoyden and Catherine Deneuve had beckoned Michael to a love nest in the South of France, he would have found it well-nigh impossible to tear himself away from the faded rose cotton of the curtains, the sand-coloured sofa, the cork floors, the deep jars of flowers placed in just the right pools of light. And the garden was coming into its own, now, too. It was really just an orchard, planned and planted by Louise, who had also sown the seeds of myriad wild flowers amongst its grasses. Bees, butterflies and tiny frogs flocked to it. To step into it was to forget the cruel city and to feel the pulse of Nature.

All this Louise had achieved. Not to mention her lovely paintings on the walls – paintings that scintillated with delight in rather the way that the Impressionists did. And as Michael inspected the tiny details of his life, Louise's hand was everywhere. A small jar of violets sweetened the air around his head as he slept. A mugful of fresh buttercups brightened up the bathroom. His shirts were neatly folded, bathed in the smell of lavender. His mornings opened with a kiss on the eyelids. His nights closed with a golden sigh in his ear.

And after all, wasn't this the way it was all meant to be? Man and his mate side by side at the centre of their universe. One of each kind. The harem is no kind of model, with its hints of slavery and abuse, and the possibility that all the wretched women are going to gang up on you and poke fun behind your back. No: one partner, one beloved face, one heart laid against your heart, and in this tableau freedom, independence and equality have their place. Mind you, there might be the odd little bit on the side now and then, but it should stay out there on the side, pass briefly like a comet in the outer sky and plunge into the darkness beneath the horizon. Not appear day after day at the marital breakfast table, thank you very much.

So how fortunate that Izzy had turned into this boy who didn't care for him! As usual he had floundered along in the dark and nearly come a frightful cropper. What possible future could they have as a threesome? None. Except some horrible voyeuristic feature in a Sunday paper. *Il Seraglio* in Muswell Hill. How much healthier for Izzy to become their surrogate daughter and by and by find herself some suitable bloke, and go off and settle down with him. Then she could swap strawberry plants with Louise, and have kids of her own, and smile dully and complacently at Michael across countless crowded rooms in the future, it all having been done and forgotten. Yes, this mating one-to-one did seem to have the sanction of Higher Nature. Forget the bulls and cows. Didn't swans mate for life, and didn't a swan pine and die when he lost his mate? Besides, he wasn't getting any younger and as the old arteries fur up there's a limit to what you can take on.

And so Michael grew not just content with his lot, but downright pleased with it. Once he started to count his blessings he more or less lost count. Sometimes he thought the only thing the human race had got going for it was its ability to change its mind.

Michael wasn't the only man to congratulate himself on escaping Izzy's attractions, either. Dick, driving south down Green Lanes, was celebrating something very similar. No more did Izzy's image buzz away at the back of his mind like a fly in a window pane, nor did a frog leap in his throat when she appeared, or tigers hurl themselves about in his chest. Dick felt much less like a wildlife park. He supposed this was falling out of love. He liked it. Why hadn't the poets praised this feeling: this clarity, this relief, this freedom? He was his own man again, and it didn't matter how much clay accumulated under his fingernails.

He lumbered fairly casually into the staff room nowadays, not searching round anxiously for Izzy's dark head. He stopped and lamented the fortunes of Manchester United with the PE bloke by the coffee machine; he submitted to Mary Greenfield's fussing over his torn sleeve; he read a publisher's catalogue which was lying about. He drank his coffee and smiled to himself. His heart was at rest.

'Dick!'

Izzy bounced down beside him. Dick gave her a complacent, offhand smile. Never again would he anxiously ply her with drinks, offer her his humble ceramics, or stumble his way towards suggesting dinner. She looked up at him with a cocked, curious expression – like a little bird.

'How's tricks, Dick?'

'Pretty good.'

'Lovely weather today – summer at last.'

'M'yeah.'

'We'd better make the most of it. It'll be winter again soon.'

'Not for me.'

'What? What do you mean, Dick?'

'I heard this morning. I've been offered – I've been accepted for that exchange scheme. So I'll be going to San Francisco in July.'

'You *what?* Dick! *Really?*'

Dick smiled privately and picked bits of dried clay off his knees.

''Sright.'

'Dick! How marvellous! How *marvellous!*'

Izzy stared at him with the rapture she used to reserve for chocolate cake. Dick was aware that he had suddenly, somehow, become delicious. He looked modestly away towards the noticeboard and idly gnawed a fingernail. Yes – he even tasted quite nice.

'But aren't you absolutely *thrilled,* Dick? I would be.'

'M – yes. It'll be nice to get away – away from England.'

'I should say so! All that sunshine! And San Francisco sounds a marvellous place. Alistair Cooke is always raving about it.' The bell rang for registration. Dick got up to go.

'Ah well,' he murmured, tossed her a brief smile, and lumbered off.

By break Dick felt about eight feet tall. It was a wonder he could get through the staff room door without stooping. He'd had a wonderful double lesson with his O level students, who, on hearing about San Francisco, had practically bowed down and worshipped him. The former, Tottenham, Dick used to feel that not merely had he feet of clay, but that the muddy substances extended upwards as far as the most remote of his split ends. The new San Francisco Superdick was 100% sprung steel. He bounded into the staff room and was instantly importuned by Izzy.

'Dick!'

'What?'

'I've got you some coffee – come and sit over here.'

'OK.'

'I want to talk to you.'

Yes, Dick thought, she wants – *wants*, mind you – to talk to me.

'Yeah?'

'Listen, Dick – I've had an idea – and I had a free lesson just now so I made some phone calls. I'm coming too.'

'You what? Where?'

'To San Francisco. With you. I'm coming with you to San Francisco.'

Dick's frog, which used to leap in his throat and had recently entered deep hibernation, was suddenly catapulted into life and flashed from his tongue to his groin and back.

'To San Francisco?'

'Yes. I rang them up. It's not too late and they're short of a drama teacher. So it's all set up. We can share a flat.'

Dick palpitated from the navel to the chops.

'Nothing wicked, of course – just good flatmates sort of thing.'

'Of c- course.'

Colonies of ants raged in his pants.

'But on the other hand – we straights must stick together, mustn't we, Dick? I'll protect you from the bad fairies, I promise.'

She did a kind of cuddling-up little dive, which set off the snakepits in his armpits and legpits. Bugger it, thought Dick, she's turned me into a bestiary again.

'But Izzy – I thought you were living with your – I mean with – with those people in Muswell Hill.'

'Oh yes. It's lovely there. But, well, in a way it's time I was thinking about moving on. You see, I've got to know them, and that's really why I – and anyway, it's not a set-up that could go on for ever. You do understand, don't you, Dick?'

Every fibre of Dick's particularly high-fibre being was boggling in an attempt to understand. He'd been fed a garbled and highly lurid account of Izzy's ménage by Hywel, and tried not to think about it. It made him feel faint.

'Yeah, um – sure.'

'All good things have to come to an end, don't they? And anyway, it was only a spur-of-the-moment sort of thing in the first place.'

Dick thought that Izzy seemed rather addicted to spur-of-the-moment sorts of thing. In fact, now he looked back on it, it appeared as if his own little escapade with her might have been a spur-of-the-moment sort of thing, sort of thing. Still, if she was so unpredictable, there was always the faint chance that – and besides, she'd wanted – *wanted*, mark you – to go to San Francisco with him, knowing full well the balmy, druggy, everso naughty reputation of the place. Well! Whatever next?

19

One faintly comatose afternoon the Muswell Hill ménage were sitting round the kitchen table polishing off some shortbread that Izzy's mum had sent from Yorkshire, when Louise had one of her strokes of genius.

'We must have a garden party this year.'

Michael groaned. Not that there was anything to groan about, but someone's got to provide the vinegar or the salad dressing will simply be too oily for words.

'It'll be lovely, Michael. Just you wait and see. Anyway, you really let you hair down last year, I seem to remember. But do you realize that Midsummer Day falls on a Saturday this year? So we could have a Midsummer Night's Dream.'

'More likely to turn into a Midsummer Night Mare.'

'Don't be silly. All we have to do is invite lots of people and get masses of food and drink into them and turn them loose in the garden. And it's always easier outdoors. If anyone gets unpleasant we can push them behind the shed.'

'No we can't, Mum! That's where my den is.'

'Oh, all right, darling. Not behind the shed. Into the nettles, maybe.'

'I think it's a lovely idea,' beamed Izzy. 'And what's more, it can be my farewell party.'

Louise's jaw dropped, and Michael's would have, too, if he hadn't been propping it up with his hand. Or perhaps not. He was finding it hard to be surprised by anything these days, as if he had already used up his supply of astonishment for the next few months. Years, even.

'What do you mean, Izzy – your farewell party?'

'Well, I'm – I'm going to San Francisco for next year, on a teacher exchange scheme. So I'll be leaving at the end of July.'

'Oh, Izzy, what a shame!'

Louise had gone quite white. Even whiter than usual. She looked aghast. She appealed, fleetingly, to Michael.

'Oh, Michael, isn't it terrible? How can you do this to us, Izzy? When it was all so marvellous having you here.'

'Well, you've both been – extraordinary and kind and made it – the best time I've ever had and – and really, changed my life, even,' said Izzy, blushing, to the shortbread. 'I mean, I even look different now. You've transformed me. I can't imagine ever having such an – an important experience again.'

That's enough, love, thought Michael; don't go on, you'll have Louise howling. But it was too late. A pearly tear was already on its way down his wife's noble nose. She took Izzy's hand.

'Dear Izzy, don't you understand, it's you that's taught me things and transformed my life.'

Now Izzy's lips too began to shake. Jack got down hastily from the table.

'Please can I get down and go and play with my interstellar nuclear war fleet, Dad?' he muttered, and ran off towards the nearest other galaxy. Michael resisted the temptation, overwhelming though it was, to follow. We must give him credit for this, if nothing else. He sat these bloody things out.

And he was turning this new development over in his mind and more or less accepting it. He noticed he was not horrified at the thought of Izzy's departure, so he couldn't be in love with her any more. Nor was he exultant at the news – so he must have got over that awful post-mortem bitterness which had eaten into his soul for a while and caused him to prune the astonished forsythia to within a millimetre of its vital pith and decapitate the dead tulips with a savage and swingeing hand. In short, he was calm. An unusual state for

Michael, accustomed as he was to oscillating wildly between exhilaration, despair, terror and shame (especially the last two).

So; Izzy was going to San Francisco. Quite apt, really. Nobody knew what sex they were over there, or cared, either. And apparently there were lots of Orientals scattered about so she could doubtless continue her martial arts programme. And as for the way it left the Muswell Hill ménage – well, it left it fine and dandy, thank you. It was one thing to accept Izzy as their surrogate daughter, but quite another to be actually mistaken for her parent, as Michael had been recently. Louise had not received this particular accolade, so her sorrow at the departing Izzy was unsullied. In fact, Michael had come to think that there was nothing sullied about Louise at all.

'Don't worry, Louise, it's all for the best.' Izzy was busy soothing that unsullied heart. 'It's a good thing for me to go while we're still all happy and before we've started to get on each other's nerves.'

Speak for yourself on that one, dear, thought Michael. His own nerves were, as a result of their little social experiment, more or less totally reduced to tapioca.

'Besides, you and Michael can come out and visit me. Christmas in San Francisco! Or Easter! Or we could go to Mexico. It'll be fantastic!'

Michael started doing the washing-up, his usual resort at times of great emotional tension. After the four cups and plates were done, though, he ran out of filthy crockery, and had to start washing up the clean stuff.

Still, pretty soon the snivelling stopped, and Louise managed to reconcile herself to getting her house back to herself, her kitchen to herself, and her husband, more grovellingly, worshippingly her own than ever before. A grisly destiny, God knows. No wonder Louise looked pale.

That night in bed the Tristrams were both wakeful. Michael was often wakeful, and on this particuar night he was counting his lucky stars jumping over a gate in an attempt to get to sleep. Louise tossed and turned a bit, lay gazing at the ceiling, then suddenly stared at Michael and finally gave an ominous sigh.

'Michael, darling.'

She wound her arms around him and nuzzled up to his collar bone. What was coming? These were the danger signals. His tired and much-abused old heart managed somehow to kick into top gear.

'What, love?'

'I hope you're not – I hope you're not too terribly upset by Izzy going off.'

'Good God, no.'

'Don't feel you have to put on a brave front with me, darling. I understand. You can tell me if you feel sad and low. I shan't mind – honestly! And if you'd like to go over and see Izzy on your own at Christmas, please do. It'll be quite all right.'

He should really at this point have got out of bed and abased himself before her on the rug, but to tell you the truth he was far too exhausted.

'No, no, Louise – it's quite all right. I'm quite all right. Honestly.'

'But really, darling, don't go all brave and stoical. It'll be much better to let yourself be upset – much better in the long run. Don't feel you have to pretend to me that you're feeling fine.'

'But I am feeling fine.'

'Oh, come on, Michael, my poor love. I know you must be feeling terrible.'

'But I'm not feeling bloody terrible, Louise, I'm feeling bleeding fine!'

Michael sat up in bed. So did Louise. She was mystified. Michael didn't want to go through all this. But what else could be done?

'Louise?'

'Yes.'

'There's something I ought to tell you.'

Her eyes widened, whitened in panic. She pulled the sheets up around her.

'What?'

'About me and Izzy.'

She looks terrified, poor love, thought Michael. He couldn't for the life of him work out what she was so scared about. That he was going to leg it over to California with the once-delectable little Assistant Mistress? Surely not. Anyway, time to put Louise's magnificent, generous, unsullied heart to rest.

'My dear,' he took her hand. 'I have to tell you. There's nothing going on between me and Izzy.'

'What?' She pulled her hand angrily away and knelt up on the bedclothes. 'Nothing? You mean you—'

'We aren't lovers any more, Louise. Izzy and I are just good friends.'

Louise's eyes blazed with anger, and she actually shook.

'How long has this been going on?'

'Not going on, you mean.'

'Don't try and escape with a bloody joke! Tell me! How long has this been going on?'

'Hush! You'll wake everybody. It's – it's ever since Izzy moved in. We've been Just Good Friends all the time she's been living here.'

'Well!' Louise hurled herself off the bed, stormed into her Chinese dressing gown and stomped up and down the room. 'This is a fine state of affairs! You might have told me! You might have bloody told me! It makes everything different. I've been completely deceived, all this time.'

Michael followed her out of bed and cornered her by the wardrobe.

'Come, come, love, calm down. How does it make everything different? Everything's just the same. I'm madly in love with you. More madly than ever. Izzy worships you. Izzy and I aren't in love. What more can you want? You've got me absolutely to yourself.'

'Ugh!' Louise threw him off with a massive whelm of strength. Those Oriental exercises were certainly having a frightening effect. 'Listen to yourself, Michael! You sound so disgustingly – so disgustingly OLD-FASHIONED! And PATRONIZING! Have you no idea what I've been going through?'

She plumped down on the bed. Michael followed, panicking. His imagination was a roaring blank. What *had* she been going through?

'What – what have you been going through, my love?' He thought she'd been going through an unequivocal triumph. That's what it had felt like to him, anyway.

'I suppose you thought it was easy for me to invite Izzy to live here.'

Crumbs. He'd been so pole-axed at the time, he'd never given it a thought at all.

'Well, I'll tell you, Michael. It wasn't a bloody picnic, you know. I was totally bowled over when she announced who she was. Then she just broke down and cried like a kid. I had no idea what to do. And if you really want to know, my motives in asking her to stay weren't altogether pure.'

'But, my dear Louise, I never suspected them of being pure at all.'

'You pig! Carl thinks my motives are pure. He thinks I've been behaving like an angel, if you want to know.'

Michael knew Carl as a thundering great pansy who taught at the same Art School as Louise. She told him, for some reason, her deepest and darkest secrets.

'I'm sure you have been an angel, love – tell me about it.'

'Take your hands off me! And don't be so bloody *patronizing*! I asked Izzy in because, if you want to know, I could see she wasn't – well, to be honest, she didn't pose too much of a threat. I mean, if she'd been devastatingly beautiful and Garboed in here and treated me with elegant disdain, it would have been different. But she was rather a nice, plump, spotty, mixed-up kid and I could see at a glance that you'd been messing her up something rotten.'

He'd been messing Izzy up something rotten? *Messing up Izzy?* A horrible chill of plausibility ran down his spine.

'Anyway, so my motives weren't exactly unmixed. I thought, in my cunning old devious way, *I can handle this kid – and knock this business on the head right now*. And so I asked her to stay. Oh, I liked her – very much, of course. There was that. Then when you sulked for weeks—'

'Days.'

'Weeks – I was terrified. Carl knows how terrified I was.'

'Never mind about bleeding Carl.'

'Well, since you were so totally uncooperative and frighteningly cold, all I could do was get to know Izzy. And of course my first impression was confirmed. She's a lovely, adorable woman. Absolutely adorable.'

'Your generosity, my dear—'

'Shut up. Anyway from the time it started being OK with us—' He seized her hand. She bit his finger. He let go.

'I just assumed it was OK between you and Izzy too. And I got such a buzz out of knowing that this woman whom I really loved was my husband's – well – was in love with you too. Don't you see? It was so hard fighting the jealousy – and dammit, I won, and won by getting to know Izzy and loving her, and I really felt I'd conquered this bloody jealousy which has made my life hell all these years. I really felt I'd won, and now you tell me there was nothing going on all the time. I put so much effort and emotion into it and all for nothing! Well, Michael, I just think it was a rotten dirty trick.'

It was time to fall on his knees before her again. Funny, it didn't seem two minutes since the last time.

'My dear Louise—' He buried his face in the Chinese dressing gown of her lap. 'My dear, dear Louise. Forgive me. I plead guilty. I was not having an affair with your best friend. Forgive me. And listen to me for just a second. The reason, or part of the reason, why the affair with Izzy just withered away when she came to live here, was that I simply couldn't help comparing the two of you all the time. And Izzy just couldn't compete. Dear Louise, you are the most splendid woman in the world.

You are truly magnificent, unparalleled and unsullied. Believe me.' He kissed her hands.

'I'm not so sure about the unsullied.'

'What?'

'I'm not so sure about the unsullied. I'm not so good or blameless as you think, Michael.'

The universe, which had been whirling, came to a sudden deadly stop. Louise's eyes, looking down into Michael's, had an evil little glint in them which he had never seen before. He leapt, unthinking, to his feet, accompanied by a deafening report from his right knee.

'Don't tell me! Don't tell me! Don't tell me! Christ, my bleeding knee! Shit! Ouch! Don't tell me!' He hopped around the bed in circles of agony so complete he could not imagine worse.

'Sit down.'

Here it came. The worse. Michael collapsed obediently on to the pillows and lay shuddering, his wounded knee clasped to what remained of his heart, and waited.

'Put the bullet in,' he whimpered, 'right behind the ear.'

'It's nothing, Michael, don't be so childish. Only I can't have you getting this Madonna/Whore complex thing. I can't have you worshipping me and putting me on a pedestal.'

'Why not? Why not? You deserve it.'

'I don't. Let me tell you. I know you've always called Carl a thundering great pansy, but he isn't. And two years ago I had a brief affair with him.'

Michael ate the pillow. There was nothing else to say or do.

'It was about the time you were having a little fling with what's her name – Maggie.'

He found a handkerchief under the pillow, and ate that, too.

'It wasn't just to pay you back, either. I was strongly attracted to Carl and he was always so kind and understanding.'

Michael devoured the duvet.

'Mind you, it turned out to be a hopeless mess. An absolute disaster. And I couldn't bear deceiving you. So I thought I wouldn't bother, another time.'

She turned to Michael and looked at him long and hard. He gave her a little peep, short and soft. Then he had another of his spontaneous whims, rolled away from her across the bed, and fell heavily on the floor. He lay quite still and didn't breathe. If he couldn't manage to bloody die at least he'd give a good performance.

'Michael, Michael?' She rattled his shoulder. 'Are you all right? Stop messing about, Michael. It was only a joke.'

Only a joke? What was only a joke? Michael cocked an ear despite himself. If playing possum was going to conjure up such unexpected information he would play it a little longer.

'Michael? Michael?'

No response. Then she suddenly jumped off the bed and darted across to the other side of the room. Michael heard a clink, and suddenly remembered the monstrous great Victorian jug and basin that was always kept on the chest of drawers: the jug always full of water. He leapt up. Crack! The other kneecap exploded.

'No! No! Not the water! Ouch, my damned knee! Please, Louise, not the water! Please! I'll lead a blameless life from now on! I'll never have affairs if you don't want me to! And I'll never have affairs if you want me to! I won't do anything! Anything at all! I'll have myself stuffed and mounted!'

'Very appropriate, too, if I may say so, Michael. A fitting end to your career.'

'Don't throw the water, please, Louise! Please! Please! You'll give me pneumonia!'

'I should have thought of throwing cold water over you long ago. And anyway – I'm not going to throw it out of spite – but just because it will make such a *lovely mess.*'

Her eyes glinted in a new, horrid and rather exciting way. Michael braced himself. An act of extraordinary heroism considering what he'd been through. The water flew through the intervening air and exploded all over him. Actually, it was tepid and quite pleasant. In fact, it had a remarkably exhilarating effect. Louise was helpless with sadistic laughter and Michael's dander, which had for so long been away on sabbatical, was now suddenly back in action and well and truly up. He leapt across at his tormentor and they fell to the floor locked in frenzied combat. She bumped her head on the wardrobe, but didn't seem to care. They were into a new era.

When they had done, they were literally steaming.

'All right, hellcat,' he snarled into her face. 'Never mention that execrable Carl's name again.'

Her face assumed a feline rictus. 'All right, big shot,' she seethed, 'and you never mention Caroline, or Sue, or Maggie, or Theresa, or—'

'Done!' cried Michael and bit her on the cheek to seal the bargain. 'Let's go back to bed now, vile fiend. The old body is seizing up and in danger of dissolution.'

'We can't go to bed yet, Michael! We're sopping wet! We'll have to have a bath first.'

He groaned and shuddered at the interminable vista of experience ahead.

'My God, my God – will this night never end?'

She paused at the door and aimed an affectionate kick at his ribs. (He was, I may add, still prone.)

'I hope not!'

20

All too soon came Midsummer Day. It always seems too
unfair to be told that we're halfway through it when it
obviously hasn't even arrived. Despite the arctic winds,
the plants still go doggedly through their numbers, poor
blighters, but we higher bipeds cling sensibly to our
woolly underwear and crouch by the radiators. *Cast not a
clout till school be out* was Michael's merry quip as yet again
he set the central heating a-thundering in mid-June. But
the day Louise had chosen for her party was different. It
wasn't exactly sunny, but it did have a certain warm,
white, clouded feel to it. Being outdoors wasn't going to
feel like a terrible penance, nor were their friends going
to cop a fatal chill in their droves.

The night before, Michael had promised to get up
early and help in the preparations, much to Louise's
scorn. He did have a habit of lying in on Saturday
mornings, turning into a kind of Egyptian mummy,
wrapped in layers of dreams. Indeed, some of his most
awful dreams had taken place on Saturday mornings.
Such as that one about the octopus—

Well, on the appointed day Michael leapt out of bed at
the crack of noon to find the women had already solved
most of the catering problems. Izzy had enlisted the help
of a green-haired youth who appeared to be called
Razors. He was dressed in a tuxedo three sizes too large
for him and he looked terrifyingly sinister. Michael ran
indoors and hid all the candlesticks, ancestral spoons and
bits of high technology. Then he ran outside bearing bits
of furniture and scattered it about among the trees.
There seemed to be an astonishing number of tables and

chairs in their possession. They all looked tipsy and slightly embarrassed to be out of doors, especially the nice Edwardian brocade number. Unfortunately the stain caused by the gerbil being sick was all too evident in broad daylight.

They frittered away the afternoon by getting in a flap and taking aspirins. Michael noticed that Jack and Razors had gone off to the shed, and he had a horrid qualm about glue sniffing, but Izzy told him not to be so stupid and he obeyed. He would always obey from now on. On the surface, anyway. The trouble was, obeying made the time pass so slowly. Eventually, however, five thirty arrived. Louise had reckoned the shindig could start at sixish, so there could be a sort of children's party bit first in the daylight. So people started arriving early – and of course, none of them had any children.

Hywel arrived first, accompanied by that dull flatmate of his whose name Michael could never remember. Gus. No, Doug. No, Dick. They both kissed Izzy like camels drinking at a water hole and it was some comfort to Michael to realize that his disgust was only aesthetic. He thought he might have been rather hard on Dick in the past. He remembered thinking of him as a door wearing glasses. On closer inspection it was clear that Dick could, in a fog, pass for a cottage: he was sound and habitable, Michael thought. Though rising damp would evidently be a problem.

'Er – I hope—' Dick seemed to be recklessly contemplating a sentence. 'I hope it's OK – I've brought a – er – friend. Michelle.'

He stood aside to reveal a rather overweight little tart with black round her eyes and red round her mouth. Michael cheered up considerably.

'Michelle! I am Michael! We were evidently made for each other. Let me get you a drink.'

''Ave yer got anythink soft? Only Oi've gorra terrible 'ead for alcohol.'

Michelle had clearly spent her deformative years in Birmingham.

'Come into the the garden, Maud,' Michael lured. 'There's Perrier there, and grapefruit juice.'

The garden looked magical. All Louise's wild flowers were blooming at once, and the bees, grasshoppers and butterflies added their delicate hums and flutters to the shimmer.

'Ooooow, it's reelly pretty.' Michelle's eyes shone through the black. 'You ent half made it noice, loike.'

'Yes.' Michael handed her a Perrier. 'We like to think of it as our little corner of *Rus In Urbe*.'

He nearly bit his tongue, but she hadn't been listening, thank God.

'Oi think it's everso noice. Reely noice. Oi loike it better than a real garden – know what Oi mean?'

He bestowed her on Razors, who listened impassively to her praise of his green hair and deadly black earring. Michael returned up the garden, and ran into Izzy by the door just as Gwyn burst through it with a sulky-looking girl in tow.

'Bonnie!' cried Izzy, and only those who know the dear girl very well could have heard that cry as the panic it was.

''Ulloa, yew darlin's, yew bewties!' Gwyn embraced everyone with impartial lust and subjected Michael to such a bearhug that his lungs wheezed like an old harmonium. 'Fuckin' bewtiful all this is, now. Another monument to middle class pastoralism, like. Grea', mon, grea'. I'll just get a few pints of Frascati down me neck and pass out in thoase buttercups.'

Bonnie fastened on Izzy.

'Oh Izzy – it is Izzy, isn't it? We met at Gwyn's and Maria's didn't we? Last New Year's it was, seems ages ago now but it's only six months, unbelievable what can happen in six months, isn't it? Dave left me – anyway I expect you've heard all about that – and of course Gwyn and Maria splitting up, sometimes it feels as if society's just disintegrating. I've been going to these Women's Group meetings Gwyn told me about, they've been really supportive and encouraging, I've been rebuilding

248

my self-esteem and of course Gwyn has been really marvellous, it's a pity he's stuck in the machismo-and-sexual-harassment mould, but I suppose to some extent he's still a prisoner of his early conditioning, and the fact is he's always ready to put your plumbing right, and as we were saying at the Discussion Group—'

'Oh, here comes Maria,' cried Izzy. 'You must tell her all about this business – I mean the Women's Groups.' She'll be thrilled.' And she bundled Bonnie off towards the luckless Maria.

Michael was rather struck by Maria's appearance. He hadn't seen her since the old red-eyed harridan days of Earl's Court. Her hair had grown somewhat, she'd put on a welcome bit of weight, and she had a new pair of New Yorkish glasses – white rimmed and smokey lensed. She was wearing a skirt, too, and it was clear that her legs were quite something. All the same, Michael thought it more politic to zoom off, for several reasons. She'd always hated him like poison, for a start. That's the great thing about your own parties: you can always zoom off and pretend to do something. Michael pretended to open some bottles.

Carl was next to arrive. He was simpering in his bow tie, and Louise and Michael exchanged meaningful looks at the sight of him. On Louise's part, mortification o'er-spread the features, whereas her husband could only provide a faintly sardonic leer. What a refreshing moment for him.

'Carl!' Michael seized his hand and squeezed it till he was sure the knuckles were splintering nicely. 'Let me get you a drink!' Michael did feel a bit sorry for Louise, though. It's bad enough to have to confront your ex-lovers after second thoughts have turned them back into frogs, but to share this experience with your spouse takes some doing. He led Carl to the wine.

'Michael! Come and meet my mum!'

Izzy's mum was everything she should have been: a dear little soul with a warm, appley face and a special shine in the eye.

'Hello, Mr Tristram. I'm so pleased to meet you.'

'Mrs Comyn! The pleasure is all mine! Let me get you a drink.'

'Just a squash, please, love, it's quite hot today, isn't it? I must sit down. I feel quite light-headed. I'm so very glad to meet you at last, Mr Tristram.'

'Well, I'm extremely pleased to meet you.'

'When I heard Izzy was moving in with a nice family, I was so happy. I didn't like to think of her all alone in that attic, and between you and me I wasn't very keen on Earl's Court. I expect I'm being silly, and it were only a fleeting glimpse I had of it once, but all the same—'

'I know what you mean.'

'Yes, well, I do think it were everso kind of you and Mrs Tristram to take Izzy in. I do hope she's been behaving herself.'

'Impeccably.'

Alas.

'She hasn't been a nuisance, at all, I hope?'

'Absolutely not. Not at all. She's been perfectly splendid.'

'Only I did have – I did have a few worries about Izzy, last Christmas. She didn't come up home for Christmas as usual, and I did think, well, maybe I'm being silly, but I did think she might have got mixed up with the wrong sort of man. D'ye know what I mean?'

'Yes. Yes, I do indeed.'

Indeed.

'You know, it were so unlike Izzy not to come. And when she's had a boyfriend before, like that nice Ben, she's brought him home wi' her. So I did wonder, well it did occur to me—' She leaned conspiratorially forward. 'I did think to wonder whether she were – you know – involved wi' *a married man.*'

'Well, I think I can reassure you on that point.' Michael felt desperately short of a drink all of a sudden. 'Izzy's leading a blameless life at the moment. I don't think she's got a boyfriend at all. And she's certainly looking forward to San Francisco.'

'Oh America!' Mrs Comyn heaved a deep sigh and leaned back. 'it's such a long way away. But it's only for a year – and Izzy says I should go over there while I've got the chance, and visit her. She says she'll pay me fare. But I don't know – what do you think?'

'A perfectly splendid idea! You absolutely must!'

She beamed at him as if he'd given her something. Ironical, really. Just then Jack came up. He'd spotted Mrs Comyn, realized she was Izzy's mum, and was all set to cross question her about the ghost of Okley Tor, which Izzy had told him about, and which her mother had even seen. Yes. Mrs Comyn looked like the sort of little woman who could see through brick walls, thought Michael. As she waved him goodbye with a secret smile, he had the distinct impression that she'd seen right through him, Fair Isle pullover and all.

Mrs Comyn had been brought by Izzy's brother, a pleasant burly chap surrounded by enchanting little girls. It's amazing what can spring from your loins if you're really lucky. His wife, he explained, was laid up with hay fever. Everyone made sympathetic noises and watched his delightful daughters dart off into the further corners of the orchard. Michael saw in a flash the moment when young Jack fell in love with the middle and most devastating one, but she was clearly already fascinated by Razors. *Take it easy, Jack, old man*, his father mentally exhorted. *Stick to the ray guns and ghost stories.* But it was no use. One cannot stem the tides of nature. Michael saw him leave Mrs Comyn's side and dawdle helplessly towards the little creature. Then the spectacle became too painful to watch: Michael looked away.

More people came, the garden filled up nicely, and Michael wandered pleasantly around, eavesdropping here and there as he filled up glasses: the welcome cupbearer. He passed Hywel talking to Izzy's mum.

'Though I'm a bit worried about the way she's lost weight, Hywel.'

''Sright, she wants to get a bit more o' yewer shortbread down 'er.'

Michael sidled up to Dick and Bonnie.

'No, really, Dick, I've always been fascinated by pottery. I do feel my creative potential was utterly frustrated by my marriage with Dave. I'd love it if you could give me some lessons say, after the end of term.'

'Er, I'd love to, but – er, I'm afraid I'm going to San Francisco.'

'Are you? With Izzy?'

'Erm – yeah.'

Michael refilled Dick's glass. 'I didn't know you were going, too, Dick.'

Dick gave a nervous, apologetic smile. 'Yeah – it's – erm, it's this teacher's exchange scheme, y'see. Izzy and I thought – we thought we might share an – erm, apartment.'

Bonnie swooped. 'Oh, I see! Like that, is it, Dick? Well, you're a lucky chap! I'm sure most blokes here would give their eye teeth to go off to California with Izzy, wouldn't they Michael?'

'It's not – it's not – erm, like that. Izzy and me—' Dick managed a look of monstrous sincerity. 'Izzy and me – are, just, erm, good friends.'

'Yes – by far the best, isn't it? Very California, too!' Michael quipped, and then sailed off towards Louise and Gwyn. He did not disturb them, for they were buried in an obviously private talk, but he hovered behind a Moor Park apricot and fiddled speciously with a corkscrew while he listened.

'Noa, Louise, whatever you dew, darlin', never – never, mind – leave Michael. No matter 'ow disgracefully 'e behaves – and far be it from me to suggest that 'e might behave disgracefully – but even if 'e does – stick by 'im darlin'! You woan't regret it. Believe me, this wrenchin' asunder business is too awful to contemplate.'

The Welsh tears were once more a-trickling.

'Poor Gwyn,' said Louise softly, her arm around his shoulders. 'It's so hard for you, isn't it? But you know – after all, it's only six months since Maria left. You might get together again, one day.'

252

'Noa, noa, noa – there's noa prospect of a reconciliation, at all. Look! She woan't even speak to me properly – just nods and walks by. She's started talkin' about divorce, now, an' she's insistin' on sellin' the flat – but never mind all these miseries o' mine, girl – just promise me that you'll never leave Michael, noa matter 'ow tempted you are – right?'

'All right. If it makes you happy. As a matter of fact, I've been very strongly tempted in the past. But I can't ever imagine being quite so tempted in the future, somehow.'

A lump rose in Michael's throat and he tiptoed away towards Izzy and Maria.

'I don't know –' Maria was sighing, and as she saw him she held out her glass with a quite genuine smile. 'Hello, Michael. Thanks – I don't know, Izzy. I feel so confused. Despite all the support I get from the Group, I still miss him like hell. Day and night. Constantly. It's like rheumatism or something.'

'Well, why don't you get together again?'

'Oh, I don't know. Hurt pride, I suppose. I've rejected him so often that he's given up trying. And I can't bear to make the first move. So we just steer clear of each other. It's too late, now, anyhow – he's all shacked up with Bonnie.'

Michael moved on, with a sigh, to the plump girl Michelle and Izzy's brother. Was he contemplating a little hanky-panky in the absence of his wife? They turned to Michael in unison, their faces full of exhilaration.

'Just think, Michael – you'll never guess what!'

He certainly wouldn't. No guessing, on principle, nowadays.

'We've just discovered that Michelle used to live in the same house as us, in Birmingham!'

'Really?'

'Well, Oi used to live in Carpenter Road, in Edgbaston, you know, about foive years ago—'

'And before that, about eight years ago, we lived

253

there. Before we moved to Edinburgh. Just fancy that!'

'The same house?'

'The same flat, even. Do you know, Oi even used to look at all these little kids' scribblings on the wall and wonder who'd done them.'

'Our girls,' Izzy's brother blushed. 'Bit of a handful when they were tiny—'

'Oh, Oi loiked it. Oi thought it was everso sweet!'

'Well, how extraordinary. Small world, isn't it?'

Night stole up. Michael leaned against the oldest of the apple trees and looked up into the dark blue vault of heaven. All the guests had clustered round the tables, and the incense-like whiff of night-scented stock crept out from the places where Louise had sown it, and stirred their souls.

Then out of the house came Izzy, carrying lighted candles. Behind her Razors, similarly illuminated. They looked like two boys come to fulfil some ancient prophecy, to bring water to the parched lands, calves to the cows and fish thronging to the rivers.

Izzy bent down at the first table and bestowed a candle on her mother and Hywel.

'Do you know, Hywel,' said Mrs Comyn suddenly, 'I think I *shall* go to America.' Her face was alive with excitement. 'And you must come too, lad! We'll go and stay with Izzy!' Hywel did the right thing. He seized her rough old hand and squeezed it. Mrs Comyn blushed with pleasure in the candlelight. Nobody had held her hand like that for years and years.

''Sright, we will an' all!' he vowed. 'We'll 'ave a romantic little 'oliday, like – jus' yew an' me, orright?'

Izzy moved on: travelling light. She placed a candle in the centre of Maria's table. Maria looked into its depths, then turned to Izzy and got up.

'I think – I think I'll just go over and say hello to him. Throw him a bun. Just for old time's sake. I know it won't – I know it isn't – But still—'

Izzy moved on, and placed a candle on the table where her three nieces and Jack were all sitting. Jack turned to

254

Kate, the middle niece. 'Will you marry me, and have four children, three boys and a girl and some gerbils?' he demanded.

Kate picked her nose, staring moodily into the candleflame. 'All right.'

Izzy moved on and placed a candle on Gwyn's table. Gwyn looked up and beyond her, to another figure arriving behind her in the dark.

'Darlin'!' he cried. His face seemed to crack open and he leapt up with arms flung wide. The candle shivered in his wake.

All around, now, human faces shone out of the night. Lips moved, eyes kindled, hands touched. Some stared into the flame, some into the dark.

Izzy moved on with her last candle down to the bottom of the garden, where Louise sat alone, watching her party. Izzy handed on the candle. Louise took it. Perhaps it was at that moment – it must have been round about then, anyway – that a few inches below Louise's heart, the two tiny specks of life that were to become her darling daughter at last seized each other and held on tight. Yes, Michael's daughter – the one who was going to cause him so much trouble.

THE END

A SELECTED LIST OF TITLES AVAILABLE FROM CORGI BOOKS

☐	24030 7	Sudden Death	**Rita Mae Brown**	£1.95
☐	12219 X	Southern Discomfort	**Rita Mae Brown**	£1.95
☐	11149 X	Imogen	**Jilly Cooper**	£1.75
☐	10878 2	Prudence	**Jilly Cooper**	£1.50
☐	10717 4	Octavia	**Jilly Cooper**	£1.50
☐	10576 7	Harriet	**Jilly Cooper**	£1.50
☐	10427 2	Bella	**Jilly Cooper**	£1.50
☐	10277 6	Emily	**Jilly Cooper**	£1.50
☐	12041 3	Lisa & Co	**Jilly Cooper**	£1.75
☐	12358 7	The Grounding	**Meredith Daneman**	£1.75
☐	11778 1	A Chance to Sit Down	**Meredith Daneman**	£1.75
☐	12201 7	Doctor Love	**Gael Green**	£1.75
☐	11980 6	Love, Dad	**Evan Hunter**	£1.95
☐	11963 6	Streets of Gold	**Evan Hunter**	£1.95
☐	11190 2	The World According to Garp	**John Irving**	£2.50
☐	11191 0	Setting Free The Bears	**John Irving**	£1.95
☐	12040 5	The Hotel New Hampshire	**John Irving**	£2.50
☐	11266 6	The Water Method Man	**John Irving**	£1.95
☐	11267 4	The 158-Pound Marriage	**John Irving**	£1.95
☐	11554 1	Tales of the City	**Armistead Maupin**	£2.95
☐	99086 8	More Tales of the City	**Armistead Maupin**	£3.95
☐	99106 6	Further Tales of the City	**Armistead Maupin**	£3.95
☐	11781 1	Still Life With Woodpecker	**Tom Robbins**	£1.50